Tears of Mehndi

01 02 03 04 05 16 15 14 13 12

Caitlin Press Inc.
8100 Alderwood Road,
Halfmoon Bay, BC V0N 1Y1
www.caitlin-press.com

Text design by Jools Andrés
Cover design by Vici Johnstone
Cover illustrations by Raqiya Khan
Printed in Canada

Caitlin Press Inc. acknowledges financial support from the Government of Canada through the Canada Book Fund and the Canada Council for the Arts, and from the Province of British Columbia through the British Columbia Arts Council and the Book Publisher's Tax Credit.

Conseil des Arts
du Canada

Library and Archives Canada Cataloguing in Publication

Sidhu, Raminder

Tears of Mehndi / Raminder Sidhu.

ISBN 978-1-894759-73-1

I. Title.

PS8637.I24T42 2012 C813'.6 C2012-900543-6

Tears of Mehndi

Raminder Sidhu

Mehndi

Commonly referred to as henna, *mehndi* is a powder derived from the shoots and leaves of the henna tree (*Lawsonia inermis*) and prepared as a dark paste. It is applied to the hands and feet as a symbol of celebration for women of various eastern cultures. For centuries Indian brides, in particular, have been entranced by its blood-rich hue.

Before it crumbles and stains the flesh, however, a bride should look beyond the artistry and between the designs that pledge eternal love and joy. There she will find a vine of *mehndi*, which begins and ends in the shape of a teardrop.

*For my mother, Beant Kaur,
for her unconditional love, wisdom,
strength, courage, faith, hope
and blessings.*

*And for those daughters who have been lost
within the depths of these pages.*

Contents

Foreword

Tears of Mehndi by Raminder Sidhu is a novel divinely inspired by the spirit of women past, present and future. It is for them and for us that this book was written from a place of inexplicable understanding. The stories are fictional. The women are fictional. Yet their pain, their longing for happiness, their search for love and their hopes and dreams are as real as our own.

I applaud my friend and former colleague, Raminder Sidhu, for having the courage to write *Tears of Mehndi* with such honesty and soul. Her brilliant debut novel brings to light the disheartening lives of women and the dangerous web of lies that can be woven by a close-knit cultural community. And although the characters in this novel portray the struggles endured by many Indo-Canadian women, their stories capture lessons with universal themes that are relevant to us all.

As each story unfolds, the robes of denial, judgment and righteousness fall, revealing the naked truth. Not just what appears on the surface, but the truth behind the facades and the illusions of success, behind the masks of gender discrimination and false pride. For these women, happiness is hard-won. There is no Prince Charming. No fairytale ending. Only the truth.

I was deeply moved when I read their stories. I felt such sorrow at what was allowed to happen to these beautiful women. Our neighbours. Our friends. Our sisters. Our daughters.

Yet amid their ashes of despair…hope rises. The heartbreaking stories in *Tears of Mehndi* have the power to set us free.

Free to live. Free to love. Free to be.

The Honourable Yonah Martin
Senator of Canada

The Incident – 1976

A crowd had congregated outside JD Foods and Music Mart. There were pieces of shattered glass scattered across the grass and wedged between the fallen leaves and damaged Hindi cassette tapes and eight-tracks. Bags of flour and sugar had been ripped open and poured onto the uneven pavement in front of the door of the shop. Slabs of meat had been removed from their packaging and flung onto the narrow road where they were drawing the attention of hungry birds. Broken pop and beer bottles lay among the remnants of smoked cigarettes and what appeared to be human feces, and streams of damp toilet paper clung to the bare birch trees and the parked cars lining the street.

On this wet and chilly morning Mrs. Gurbaksh Dhillon, known by everyone as Baksho, owner of the desecrated corner store, marched down the street toward the scene. Her brown polyester pants were tucked inside her green rubber boots, and her shawl slid off her shoulders, exposing her flannel pajama top. She was returning from her home four blocks away where she had gone to retrieve two brooms, a box of black garbage bags and a dustpan. There were more cleaning supplies inside the store, but it was impossible to get in past the barrel of bulk *daal* that had been upturned in front of the entrance. She had come to expect depredations of this kind on Halloween. Her friends had warned her to put up metal bars on the windows and door, but a widowed mother could not afford that kind of protection.

After removing all the glass and littered garbage from the property, most of the neighbours had dispersed by the time Baksho's concerned friend, Mrs. Gill, arrived. She walked quickly, the clatter of her gold platform sandals echoing behind her. When Charnjit Gill first came to the community, Baksho had referred to her as *Mrs. Gill* to mock her profession as a Punjabi teacher. Eventually the whole community had joined in, and now everyone forgot she even had a first name. Mrs. Gill and her husband lived six doors down from Baksho's shop.

"Don't worry, Baksho *panji,* we will get it all cleaned up," Mrs. Gill comforted her friend. "My husband is coming with plywood to board up the windows. Have you called the police?" Baksho was almost old enough to be Mrs. Gill's mother, so as a sign of respect, Mrs. Gill called her *panji,* meaning "older sister," but only when addressing her directly.

"What would the police say?" Baksho asked. "The neighbours called them at two-thirty this morning when they heard the screams and laughter outside, but the police didn't arrive until three hours later. By then those *kuttay goray,* those little white bastards, were already gone! Did the police expect that those hooligans would stick around to be arrested? Anyway, it was that same bald *sarda macha,* that mean police officer. He doesn't care. If he did, he would have kept guard or at least driven by, knowing this was likely to happen! He just said it's probably that same group of teenagers that's always causing trouble. There is nothing he can do. And I saw that dirty dog smirking when he read the words on the side of the wall!"

Mrs. Gill walked to the corner of the old stucco structure and peered around the side. Three empty cartons of chocolate milk had been missed by the cleanup crew, the liquid saturating the earth and splattered on the side of the building. The black spray paint above it read *Hindu breast milk for free*—with breast spelled *brest*.

Mrs. Gill's husband drove up with another neighbour, Lloyd Wilson, in the passenger side of his blue Datsun pickup. Mr. Gill jumped out and headed down the street behind the store while Lloyd began to unload supplies from the back of the truck. "So sorry this has happened again, Baksho," he said as he carried some empty boxes toward the store. "I heard there were some men out patrolling the neighbourhood until about one o'clock, but I guess they missed them. I sure hope the police catch those kids."

"Fine, fine. You can leave that for now!" Baksho called from inside the store. Some of the neighbours had managed to move the barrel of *daal* and she had cleared a pathway through the mess that obstructed the doorway. "I want you to fix up the outside first!"

Lloyd put the boxes down inside the door and headed out to tackle the damage to the exterior of the building. Mr. Gill had walked around the corner to the *gurdwara* and returned in mere minutes with reinforcements, a group of men with long hair and sideburns, as was the current fashion. They would be sufficient to restore the shop to its original form in minimal time.

Baksho was carrying a bucket of soapy water and a scrub brush to the front sidewalk but stopped as soon as she saw Manjeet approaching the corner.

"B-b-baksho *panji*, I c-c-came as soon as I heard!" Manjeet said. She and her husband and daughter had moved down the street from Baksho's house only a few weeks before.

Baksho handed the scrub brush and pail of water to Manjeet and pointed at the swastika sketched in red crayon on the pavement. Manjeet shook her head as she stared at it. Had it been resting flat and not at a slant, it would have been the ancient Hindu symbol representing good fortune. She pulled up her plaid trousers, squatted on the sidewalk and poured the soapy water onto the symbol. She scrubbed until her hands were red and the swastika had vanished.

After instructing Manjeet to take a walk about the building with the water hose, Baksho went back inside where Mrs. Gill was busy restocking the shelves with what was left of the products.

"The *masala* packages have been torn, but most of the smaller dry items are salvageable." Mrs. Gill wiped her hands with some paper towels and headed toward the cash counter where she picked up Baksho's baseball bat, which had most likely been used by the intruders. "It's good you didn't leave any money in the register!" The machine was lying open on the floor. It had been smashed against the small freezer.

Baksho dropped to the floor and started to weep. She was a strong woman, and it was rare to see her so exposed and vulnerable. "Why does this keep happening to me!" she cried. "Just when it seems things are getting better these stupid boys try to destroy everything I've worked for!" Although she had not assumed the white clothing of a traditional widow, Baksho did stay away from most cosmetics. Her dark and heavy kohl liner was all that was evident of her life before the loss of her husband, and now it streamed down her face with her tears.

Mrs. Gill knelt beside her, adjusting her skirt with both hands. Baksho's knees could not support her heavy body so she had stretched her legs out into the puddle of mustard hair oil on the floor. Her sobs got louder.

"Let me get Manjeet. Where is her husband? I'm sure he will help, too!" Mrs. Gill needed backup.

"She's outside," Baksho said. She pointed to where Manjeet was quietly holding the ladder for one of the men while he painted over Baksho's sign, to which had been added with spray paint: *No Hindus Allowed.*

But Mrs. Gill had accidentally fumbled onto a topic that would distract her, and Baksho took a deep breath, unfastened the chiffon *dupatta* that had been wrapped around her neck and carefully tucked inside her pajama top, and wiped her tears and nose on the edge of it. Just as she leaned against the wall in order to pull herself up, Daisy Kang from next door barged in with a thermos and plastic cups. Her husband, Bittu, had been the one who called the police. He had been living beside Baksho's store for four years and was familiar with the events that had unfolded. He waited to call Baksho until early morning, as he was worried she might endanger herself by charging down to the store and confronting the vandals.

As Daisy poured the milky tea for the two women, her red *choora* jingled on both of her *mehndi*-adorned arms. It was a bad omen to remove the bangles until at least five weeks after the wedding, but they were an odd fit with her braided hair, pink *parandi,* beige sweater and navy blue bell-bottoms.

Within seconds, the strong but sweet aroma of cardamom, cloves and cinnamon filled the air with warmth, and as Baksho took her first sip, she said, "Now this is real *cha*! Those *goray* call it tea when they throw a tea bag into a cup of boiling hot water!"

"You are so brave, Baksho *panji*!" Daisy said. "Running this store all by yourself for almost four years! Your son was so young when you lost your husband. How did you do it? I can't imagine living life without my Bittu."

"What else could I do? It wasn't easy, but I had to raise my son. My husband pinched every penny so he could one day open his own shop in Vancouver. I tried not to touch his savings for several years. I scrimped and saved, working on the berry farms and renting rooms to new immigrants, but as Jagdeep grew older and his expenses increased I decided it was time to fulfill my husband's dream. So I poured everything we had into this!" Baksho pointed to the mess around her. "I should never have let him return to India, at least not alone."

Baksho waved Daisy away as the young woman tried to refill her cup. She had no desire to rehash old disappointments. She wanted Daisy to leave so she could talk to Mrs. Gill.

"I don't let my husband out of my sight," Mrs. Gill stated. "My mother taught me three things: marry a man who is less attractive, loves you more and then never allow him to stay away from you for too long."

Baksho nodded in agreement. She wished she had been given that advice before she married her late husband.

"By the way, Mrs. Gill, your new hairstyle is very pretty," Daisy said. "The shorter length suits you."

Mrs. Gill blushed and tucked a loose strand behind her ear.

Daisy smiled, screwed the lid onto the thermos and went outside to return the remaining cups to her landlady who was waiting at the edge of her driveway in anticipation.

"Is everything all right in there?" The woman asked as she shoved the cups into a large brown paper bag and accompanied Daisy to the front door of their home. "Do tell me, what was Mrs. Gill wearing?"

"Do you mean *Miss Perfect*?" Daisy asked.

The woman looked at her, confused.

"Well, that's what the young girls at the *gurdwara* call her!" Daisy whispered. "These Canadian-born girls idolize these women they call *stylish and modern*. I overheard Kiran, Manjeet's daughter, telling her friends that all the young boys in the neighbourhood are in love with Mrs. Gill's beauty and hourglass body!"

"They say her father is a well-respected politician in India. I think she's originally from a big city and not from a village like us. Her family must be very wealthy! No wonder the girls think she's perfect!"

The two women, ignoring the cleanup effort that continued behind them, did not even notice the mild drizzle.

"Anyway," Daisy continued, "she had on her usual—a tiny fitted skirt and a low-cut blouse. I could see everything when she bent forward. My husband would never let me dress like that. I don't know why she can't cover herself in more conservative western clothing like the rest of us. I know it's asking for trouble to wear traditional Indian attire when leaving the house, but she doesn't have to expose so much skin!"

"At least she has enough sense to wear a *salwar kameez* when she teaches the Punjabi classes in her basement. Did you know my younger son wanted to take an extra tutorial class with her? But I refused. He had no interest in the language before she arrived and now all of a sudden he wants to be fluent!" The woman laughed.

"He's not alone. Baksho was just telling me a couple of days ago that her son doesn't help out at the store anymore because he's busy learning Punjabi, too. He's only a few years younger than Mrs. Gill and at his age young boys don't think with their heads. But Baksho is too proud of her son to notice these things. And Mrs. Gill is her dearest companion," Daisy said.

"I just don't see the connection between the two. Mrs. Gill is so young and glamorous and Baksho is boring and old-fashioned. She must be in her late thirties at least. What could those two possibly have in common?" The woman was baffled.

"Who knows?" Daisy sighed.

Just then the women heard a thud and turned their attention back to the store. One of the men had dropped his ladder onto the pavement. Manjeet was fumbling with the hose nearby. Daisy and her landlady quickly moved indoors before they were called over for assistance.

Meanwhile, inside the store, Baksho was all business. She had dragged over a wooden chair that was lying in a mess of salt, wiped it down with her shawl and firmly planted herself on it next to where Mrs. Gill was cleaning.

"Do you know what happened with Manjeet's husband?" She did not wait for Mrs. Gill to respond. "He lost his job at the sawmill and it's so difficult to get a job there, too!" Baksho leaned over, picked up a bag of potato chips, dusted it off with her shawl and placed it back on the rack.

"My husband told me it wasn't entirely his fault this time," Mrs. Gill replied.

Baksho raised her eyebrows. She had heard bits and pieces but not the whole story.

"Well, his first day at work," Mrs. Gill said, "he found the words *stop stealing our jobs* scribbled in black marker on the table where he'd left his lunch kit. My husband complains about this kind of little stuff sometimes, even though most of the workers at the mill are Indian. But this one *gora* worker just wouldn't stop picking on Manjeet's poor husband. During his second shift, the worker blocked the washroom door and wouldn't let him go in until he saw the foreman approaching." Mrs. Gill was revealing each detail in the exact manner her husband had relayed the information to her. "And on the third day," she paused to pull out a small box that had fallen behind the shelf and then continued, "as Manjeet's husband walked into the parking lot, he noticed one of his tires had been slashed."

"Don't stop! What happened next?" Baksho had opened up a package of almonds and was popping them into her mouth three at a time.

"He lost his temper, of course, and challenged the *gora* he knew was responsible. They had a terrible fight in the lunchroom, yet only he was dismissed. It was so unfair."

Baksho smacked her hand on her forehead. "Didn't anyone vouch for him?"

"What could they say? A few of the workers tried to get involved but the management said that it was Manjeet's husband who had thrown the first punch. If any of them continued to make an issue out of it they would have fired them, too! No man can afford to jeopardize his own livelihood in this country!" Mrs. Gill kicked at the roll of toilet paper jammed between two racks.

"*Bechari* Manjeet. The poor woman! She was cursed at birth. A dark complexion and a speech impediment, who else could she marry?" Baksho shook her head.

"You can't blame Manjeet for what happened with her husband!"

"But it is her bad *kismet*!"

"What do you mean?"

"Look at her husband—does he look suitable to you? The poor woman was married off to a man old enough to be her father. She's no more than thirty but he's long crossed fifty. He's almost twice her age and two inches shorter!" Baksho threw the empty almond package toward the trash bin but it missed and landed on the floor.

"I agree she isn't attractive but her stutter isn't that bad. It comes and goes."

"Yes, but when she's under pressure, her stutter is worse. It only disappears when she's calm and comfortable in her surroundings," Baksho explained. "I bet you anything, when her family tried to arrange her marriage, she got nervous. That's why she ended up with him!" Baksho had only known Manjeet a few weeks but had already come to her own conclusions about her life.

"I feel so sorry for her. She must've been ridiculed as a child."

Baskho shushed Mrs. Gill as she saw Manjeet heading into the shop.

"I can only stay a little longer," Manjeet announced. "My Kiran will be awake soon."

"That's fine. You can go, Manjeet. I don't know why you're out there with the men in the first place! Jagdeep, my son Jugga, will be here soon to help. And I'm sure the other ladies will come as soon as they can, too." Baksho paused and then added, "*Bechari* Kiran, poor girl. An only child and a girl! I'm so lucky. At least I have a son, and it's so much safer for him. He can take care of me, but *you,* Manjeet, you have a daughter and the responsibility for a girl never ends. Daughters are such a burden."

Manjeet lowered her eyes and rushed out of the store, pushing an empty crate to the side as she hurried away.

"Oh no, I forgot to tell Manjeet to send her husband to help out!" Mrs. Gill started to chase after Manjeet but Baksho called out to stop her before she was out of the store.

"Don't you know?" Baksho walked up to Mrs. Gill and pulled her closer. "Manjeet and her daughter are home alone. Her *budda,* her old man left for India two days ago. There's something going on there."

"Maybe he has some family function." Mrs. Gill moved to another aisle that needed attention.

Baksho reached down to pick up a piece of Bazooka bubble gum off the floor, unwrapped it, peeked at the comic strip inside and then chucked the red, white and blue wrapper back onto the floor. She chewed for a few seconds with her mouth open and then carried on. "I asked Manjeet but she wouldn't say. She was being very secretive. I think there has been a death, maybe his mother! They received a telegram. She also mentioned a name—what was it? Satwant, Satya, Satinder, something like that..."

"Manjeet doesn't say a word unless necessary, but it's a bit odd to keep a family death a secret. And she would never call her mother-in-law by her name!"

"Exactly, that's why I think she's hiding something. That *budda* of hers must have a past!"

Mrs. Gill noticed her husband and the others had finished the repairs outside and were ready to board up the door area.

"Now isn't the time to discuss these things," she said, bending to pick up a pile of Twinkie boxes. "Let's get this place back together. We'll find out soon enough what's going on."

"I don't know, Mrs. Gill, I'm telling you there's something strange happening. Maybe it's something to do with Kiran. I count my blessings everyday that I don't have a daughter. You will learn too, Mrs. Gill, when you have your own children. Start praying for a son now, and in a year you too can be grateful!" She lowered her voice. "Hear me now—that Kiran will be trouble. All pretty girls are!"

Baksho examined Mrs. Gill's face for a reaction, but Mrs. Gill's expression did not change. Instead she said, "Well, I don't know about Kiran. She's only twelve so it's too early to say, but she's a little overweight, don't you think? And fat girls are even more unlucky!" Mrs. Gill smirked and placed the last undamaged Twinkie box on the shelf.

Satinder – Truth

❧

"Go outside, Kiran!"

My feet were planted solidly on the floor. I could not move.

"I said get out!" My father only spoke English when he was drunk, immersed in conversation with *goray* or when he was furious. Right now he was so angry his eyes were bulging out of their sockets.

A few minutes earlier he had stormed through the door and swung his lunch kit at the wall, narrowly missing my face as he headed straight for the kitchen. I watched in horror as he grabbed Satinder by the hair, dragged her into the living room and threw her down on the floor. My mother, Manjeet, had gone to the grocery store and I had stayed behind with no knowledge of what lay ahead.

"KIRAN, LEAVE NOW!" he yelled at me again, so I ran into my room and peered from behind my door, unwilling to be shut away from the storm that was about to engulf our household.

"*Kanjree*! Whore!" he bellowed.

He kicked her so hard in the stomach that her scream must have echoed throughout the neighbourhood. I was terrified. I wanted to stop him, to yell at him. I wanted to tell him he was crazy but I could not. I could hear my heartbeat thumping louder and louder.

It was like the dream I had so often. I would find myself in the middle of a jungle with someone chasing me. It would be daylight one minute and the next minute I could not see my shadow. And then I would be surrounded by people, but their faces were blurred and unrecognizable and I was terrified. Just as I closed my eyes to surrender, I would awaken. Watching Satinder now, I felt as helpless as I did in my sleep.

Luckily my mother arrived at that moment and was able to stop my father just as he began pummelling Satinder with his bare hands.

My mother dragged him out onto the balcony where she knew he would not want to cause a scene in front of the neighbours and he would calm down in the fresh air. Satinder remained on the floor where he had left her, her body motionless. I ran into the kitchen, grabbed a wet towel and gently wiped the blood from her face and then helped her walk down the stairs to her bedroom in the basement. I did not ask why my father had attacked her. She did not explain. I went to my own room and stayed there, pretending to do my homework, until I heard my father leaving the house. When I came out, my mother was sitting on the sofa. She was staring at the television, entranced by a talk show, but the volume had been muted.

When Satinder came to stay with us, my family had been living in our new three-bedroom Vancouver Special for almost two months. It was 1976 and I had just turned twelve.

The interior of our white stucco house with its partial wood siding and its brown trim resembled the inside of every other home on our street. My mother had cut pictures of Sikh gurus, *gurdwaras,* and other Indian monuments from calendars and newspapers, framed them and hung them on the walls of each room. She had also lined the red shag carpet on the stairway with plastic and laid beige crocheted covers on the sofa and coffee table. Not a single room had escaped being adorned with Indian furnishings.

We were the newest residents of Little India. In our old neighbourhood the smell of my mother's elaborate Punjabi meals had distinguished our home from our neighbours' homes. Here the potent odour of *tarka,* a mixture of spices, onions, ginger, tomatoes and garlic, permeated the entire block. There could not have been a more suitable environment for fifteen-year-old Satinder to reside in. My father had explained that she was a distant relative whose parents had been killed in an accident. Since she had no other surviving relatives in Punjab or anywhere else, he was compelled to bring her to live with us.

"She has no one," he said every time my mother had asked him why he didn't just leave her in India. It was solely his decision to bring her to Canada.

Satinder was a very shy and simple girl, but while she had a sweet demeanour, I saw glimpses of resentment in her large, wide-set eyes.

Her face was round, her skin was fair like milk, and she wore her long hair in two tight braids. She was short but voluptuous. Though not gorgeous by any means, she was what my mother called "Indian pretty."

In the first weeks after her arrival, Satinder remained distant from our family, even choosing not to accompany us to our regular Sunday prayers at the *gurdwara*. She scarfed down her meals and quickly excused herself from the table. She often put a damper on my Hindi movie nights because if Satinder was too tired to view the three-hour film, my mother thought it was in my best interest to go to bed early as well. In fact, Satinder managed to have a headache, stomach pains or a fever every time there was the remote possibility she would need to interact with the family.

"It'll take her some time to adjust to a different country, strange language and unfamiliar people," my father would reassure us.

My parents tried hard to please Satinder. The only time I had been to Stanley Park had been on a school field trip, but for Satinder my father planned a special outing. However, she sauntered through the park as if she had been there a dozen times, turning her head away when he would point out new sights. My father seemed hurt, but he would always try again. He took her to the Capilano Suspension Bridge and Chinatown, but to no avail.

My mother was not one to show affection, but she made many attempts to help Satinder feel at home. She served *jalebis* and other sweet, fried desserts with Satinder's morning tea, although I was not allowed to consume any sugar until the afternoon. While I had to eat all my *daal* and *roti* so I had no room left for treats, Satinder was told to pace herself so she could also enjoy the *kheer*. Then, since Satinder did not like to go shopping in her unfamiliar surroundings, my mother would make trip after trip to Woodward's until she found clothes that were the right size and fit for Satinder. And just when I thought she could not get any more special treatment, my parents moved her from the small bedroom upstairs down to the suite on the ground level of the house, so she could have her own space.

"Guests are a reflection of God," my mother would say. "These are our Punjabi values, and they'll not be c-c-compromised!"

Where Satinder was involved, my father would dispense cash as if he were the maharaja of Vancouver, though my mother still constantly reminded me that we could not afford to spend on meaningless luxuries. One year for her birthday I had used my savings to buy her a bottle of musk oil perfume. She was furious. She did not care that the essence of fish, spices and curry always lingered on her skin. She lectured me for an hour on the value of money and then sent me back to the department store to return the gift.

My mother was diligent in looking after our household—cooking, cleaning and catering to my father's ongoing demands—but she also worked forty hours a week at a fish cannery, even though she was a strict vegetarian. My father did not approve of my mother working, but with a new mortgage and an extra mouth to feed he was left with no other option. Although he had recently found a part-time position at a plastic factory after he lost his job at the sawmill, money was still tight. But no matter how exhausted or overworked my mother was, she never complained, and if she felt any resentment toward Satinder, she did not divulge her feelings.

After Satinder had been in the country for more than five months, the only English she had learned was *"hallo, see joo, gud bye"* and *"stuped."*

My mother decided it was time for her to attend high school. "If she's going to s-s-survive in this city she has to l-l-learn English. She can't live off of us f-forever!"

When Satinder arrived home after her first day of school, she threw her notebook on the table. "*Kuttay goray*!" she yelled and began cursing white people in the same manner my father did.

Apparently she had been called a Hindu and a Paki, and she was furious. "I'm not a Hindu, and I'm not from Pakistan. I'm a Sikh! And why are these stupid people referring to us by religion? These *goray* don't even understand that we are Indians from the state of Punjab!"

"It doesn't matter what you are," said my father. "It's what you're not that matters! And just be thankful you didn't understand everything they called you."

I put my arm around Satinder's shoulders as my mother had often done to me when I had been bullied at school.

"Here, have some hot m-m-milk," my mother said. "It'll make you feel b-b-better."

Satinder took the mug from my mother and quickly wiped her tears away. It occurred to me that she must have cried many tears when her parents died. She had endured that tragedy alone.

As usual, my parents thought I was too young to listen in on the rest of the discussion and I was sent to my room. But I listened from behind my partly closed door as they tried to console Satinder, though mostly they discussed the unjust realities of this new land we called home.

"Tomorrow will be the same," said my father. "And the next day may be even worse. But we have no choice. You will have to discover for yourself how to be better than them. It's only *apnay lok*, our people, who will give you a helping hand."

At first Satinder was reluctant to go back to school, but six hours of name calling, braid pulling, tripping, pushing, taunting and teasing were far more bearable than the anger in my mother's eyes if she refused. I never knew if her situation improved at school or if she just decided to persevere, but by the end of the year her circle consisted of a handful of Indian girls. These friends couldn't teach each other about western culture since they all had limited knowledge, and they couldn't improve their language skills since they only conversed in Punjabi.

However, Satinder's newfound sisterhood did not last long. The other girls' parents began to withdraw them from school one by one, probably believing, as many Indian families did, that their time would be better spent earning wages at nurseries, berry farms and greenhouses rather than trying to assimilate into Canadian culture. Baksho had often talked to my mother about how Canadian education was restricted to those who were willing to integrate completely into mainstream society. And to her, assimilation meant the loss of Indian culture and the vanishing prospect of having *pure* Indian children.

When my father, who had softened after so many months of seeing Satinder suffer, even mentioned the possibility of Satinder joining the working world, my mother would announce firmly, "I'm not p-p-pulling her out of s-s-school! What will people say? I can hear the *khusar-phusar* now! The gossips will accuse me of not treating Satinder as I do my own daughter. They will say we had n-n-no intention of giving her a better life, that we sponsored her only for the extra income. They'll damn me to hell for treating a m-m-motherless daughter as a s-s-servant!"

After hearing this same diatribe over and over again, my father would retreat and Satinder would return to school. She seemed to descend into a state of depression. Since her friends had left school, she was only allowed to make contact with them by phone when they were able to take time out of their busy ten-to-twelve-hour workdays. She was afraid of all the *goray*, and she was not permitted to socialize with people outside of school. Extracurricular school functions, dances and sporting events were also off limits. School was simply for academic purposes, as my parents and their friends believed that these other activities steered young girls toward corruption.

When Satinder questioned these rules, my mother would say, "Satinder, you're a woman. Women need to learn the responsibilities of a household. There's no need for us to have friendships."

Satinder would rarely put forth her opinion but that didn't stop me. "Mom, we aren't in India. You shouldn't think like that anymore."

"Just because we're not in India," she would say, "it doesn't mean we're not Indian. Living in Canada doesn't make us *goray*."

Once Satinder asked permission to go to the mall to meet one of her working girl friends.

"Women from respectable households don't go gallivanting to the mall. Kiran's father would n-n-never allow it," my mother replied. She never addressed my father by his first name. To do so would be falling into an awful western habit.

"We're not like the *goray* or even like those irresponsible parents who think they're white with their foreign clothes and their bob cuts. They can act as western as they want and they can erode the minds of their children, but every time they look in the mirror they'll be reminded of who they really are. Their skin is b-b-brown and that's something they'll never be able to h-h-hide." It was the same speech she had heard my father giving me so many times. Then she rushed back to the kitchen sink to wash the dirty dishes. The bangs and clatters could be heard throughout the house.

A few months before Satinder's final year of high school she tried desperately to convince my mother to grant her permission to get a job. "Oh please, Aunty *ji*! The extra money will help you." By adding *ji* to Aunty, she hoped to show her respect toward my mother. But she had unknowingly put her hand down the mouth of a cobra.

"We don't want or need your m-m-money," my mother snarled. "How dare you insult us this way, you ungrateful girl! Is this how you thank us f-f-for our k-kindness? Why didn't you just s-s-slap me in the face? It would've been far less d-d-degrading!"

My mother was not one to lose her temper, but when she did, I usually preferred to be out of the vicinity because she did not just tackle the issue at hand but brought up every incident that had disturbed her in the past. Sometimes it went as far back as her childhood. That was the last time Satinder asked for anything.

However, Satinder's silence must have gotten to my mother because when Satinder no longer asked, my mother made her an offer. "Do you know the young family who lives in the basement suite next to the corner store? Their last name is Kang." Without waiting for a response she continued. "They're looking for a babysitter. Are you interested?" My mother did not look up from the counter where her hands were occupied with the *roti* dough.

"Oh please, can I?" I begged, with both my hands pressed together. I had just discovered makeup and my mother would never grant me consent to paint my face, let alone buy the products for me. Babysitting money would secure plenty of pink lipsticks and shimmery eyeshadows, and I would no longer have to sneak out of the house early and meet my *gori* friends in the school parking lot to borrow their cosmetics. And I wouldn't have to endure their teasing when I washed it off before I went home.

"No, n-n-not you, Kiran. I meant Satinder!"

Satinder's face lit up.

But before she could answer, my mother read the expression on her face. "Good. I will talk to Daisy tomorrow."

It had been a long time since I had seen Satinder smile.

The first month she cared for the Kangs' young twins she was only needed for a couple of hours a week, but soon Satinder's evenings and weekends were spent at their home while Daisy Kang worked at her new job as a dishwasher for a restaurant downtown.

Although my parents did not take any of the money Satinder earned, they did encourage her to save. They believed living paycheque to paycheque was not the way to build a life. It was important to suppress one's material desires in the present in order to ensure a successful future. Satinder, however, spent her new income on jewellery and clothes.

Then one weekend when Satinder was given time off, she announced that she wanted to hang out with me. This was unusual because we never spent any time together. Like most teenagers, she felt she was much too mature to have a child three years younger tagging along.

"I got paid yesterday. Do you want to go for ice cream?" she asked.

Although I was curious about her intentions, I accepted the offer. Perhaps she had realized I was growing up and not an embarrassment after all.

"I'll go but you have to ask Mom."

"Fine," Satinder replied.

She wandered over to my mother, pretending to show an interest in the way she cut the vegetables for the cauliflower *sabji*.

"Aunty *ji*, can we please go for ice cream? We won't be gone long."

"You can go, but hurry back. Kiran's father will be home soon. The laundry is piled up. The sinks are overflowing with dishes and he's going to demand dinner as soon as he walks through that d-d-door."

I did not believe my mother's mind had absorbed Satinder's request because she constantly monitored my sugar intake. She was worried that if I put on any more weight at such a young age I would never slim down. God forbid anyone would want to marry a fat girl! But she was inundated with the household chores as usual—and my sweet tooth was grateful.

The closest Dairy Queen was eight blocks away, and by the time we made it through the pouring April rain, I was ready for my treat. I didn't question why Satinder craved ice cream on a day like that. I was too concerned with the amount of fudge the clerk was adding to my sundae.

"Hello...Satinder?" a low voice greeted us from behind.

I turned to see who could have possibly befriended a girl who rarely left her house. He was tall and dark, his teeth were a little crooked and he had one lazy eye. He looked like he wasn't sure if she was the right person.

"Yes, hi," she said almost eagerly. She placed a hand on my shoulder to turn me toward the counter. "Look," she said. "Your sundae is ready."

I pretended to be interested in my ice cream but when they thought I wasn't looking I saw the man quickly slip Satinder a note, and she hid it discreetly in the palm of her hand. He said a hurried goodbye and disappeared in the crowd of fast food patrons, not stopping to make a purchase.

Later I mentioned nothing of this meeting to anyone, not even my mother. I was convinced that she would only draw attention to my inability to keep secrets and then lecture me on the importance of minding my own business. "You're a child," she would say. "There's no need for you to meddle in adult affairs. You'll have plenty of time to gossip when you become a woman."

It was not long after that meeting at the Dairy Queen that my father assaulted Satinder and probably would have killed her if my mother hadn't intervened. But I waited a few more days before I finally mustered up the courage to ask my mother why he had behaved like an animal. In the back of my mind I knew that asking was not a bright idea, but I had to know.

Smack! "*Kasama nu kahni, chup kar*! Sh-shut up! D-d-don't ever ask me again or you'll be the next one to get a b-b-beating. What goes on inside these f-f-four walls s-s-stays within these w-walls. D-d-do you understand?" she asked, giving me a firm shake. Then she announced that I was to give Satinder the silent treatment from now on. In our world Satinder was now a stranger.

I nodded, my mouth too dry to swallow, and turned up the television to drown out the silence.

Several days later my mother made another announcement. "Your father and I are going away for a few days. Mrs. Gill will be staying with you."

If this had been any other time, I would have asked a thousand questions and then I would have pleaded to go with them. But this was different. There had been so much tension in the house lately that the change was welcome. Besides, Mrs. Gill would let me try on her heels and maybe even teach me how to comb my hair all fancy like she did. And I would be able to talk to Satinder again, and she could finally tell me what had happened to make my father so angry. I knew I would never get it out of Mrs. Gill. My parents had most likely crafted some kind of story to settle her curiosity because, if anyone in the neighbourhood, including Mrs. Gill, had discovered the truth, no one would ever confess. They would just circulate the story throughout the community without my family ever knowing. But clearly Mrs. Gill had been their best option. They would never have asked Baksho because she would have talked my ear off trying to find out what had really happened.

The next morning when I woke up I found Mrs. Gill asleep on the sofa. My parents had left in the middle of the night and taken Satinder with them.

They did not return for two long weeks, and by then Mr. Gill had also started staying overnight. But Satinder did not come back with my parents. I was told she had returned to India to live with other relatives, which was strange as I thought the only reason Satinder had come to live with us in the first place was because she had no family in India. But I dared not ask because as far as my father was concerned, Satinder had died on our living room floor that horrific afternoon.

Satinder's Diary

10 July, 1975

When my father abandoned Mother and me, he never thought twice about leaving us at the mercy of his wretched mother. He lives comfortably with the other wife and daughter far away while we live in fear each day that the *churale,* that witch, will put us out on the street.

All these years she has hated us. Mother has to hear daily how she did not bring a sufficient dowry with her when she married that woman's son. But it is not only the size of the dowry that eats away at that greedy old woman; she blames Mother for not producing a boy. They tried for many years before I was born, and he married that other woman only two years later. I guess my mother was out of chances.

Now beating Mother no longer satisfies my grandmother's evil soul. Her tongue has also become the home of Satan. And still Mother says my father is a good man and did not want to re-marry but was forced to. She continues to love this man regardless of how he betrayed her. Her life purpose has been to worship her husband as if he were her lord. When she was very young, her mother imbedded the belief into her brain that not only is she to love him until death separates them but she is also to serve his family even if it kills her. The *churale* never touches me, saving her wrath for my poor mother. She simply pretends I do not exist.

I have always asked why we pretend that everything is fine. Why does it matter so much what the villagers think? Mother always gives the same disheartening speech: "Once a woman is married, she only leaves her husband's home in a coffin. No matter what the injustices, we must be obedient. It is our duty. When we are young, we are our fathers' property, and once we marry, we belong to our husbands and their families. You will understand when you become a wife and mother. A woman's second name is sacrifice."

4 October

I came home from school today to find Mother curled up in a corner of the kitchen. The *churale* had whipped her with a rolling pin after Mother burnt the *kheer* because she was busy dusting the *churale*'s room. I do not know how much more of this she can take. I am not permitted to fetch a doctor. Mother fears that people will talk, which will only result in more beatings. She says that even those who want to help will not.

I must go now. I hear Mother crying softly, hoping I will not notice. I usually cry louder than that when I cling to her for comfort. I try to convince myself that this makes her feel she is still needed and loved. But this time I am afraid to hold her. Her body is the colour of day-old *mehndi* from head to toe.

21 February, 1976

The *churale* struck Mother with a broomhandle today. Mother was feeling ill and had gone to lie down for a while. I sat with her in case she needed anything. She had not been gone longer than fifteen minutes when the *churale* poured a bucket of cold water on Mother's face. Then she dragged her by her hair down the stairs to where the dirty dishes were waiting.

"Who will do this work? Do you think your cheap father is going to come and clean after you? I feed you and you cannot even pick up the dirty dishes. *Kutti,* you bitch!"

"I am sorry, *Bebe ji*. I was feeling nauseous…"

She did not let Mother explain. She reached for the broom that lay next to her foot and smacked her with it. Mother fell to the floor after one blow. Her hands went up to protect her face and she pleaded for the attack to end but it did not. The *churale* threw the broom down, the handle just missing Mother's eye, and began to kick her in the stomach. I tried to stop her. I yelled and screamed only to get the brunt of her anger across my face. Then she picked up the broom, hit Mother one last time and retired to her room for the evening. As soon as she disappeared behind the dark curtain, Mother yelled at me for getting in the way. Afterwards she wiped away my tears and told me I was a strong, brave girl, and I helped her wash the dishes.

I often have dreams of strangling the *churale* in her sleep. I hope I have the courage to do it soon.

4 June

It has been three days since she locked Mother in the storage room. I am not allowed to see her. If she catches me sneaking food to her, the *churale* will lock me up too and leave us both to rot.

Every night I go to the door of the storage room and listen to Mother's whimpers. I call out to her once in a while just to make sure she is still alive. She tells me to go away. I know the *churale* will let her out soon because there is housework to be done. And she will not let Mother die because she does not want her to have an easy way out.

5 June

Mother has not eaten in days. I tried to pry open the door when the *churale* was bargaining with the vegetable vendor across the alley, but I was unsuccessful. She tells me not to worry. She says she is fine, but I know better. I have asked her several times why she has been locked away but she does not answer. Every time I close my eyes I see Mother's bloody, bruised body, her eyes barely open behind the swelling, sitting on the cold, hard, concrete floor.

31 October

If only I had come home from school a little earlier! The villagers say it was a kitchen fire, but I do not believe this story. The *churale* must have tried to burn Mother alive, and somehow things got out of control, and the fire devoured her, too. I know I should not think such thoughts, but sometimes I wonder if it was Mother who tried to kill the old hag. What if she set the fire? But she promised she would never leave me.

I have been staying with Mother's sister and her husband. They have four daughters of their own.

The bastard father is coming tomorrow to take me to Canada. I wish I had died in the fire with Mother.

14 November

I should have known the bastard would not accept me. I am not allowed to reveal my true identity. I must pretend there is no blood bond between us. I am grateful Mother is not alive to see this day. Deep down in her heart, she always believed the bastard loved us. Her life would have been in vain if she had known the truth.

The stepmother, Manjeet, tries to be nice to me—I call her Aunty and him Uncle, greetings we use to be polite to strangers—because I know she will never treat me as her own. I cannot believe he chose her over my beautiful mother. She stutters when she speaks, and she is dark and ugly. She has a short, stubby nose and a long face.

It is quiet here but I do not feel safe, not the way I did in Mother's arms. Although most of our intimate moments were filled with tears and sorrow, at least they were real. This life is a lie. My soul will never be at peace here.

19 December

I have to be careful with my diary. Back home I did not need to worry. The *churale* could not read or write and I had nothing to hide from Mother. But here in Canada, it is different. These people can read Punjabi, and I would never want them to see this. I will have to keep my diary locked in my bedroom or with me at all times. I have no choice. There is no one else to confide in.

6 January, 1977

I keep my distance. Sometimes Kiran acts friendly but I know she would turn on me if she knew who I was. I will never forgive the bastard for leaving me and Mother with that old miserable woman, and now that we are together we are even farther apart. He can say what he wants, but his words cannot hide his actions.

30 April

The *goray* at school are cruel to me. They can never be as callous as the *churale* was to Mother and me but it still hurts. I have never said or done anything to hurt them. Why do they hate me?

1 June

A few of the Indian girls at my school have asked me to sit with them at lunchtime. They seem very nice. For once I feel like I am not alone.

19 September

I met two new girls last week! Lakhvinder lives here with her brother and sister-in-law. They are not kind to her. Mona lives with her family in her uncle's house, but they have overstayed their welcome. It disheartens me to learn that people in Canada are no happier than people in India.

But I do not get to spend much time with any of my new friends. We only get to talk in school or on the phone. The bastard and the stepmother do not think it is necessary for me to socialize. Sometimes I think the people in India are better off. At least they do not even have a hope of a better life.

10 January, 1978

One by one, my dearest friends have left the school. Lakhvinder and Mona do not come to class anymore and I am not permitted to go to work with them. I am very lonely. Although no one ever says anything and the stepmother makes tireless attempts to make me feel comfortable, I know she only does it because she feels sorry for me because she is a mother of a daughter herself. It is a bad omen to give birth to a daughter.

If it had been Mother who had to take in Kiran, she would have fed her first even if it meant she would go hungry. Then there are mothers like the *churale*. She did not need to be kind or loving or considerate because she gave birth to a son. And she forgot that she, too, was someone's daughter. If she did not die in that fire, eventually I would have killed her.

19 February

I am so happy today. I will start my new job tomorrow. I cannot wait to go to sleep and wake up so I can earn money. I will never have to hold out my hand in front of anyone again, not the way Mother had to.

I often wonder how the bastard would feel if he had to beg for money from his wife. But that would never happen. What a man wants he gets, and no matter what the circumstances he will always be superior.

20 February

Today was the first day I felt like I was actually free. The babies are so sweet. I want to have my own some day.

Daisy is very kind. She tells me to make myself at home. I have not seen much of Bittu yet because he is always at work. They seem like such a nice family.

15 May

I know it is a sin, but I think I am in love. When I went to the Kang house today, I walked in on Bittu and his children. He was cuddling them, holding them, laughing and smiling. When he saw me watching, he got up to greet me, and his smile sent chills down my spine. We were only together for twenty minutes but it felt as if I had known him forever.

I always knew that one day someone would come to save me.

18 June

Bittu says I am a very pretty girl, the envy of many on his street. "If I was not married," he said, "I would court you for as long as it took to win your heart."

He is so sincere. I am crazy about him. I wonder if he feels the same way about me. Today I offered to make his lunch to take to his job at the factory. As I was pouring the *cha* into the thermos, I watched him dress through the gap in his bedroom door, and I was so preoccupied that I spilled the tea everywhere.

If only Daisy was not in the picture. She does not treat him with the admiration and love he deserves. And she works so much...I can take care of the babies better than she can.

23 July

I think I have died and experienced my first taste of paradise. I fell asleep on the sofa waiting for Daisy to come home. To my amazement, it was Bittu who gently awakened me as if careful not to chase away my sweet dreams. As he reached over to quietly whisper into my ear, I kissed him. At first he pulled away and stared at me, and I thought I may have mistaken his courtesy for love. But he could not deny the chemistry between us, and he willingly brought his lips to mine.

30 August

Bittu surprised me with a gift of jewellery today. Other than Mother, no one has ever bought anything for me. When the stepmother buys clothes for me, it is just because she feels guilty for taking my father away from Mother, so her gifts do not count!

Bittu told me not to tell anyone who gave me the earrings. He says people will be jealous of our love. He wants me to give myself to him completely. I want him to leave his wife, but he says he feels sorry for her. She has nowhere to go.

6 September

Bittu says if I really love him, I would consummate our love. He does not have the heart to humiliate his wife. She has given him two sons. Despite my wishes for him to leave her, I respect his sense of honour and I know he will never harm me either...because he loves me.

10 October

Today Bittu and I became one. He says his feelings for me are deeper than I could ever imagine. He promises to leave his wife soon.

19 January, 1979

Daisy has cut my hours. She is suspicious. Good! I want her to find out. Bittu does not want me to come to the house anymore so it will be easier to keep our secret from his wife. He will ask his friend, Sukha, to deliver messages to me somehow. He says he will tell Daisy when the time is right. I know it is wrong of me to pressure him like this but I am getting impatient. I can smell her jasmine perfume on his skin.

22 March

Bittu is confused. He is going through such a difficult time. He worries about his children and what will become of them. He says if I really love him I should do as he asks.

13 April

I do not deserve happiness!

How could I have thought that these people would let me live my own life? Bittu was right—they are jealous of our love.

The bastard must have found out somehow. I may have left a note lying around. Perhaps I even hoped we would get caught. But the beating and the cursing the bastard gave me are far less painful than the separation between Bittu and me. I am forbidden to leave the house. I have been phoning his home but Daisy keeps picking up. She is so resentful of me because she cannot give Bittu the love he needs.

27 April

We are in India, the home I once longed for, only now it seems like the foreign land I once dreamed of escaping. The bastard and his wife woke me up early three mornings ago. They did not tell me where we were going, but the bastard insisted I obey or there would be dire consequences.

"We trusted you and you have disgraced us," the bastard told me. "This is your only chance to ask God for forgiveness. You must do as we say or your mother's soul will not rest."

The memory of Mother's life of torture forced me to cooperate.

Although they are being very discreet, I know they have something dreadful planned for me. I have been forbidden to leave my room but through the barred window I can see them talking in the courtyard.

The stepmother has told me to forget about Bittu. She says he does not love me, that he has taken advantage of me. She says the bastard overheard Bittu at the plastic factory bragging to one of his friends about how I satisfied all his manly needs. I do not believe her. She has made up these lies just to break me. She wants to manipulate my mind so I will trust them and not Bittu.

I did not expect this from her. She is the mother of a daughter.

1 May

The evil stepmother left a crimson wedding *lengha* on my bed today. She told me to put it on, wipe my tears and prepare for a new beginning. A life with a man I do not even know. It is to be the end of all my fantasies of a life with Bittu.

5 May

He is nearly forty. His hair has been coloured to hide the grey. He is missing enough teeth to notice and his eyes are deep and dark. The bastard told him I am very reserved, and although he has not said much to me, he has been watching me carefully. Every time he looks at me, he undresses me with his eyes. It makes me want to bathe in disinfectant.

17 May

For days I have been avoiding him. He tries to grope me every chance he gets, but I busy myself with housework so he will not touch me. I pretend to fall asleep before he enters the bedroom, but I wonder how long I can fool him. Last night I could feel his heavy whisky breath upon my face as he rubbed his body against mine.

Only a few weeks ago I was watching Rishi Kapoor romancing Dimple Kapadia in my favourite film, *Bobby*. Bittu sang along to the tunes and danced with me in his living room. And today I am the tormented *woti* of an aging, alcoholic bridegroom. I wonder if the stepmother and the bastard know what they have done to me.

23 May

I have been slipping pills into his drink. I told the village doctor I was homesick and had trouble sleeping and he gave me some tablets. I have conveniently misplaced two bottles of them in the last four days and he gave me more. But I do not know how long I can continue to trick him. The thought of that grotesque man on top of me, inside me, makes me tremble. If his family did not keep such a close eye on me, perhaps I could do something.

This place is hell. There is not even electricity in this tiny house. I go to the well with my sister-in-law every morning to fetch water. The bathroom is an outhouse around the back and is shared with two other families. There is no stove, just a *chulla* where we cook our food over the fire. To purchase any goods, my brother-in-law has to go into the town. I do not even know what town it is because I never set foot outside my village before I left for Canada.

29 May

His family guards my every breath but no one asks me any questions. They wait for me to make the first move.

Unfortunately, my new bridegroom is losing patience.

5 June

He must have become immune to the pills. I lie in bed as if a corpse in a coffin, his body too large for me to push away, my cries and screams unheard. I close my eyes and hold my breath in hopes I will pass out or at least reach the point of numbness.

18 June

It is the same thing night after night. In exchange for three meals a day and a roof over my head I sacrifice my body to a drunk. I want to destroy him before he annihilates the rest of me.

23 June

There was a wedding in the village today. I was allowed to go as long as my sister-in-law accompanied me. Suddenly I remembered the story

Mother told me when I was just a little girl. We were on our way home from a neighbourhood wedding that day, and I told her to forget about the bastard and to take me away from the *churale*. I begged her to take me to her parents' house. She had not returned to her maternal home since she married the bastard and no one had come to visit her in all those years. That was when she had scolded me and forced me to listen very carefully to the folklore from her hometown, a tale about a girl named Mehndi.

> One day thousands of years ago a little homeless girl was caught stealing from the glass palace of an evil raja who tormented and killed innocent villagers. This raja gave orders for the girl's hands to be cut off. Her mother begged him to forgive her daughter. She pleaded with him to take her life instead, but he would not listen. The whole village was forced to watch as the girl's hands were amputated. The girl, too weak to withstand the shock, died in her mother's arms.
>
> The mother held up her daughter's two little hands and cursed the raja's family for eternity. The raja had stained the soul of a mother with the colour of her child's blood and would not be forgiven by the Gods. He had stolen the right of a mother to see her daughter as a bride and the same punishment would be bestowed upon him. Never would a member of the royal family see the day their daughters would be adorned with *mehndi*. And if a daughter of the raja did happen to survive her birth, she would be confined within the four glass walls of the palace. She could never leave because in the real world she would die.
>
> At first the evil raja laughed and dismissed the curse, but soon he realized that the woman's premonition had come true. His wife gave birth to seven daughters, and not one of them lived beyond a few minutes.
>
> The raja had never been defeated and would not publicly bow his head in front of a poor and helpless woman. He commanded she remove the spell, and when she would not reverse her decision, he ordered that she be put to death.
>
> One year after her execution the raja's wife gave birth to a baby girl. The girl survived for days and then weeks. But the raja knew very well that the curse had not been broken. He knew that his daughter would never be able to marry and leave the palace. He

chose to name her Mehndi.

The raja managed to keep the girl inside at all times, but as she grew older, it became difficult to stifle her curiosity. She watched the other girls playing outside the palace, but when she asked the raja if she could join them, he would tell her that, although she could see through the glass walls, what existed beyond them was only an illusion. She was forbidden to go outside.

But Mehndi did not listen. Late one night when everyone was asleep, she slipped past the raja's chamber and through the front gates. But she was stunned to see what lay before her. It was not as she had imagined. All that she had admired from inside the palace must have been a hallucination. The land was barren, almost desert-like and there were no signs of life. She looked back, hoping to return to the palace, but she saw the raja's men locking the gates behind her. She banged on the bars, screamed and yelled, but the raja did not come out to rescue her. He had turned his back on her perhaps the very moment she went astray because the raja knew that only bad things would happen to his palace if he allowed her to return. Mehndi sat outside the palace walls day and night, cold and hungry. And then one day she just vanished. Some said wild beasts dragged away her withering body, tearing it apart bit by bit. Others believed the demons beneath the earth swallowed her up. All that is known for sure is that the raja never forgave her for disobeying him.

I was not impressed with Mother's story. I thought it was a silly fairytale that made no sense. I told Mother it was the raja who should have been punished, not Mehndi. He was the reason why the poor woman's child had died and why he had been cursed. Mother had shaken her head and told me that kismet could not be rewritten. It is women who pay for their own mistakes and for those of their ancestors, not the men. And women who do not oblige and neglect their duties ruin all they leave behind and destroy all that is still to come.

5 August

I think I am pregnant. What if it is a girl? I am very unlucky. I will not give birth to an innocent daughter who will live the same fate as me. If I leave this world before she enters, no one will ever notice.

Mother was right. A woman's second name is sacrifice.

Sunday Langar – 1979

The brightly decorated temple in the heart of Little India was a converted church. On the main floor the worshippers sat shoulder to shoulder, men on the right and women on the left, cross-legged, heads covered, all deeply immersed in prayer. In the communal kitchen in the basement, Baksho, Mrs. Gill and a few of the other faithful devotees from the neighbourhood prepared the afternoon *langar*, the free vegetarian meal.

"That *roti* is burning, Mrs. Gill! Where's your mind today?" Baksho demanded.

"Sorry, Baksho *panji*! I've been thinking about Manjeet. Usually she's the first one to help in the kitchen, but she hasn't been coming to the *gurdwara* lately. And her daughter Kiran hasn't been attending my classes."

"If anything was the matter, would Manjeet not tell you?" Baksho inquired as she placed another *roti* on the *dhava*. "I thought you two had become close friends."

"Hurry up, *panjis*!" yelled Prakash Kaur from the *langar* hall where she had served her last *roti* to an elderly gentleman seated at the table. Prakash Kaur referred to all women as her dear sisters.

Prakash Kaur's family had immigrated to Canada when she was a teenager. Now, although she was ten years younger than Baksho, her presence was strongly felt in the community. Well respected and a true devotee of the Sikh faith, she had all the qualities of a virtuous woman: she was honest, kind, helpful, sincere and content. Prakash Kaur was a good wife and mother. Her best trait, however, was her ability to keep herself detached from the soap operas in which Baksho and the other women indulged. And perhaps it was this reluctance to engage with these women and their dramas that made her unpopular with Baksho's crew.

"Since Prakash Kaur's husband has become the president of the *gurdwara comaity,* she's become so bossy. What an attitude! She thinks she's the maharani of the *gurdwara*!" Baksho laughed at her own joke and then turned the burner on the stove down so Prakash Kaur would have to wait longer to serve the rest of the devoted temple-goers who had started pouring into the hall. Baksho smirked as she prepared the dough to roll out the next *roti*. "Actually, Mrs. Gill, I didn't really want to say anything, but I heard some *khusar-phusar* about that girl who was staying with Manjeet."

"Really? Like what?" Mrs. Gill tossed her head so that her long, layered and feathered hair would move away from her face. She then gently pushed the bangs off her forehead with the back of her hand, exposing her finely tweezed eyebrows.

"You're trying to fool me, Mrs. Gill. I know you know everything so I'm not going to say anything or later everyone will be saying that Baksho likes to gossip." Baksho's face had turned cherry red and it glistened with sweat from the heat of the stove. She stopped rolling the dough to re-fasten her apron around her large waist.

"No, really! I don't know anything, Baksho *panji*. Manjeet is very private. She doesn't breathe a word about her family life. I only know that a while back she asked me to look after Kiran because they took that girl...what was her name?"

"Satinder!"

"Yes, yes. That girl Satinder to India to arrange her marriage. They're such good people. These days no one does so much for strangers. They took the girl in, took care of her and then found her a nice match." Mrs. Gill transferred the *rotis* from the counter to the empty basket Prakash Kaur had placed next to the stove while they were immersed in conversation.

"You're so trusting, Mrs. Gill! I heard that Daisy Kang's husband..." Baksho's voice trailed off as she saw Prakash Kaur returning for the basket.

Mrs. Gill touched her swollen belly discreetly. She was still in the first trimester and had not told anyone that she was expecting her second child as she did not want anyone to jinx her. She already had a year-

and-a-half-old daughter, who she had sent off with her in-laws, months earlier, on an extended trip to India. And no one, not even Baksho, had noticed that she had been wearing a silk *sharara,* a tunic paired with pleated flare pants, to places other than the *gurdwara.* In fact, no one had seen her in a miniskirt for weeks.

"Don't make any more *rotis,*" Prakash Kaur directed. "I think this should be enough for now. You ladies should go and eat, too. You've done lots of service to others today." The women sensed the sarcasm in Prakash Kaur's voice. She had often been heard to say that God would hear their prayers sooner if they spent more time singing hymns rather than dissecting the lives of their neighbours.

Baksho and Mrs. Gill washed their floury hands and went to sit at the most distant table in the room. The only interruption here would be from the servers who would visit them occasionally with *daal* and other dishes.

"*Lorra, aini mirch*! It's so spicy!" Mrs. Gill said, motioning the water boy to hurry over to her table. "Someone really needs to give Prakash Kaur some cooking lessons. Just because her husband is president, it doesn't mean she can do whatever she wants with the food. And we can't even complain. The last time I mentioned there was too much salt in the potato and pea *sabji,* she made me come with her at five in the morning to prepare it."

Ignoring Mrs. Gill's complaints about the food, Baksho continued the conversation she had begun earlier. "As I was saying," she began, adjusting her parrot green *dupatta* over her outdated beehive hairdo, "that Satinder girl, she was having an affair with Daisy's husband. And I heard she was also pregnant with his child. Apparently she'd moved right into the Kangs' house. She and Bittu would make Daisy sleep on the floor of the bedroom while they did God knows what on the bed!"

"That's disgusting!" Mrs. Gill shook her head. "I just don't believe it!"

"It's true! Now would I lie to you in the house of God?" Without waiting for a reply, Baksho carried on. "Of course, someone else told me that Manjeet was the one who put the girl up to it, and when the girl couldn't take the torture anymore, she returned to India to live in an ashram." She paused then added, "I don't really believe the bit about Manjeet though—she's not *that* kind of lady. But only God knows the truth."

"It's hard to believe such uncivilized people are able to get visas to live in this country these days!" Mrs. Gill shook her head again and waved the boy serving the water back to their table.

"Ah, Mrs. Gill, you come from a cultured family like my own. You're not one of these *unpar lok*, these uneducated people. You're too sophisticated to understand the goings-on in this village-mentality neighbourhood."

Mrs. Gill shushed Baksho when she noticed Indu and her daughter, Nikky, headed in their direction, food trays in hand.

Indu lived right across the street from Baksho, and hers had been the first wedding Baksho attended when she came to Vancouver. The bridegroom had been Indu's older brother's best friend, and when her parents learned he was preparing to go to Canada, they had accepted the *rishta,* the wedding proposal from his family. Everyone, including their parents, believed the union had been arranged, but Indu and her husband knew different. They had been writing each other love letters since she was in the ninth grade. Once her fiancé was settled in his new country, he had sponsored her and they got married shortly after she arrived.

But although Indu was clearly cherished by her husband, she was plagued by despair because she could not give him sons. At the age of thirty-five, with the burden of four daughters, she looked as if she was in her mid-forties. She was very thin, her face sunken and sallow, and permanent darkness encircled her eyes. No one could remember the last time they had seen her laugh.

"*Sat Sri Akal,* Indu." Baksho greeted her neighbour with the most welcoming of smiles.

Nikky was so busy scanning the area for space at some other table that her over-filled tray had become a mish-mash of buttermilk and *daal.* But before she had a chance to bolt and sit with the other teenage girls at the table parallel to the young men, her mother directed her to the seat next to Mrs. Gill.

"*Kuray,* Indu, have you spoken to Manjeet lately?" Mrs. Gill's attempt at a subtle approach failed when her spoon slipped out of her hand and landed on the floor. She was not yet a professional gossip like Baksho, though she had been learning quickly since Baksho had taken her under her guidance.

Nikky rolled her eyes and began to eat the food on her tray as quickly as she possibly could. The excessive amount of spice in the *daal* did not seem to bother her.

Baksho patted the girl's head to slow her down, but the greasiness of the coconut hair oil made her remove her hand quickly.

"Her hair is so coarse and so thick and dry that I have to massage the oil right into the roots before I can weave it into a braid," Indu apologized.

Baksho, wiping her hand on her *kameez,* asked, "So, have you heard anything?"

"I have no *time-shime* for anything—first it's work then it's household chores." Indu had acquired the quirky habit of inventing rhyming words to add rhythm to her speech.

This was not the answer Baksho had hoped for.

"Oh, Indu, you're always complaining," Mrs. Gill chided. "We all know you're well taken care of, so why do you do this *maru maru* all the time? You act like your life is so miserable!" Mrs. Gill pulled out her compact to check if any of the mustard leaves from the *saag* had caught between her teeth.

"And you should not complain either, Mrs. Gill," Baksho said. "Everyone knows your husband listens to everything you say. And I hear he is very romantic, too!"

"Well, I'm the mother of daughters," Indu said. "I have to worry about marrying them off one day." She was watching closely as Mrs. Gill reapplied her peach lipstick and placed her compact neatly back into her designer bag.

Baksho made one last attempt to coax Indu and Nikky into her confidence. "You're right, Indu. Daughters are a real problem." She gestured toward the teenagers whose voices had now grown louder. "You should really think about the young people you let Nikky keep company with."

"It's God who writes our destiny, Baksho. He hears all and sees all. Who are we to *judge-vudge*?"

"Speaking of destiny, how is that fortunate son of yours, Baksho *panji*?" Mrs. Gill inquired. "I haven't seen your Jugga in months. He never comes to Punjabi classes anymore. What is he up to these days?"

"We often forget you even have a son, Baksho, you say so little about him." The voice belonged to Prakash Kaur, who was walking past their table with a damp dishcloth in her hand. "He must be in college now, *no*?"

"Yes, yes, my Jugga is such a good son! Soon he will be ready to get married," Baksho replied, loud enough for everyone around them to hear. Prakash Kaur moved on to wipe the table next to them.

"Of course, Aunty, your *munda*, your darling boy is such a *heera*, such a diamond!" Nikky couldn't keep her comments to herself as her mother had instructed, but before she could make any more sarcastic remarks, Baksho began to rattle on about Prakash Kaur's skin-tight *salwar kameez*. Mrs. Gill and Indu continued with their meals while Nikky sat quietly watching the clock. She had finished most of her meal and hidden the rest under her napkin so her mother would not comment when she got up to take her tray to the sink.

Preet – Love

"Hurry up, Nikky. We're going to be late for the *gurdwara*!" my mother, Indu, screamed from the bottom of the stairs.

"I'm coming, can't you hold on for one minute?" I grabbed my *dupatta* and followed her outside to our car. If it were any other Sunday I would have taken my time getting dressed, and my mother would have eventually lost patience and left without me. But this Sunday was special. Baksho's new daughter-in-law would be on display, and I wasn't going to miss that for the world.

As we drove off, I glanced at the house across the street. It belonged to Baksho—or Aunty Bullshit as I preferred to call her—and I could see that she was planning on changing the name of her shop. The delivery truck had unloaded a large sign and left it against the front of her house rather than at her store. What used to be JD Foods and Music Mart was now to be known as JD Meat, Sweets, Music, Gifts and Movie Mart.

"Did you see it? Why would she do that?" I asked

"Yes, I saw it," my mother replied. "It's because she's selling imported sweaters and Beta and VHS movie collections now."

"But it's stupid to give the store a new name," I said.

"She is on her own and has no one to offer her any sensible advice," my mother said.

Baksho's husband had died shortly after I was born, but I was sure he had taken his own life because I could not think of one man who would want to spend his days with her.

But according to my mother, he had gone back to India on a visit and had been killed there. Baksho was told he had died in a car accident after consuming excessive amounts of alcohol, but Mr. Dhillon did not drink. So, unconvinced by the explanation she was given, Baksho had launched her own investigation into the death.

There were many rumours, but the most bizarre yet likely version of what happened to Mr. Dhillon did not come out until years later when one of Baksho's distant relatives immigrated to Canada. This woman told Kamal Brar, who was a regular customer at Baksho's store, that before Baksho married Mr. Dhillon she was betrothed to the son of a *goonda*, a thug, known to have ties with the Indian underworld. But then Mr. Dhillon showed up. At the request of his parents, he had gone back to India to pick out a suitable bride. He spotted Baksho at the wedding of a mutual friend and instantly fell in love. Of course, Baksho's family pounced on the opportunity to send their daughter to Canada. There was no resistance on Baksho's part, and she married Mr. Dhillon in a private ceremony and went to live with him in her in-laws' home in another village. He stayed in India for a month after the marriage but he remained oblivious to his wife's earlier betrothal.

He didn't know that Baksho had been secretly rendezvousing with the son of this *goonda* for several weeks before the announced engagement. Of course, a *love marriage* was unacceptable in those days, but to back out of a commitment was a heinous crime, and that is exactly what Baksho had done.

After Mr. Dhillon sponsored his new wife to Canada, Baksho's parents notified the mobster's family that their daughter had eloped with another man, and since she had disgraced the family, they assured the mobster that she would be killed if she ever returned. Since the wedding had been a small function, Baksho's family was able to conceal her whereabouts for some time. Eventually, though, the facts were revealed and the *goondas* were out for blood. Killing a woman was beneath them so instead Mr. Dhillon became the target. Someone leaked the news regarding Mr. Dhillon's visit to India, and in the middle of the night they raided his village. They stripped and beat him and then they set fire to his house and forced him to watch as his family perished inside it. The fire had not yet died out when they tied a rope around his legs and dragged him behind a horse for miles. His body was never recovered.

Apparently it was to spare Baksho the gruesome details surrounding her husband's death that the police and her family had devised the tale of the accident. But according to Kamal, there was talk in Baksho's village that Baksho had masterminded the conspiracy. They said she wanted to have her husband killed for the insurance money, and once the legalities were out of the way she would send for her former lover. Some villagers went as far as accusing Baksho of infidelity, even referring to her son as a bastard child. But this was all speculation. No evidence was ever found linking Baksho to the tragedy.

A few years after her husband's demise she opened her corner store. My mother said that the loss of her husband had left Baksho feeling alone and insecure, perhaps even resentful that life had dealt her such an awful fate. It was not widely accepted for widows to remarry at that time, no matter how young and especially not those widows who already had children from the previous marriage. So Baksho learned to preoccupy herself with the lives of others, and she became an expert in everyone else's business.

Within moments of her arrival at the *gurdwara,* Baksho's daughter-in-law was overwhelmed by the stares and endless greetings.

"What a beautiful *woti*! Jugga's wife is so pretty! Your Jugga has done well," Prakash Kaur said, following a thorough inspection of Baksho's choice of a bride. Everyone knew Prakash Kaur was pregnant. She tried to cover her stomach with her shawl but such a large bump was hard to hide.

Baksho ignored her comment. It was obvious she didn't like Prakash Kaur. Some of my teenage friends in the neighbourhood believed Baksho had a crush on Prakash Kaur's husband because there didn't seem to be any other logical reason for her to dislike such a sweet and polite lady.

"*Hai aini sohni*! She's gorgeous!" Mrs. Gill exclaimed, while my mother looked on with her mouth wide open in admiration.

"*Nazar na ladayo,*" Baksho said, requesting onlookers not to cast an evil eye on her lovely daughter-in-law.

As though the girl, Preet, was invisible, the women talked among themselves and whispered their concerns for her future. They asked questions about her life, probably hoping to find flaws or faults that would make her beauty more acceptable.

But Preet seemed like a complaisant girl who did not have much to say. When they spoke to her, she answered politely, and when they talked about her, she listened quietly as if it was customary for people to appraise her value.

Preet's new husband, Jagdeep, known as Jugga to close family and friends and as Jack to native English speakers, was a complete disaster. Even though Baksho praised him and referred to him as a godsend, everyone in our neighbourhood knew he was a bad character. Jack was spoiled and disrespectful and had some major problems, although my mother always insisted Baksho could not be entirely blamed for that. She said that raising a child between two very different cultures was challenging when there were *two* parents and Baksho was a single Indian mother. She was never able to spend much time with him because she put in such long hours working to pay the bills.

He started getting into drugs at an early age, and by the time Baksho intervened it was too late. He dropped out of school in tenth grade and couldn't hold down a job. Jack never worked at any one place for more than a few weeks, and even ended up in jail once when he was eighteen. There was a rumour that he became so desperate to support his drug habit, he began to steal from his mother. It would have been no surprise if he had sold every last item in the house. The entire community was apprehensive about letting him into their homes, afraid he would ask for money or worse, help himself.

Baksho told everyone he had gone away to college, but we all suspected she had forced him into a rehab centre. He was still seen drinking and smoking, so it was no wonder Baksho had convinced him to marry. She probably thought a wife would help him settle down. And it would be an arranged marriage in Punjab, *of course*, although she claimed she had been brought many suitable matches but decided she did not want her son to marry a Canadian-born Indian girl.

"These girls have no respect for their culture or their elders. They drink, they smoke, *chi chi*. They don't know how to do housework. They don't want to cook and clean for their husbands. I don't want my son controlled by this kind of clever woman. He needs a *good* girl who will be able to get along with him."

But the truth was, no Canadian-born girl would want him. And the Indian community was so tightly knit, interested parties could get information on Jack from anybody they asked. But a girl from India would love to come to Canada, regardless of Jack's reputation. She would not only worship and obey her husband but also her mother-in-law. I figured Baksho didn't just want a wife for her son, but a robot to control. Preet was the perfect bride for Jack.

After that Sunday at the *gurdwara*, Baksho would often bring Preet on visits to our house. I felt sorry for her. Other than Baksho and Jack, she had no family in Vancouver, and although my sisters and I had nothing in common with the new bride, we would ask the same tired questions about her life in India every time she dropped by, and reassure her that she would grow to like Canada.

"Life was so simple in Punjab," she told us. "Here there's so much hustle-bustle! Everyone is so busy. No one has time for anyone. People work like machines in this place, but back home everyone is content with what they have." And she would repeat this speech over and over, varying the details each time. She spoke so glowingly of her old home in India, and it was obvious she had led a naïve and sheltered life. She possessed no skills that would prove useful in Canada. But I often tried to ask her why she chose to come to Canada if life in her country was so wonderful. Why did she marry Jack? But one of my older sisters would change the subject and I would be left to answer my own inappropriate questions.

As the weeks passed, Preet's appearance began to change, aging from a beautiful new bride to a sombre middle-aged woman. The enthusiasm she expressed about her homeland was now replaced with resentment of Canada. The excitement with which she spoke about her husband in the first days after her arrival vanished at the mere mention of his name. The honeymoon period seemed to be over.

Jack was rarely seen with his wife at the temple or other community events. She seemed to spend all her time with her mother-in-law. Baksho, however, did not seem to mind at all that her daughter-in-law was more attached to her than to her son.

More than a year after her introduction to Canada, Preet finally got pregnant. There had been chatter in the neighbourhood that she was infertile because most brides who came from India arrived not only with their luggage in hand but also with the "seed of love" planted in their wombs. Preet did not seem nearly as sad now that there was a child on the way.

"My grandson is going to be such a loved baby. I can't wait!" Baksho exclaimed.

"Do you know for sure it's a boy?" my mother asked.

"I know it will be a boy. I can feel it, Indu! I've forced Preet to drink three glasses of milk a day since we found out. God will have mercy on my family." She paused for a moment and then added, "I don't know what I'll do if it's a girl."

Baksho snatched up the last *samosa* from the Corelle plate she was holding and shoved the entire thing into her mouth. She was not one to control her appetite. Her five-foot frame carried over two hundred pounds.

"Baksho, these days it's the daughters who look after their parents," my mother said. "Once the sons are married, they become their wives' *chamchas*, they get *wrapped-shrapped* around their fingers." As she spoke those words, I knew she was trying to convince herself, rather than Baksho, about the advantages of having girls. My mother had been cursed with four daughters. My sisters often reminded me that our parents loved them more as I had been their last hope for a son. Instead, I brought colossal misfortune into their lives. Instead of a Ramnik *Singh*, the middle name meaning lion and given to each Sikh boy, my parents had to settle for a Ramnik *Kaur*, a princess—though in name only.

My birth had devastated my mother, causing her to lapse into a state of depression and, according to my sisters, she had spent several weeks in an institution. She wanted to try again for a son but the doctor advised against it. Regardless of his concerns, my parents continued their attempts, but after two miscarriages they gave up. The birth of four daughters was seen as penance for sins committed in a previous lifetime.

"What's so bad about girls, Aunty? You're a female. Do you hate yourself?" I asked, hoping Baksho would spill hot tea on herself. I wanted the burns to scar her as much as her comments about being a girl cut into me each time I heard them.

"It's difficult for women in this world, Nikky. They're always worrying about protecting their reputations. What if they run away with a boy or get pregnant? *Hai Rabba!* Dear God! The shame daughters bring upon their families."

Baksho had ignored the second part of my question, but I was not one to back down even before my mother's disapproval.

"But Aunty, the boys who impregnate these girls or persuade them to run away, aren't they anyone's children? Shouldn't they be disowned the way the daughters are once they've been *ruined*?"

"Silly child, no one blames men for anything. They're never at fault. A woman can do one wrong and she'll be persecuted. A man can do a thousand wrongs, a hundred times worse, and he'll be forgiven."

"But it's always women who point *fingers-shingers* at other women," my mother said, directing her comment toward Baksho. "And women are the first to forgive the guilty men."

Baksho disregarded my mother's comment and turned her attention back to me as she carefully placed her cup next to the plate she had just licked clean. "You'll understand when you're older. When you have a son of your own, you'll realize how dear they are compared to daughters."

"That's bullshit!" I paused for a split second and then added, "You should be ashamed, Aunty! Not for being a female but for being so stupid!"

That was when my mother smacked me across the face and sent me to my room.

"*Satyanaas*! That youngest daughter of yours is going to be trouble, Indu," Baksho said, loudly enough for me to hear as I stormed down the hall to my room. "This is what I mean about girls, especially *Kanayda*-born. They think they know it all. What will happen when she's married and passed on to her rightful owners? What will her mother-in-law say? She'll think you have taught her nothing."

My mother was already furious with me, and Baksho's critical assessment of my behaviour was an implied insult about her inability as a parent. She didn't speak to me for days.

In our community everyone felt it was their business to make sure they knew what was going on with everyone else. The lack of sightings of Jack had heightened people's curiosity. No one, it seemed, had seen him for months. It was said that this was because he no longer associated with members of the Indian community, and my sisters and I began referring to him as a coconut, brown on the outside and white on the inside. Baksho was being quite secretive and did not let out a word regarding his whereabouts, and sympathy for Preet's situation forced the women in our community to keep their comments to themselves. Then, although Preet emanated a healthy pregnant glow, the doctor ordered her to bed rest for the last trimester. Baksho insisted it was just a precaution, but my mother heard that Jack was in jail again. Preet, unable to deal with this type of stress, nearly lost the baby.

Since Jack was not around to help, my mother offered my services to the Dhillon family. "If Preet needs anything, anything at all, don't hesitate to ask. Nikky can come and stay with you after the baby is *born-shorn*. It'll make it easier for you two to have an extra set of hands."

That is something I have never understood about women. In times of need we swallow our pride and do everything to help those who are less fortunate. We will even turn an enemy into a friend. But it is these same people we backstab and gossip about once the difficult times have passed.

Regardless of how I felt about Baksho, my mother left me no choice.

"What'll I do there?" I asked. "I'm just a kid."

"Don't be so selfish, Nikky. You're fifteen. In India girls your age are raising children all by themselves. You need to learn to be responsible. And one day Baksho will be very useful to us. She knows lots of people. Maybe she'll bring us good *rishtas* for you and your sisters. Plus, you can make *cha-choo* and translate if necessary."

"Aunty Bullshit can speak English. She doesn't need me to translate."

My mother dismissed my complaints and hurried me over to the Dhillon's house where Baksho was helping Preet into the car.

"Oh good! You're here, Nikky. Get that overnight bag from the top of the stairs. Quickly, the pain has started."

Yes, the pain had started. I knew it was going to be unbearable sitting with Baksho in the waiting room because I would have to listen to non-stop praise about baby boys. All I could pray for was a quick delivery—for Preet's sake and my own.

Preet's water broke in the car. When I asked Baksho what was happening, she told me she had washed the car earlier and accidentally left the window open. She disregarded the rest of my questions. My knowledge of sex and pregnancy was actually quite vast, but annoying Baksho was fun. When we got to the hospital, the nurses led Preet to a small room and promised to return to check on her. After delivering what seemed like an eternity of rubbish, Baksho asked the nurses if she could join Preet in the room. She was told that it was entirely the patient's decision, but Preet really did not have a say in the matter. She would do as a *good* daughter-in-law would do and abide by Baksho's wishes.

After a while I developed a cramp in my leg from sitting on the hard plastic chair so I went for a stroll around the ward. It had to be short because, if Baksho returned and I was nowhere around, my mother and I would never hear the end of it.

As I walked down the hall, I noticed that all the new mothers looked exhausted. Some were holding newborns, others were nursing and a few were showing off their gifts of joy to visitors. Then, slipping into a room to avoid a nurse who would surely escort me back to the waiting room, I heard a soft whimper coming from behind a curtain.

"It's okay," a man's voice said. "Everything will be all right."

I assumed the woman had given birth to a daughter and I turned away with a taste of repugnance in my throat.

"Don't lose hope," the man continued. "One day we'll be granted a sweet little boy or girl. You'll see."

A sharp pain pierced my body. I was no different than Baksho and her ludicrous stereotypes. This poor woman had just lost her child. My guilt accompanied me back to my seat.

A few minutes later Baksho came bolting down the hall with her arms raised high as if she had scored the winning goal in sudden-death overtime.

"It's a boy!"

Her tears of relief focussed my attention back to the woman in the room. I had not seen her face or heard her voice, but I knew she would make an excellent mother one day. She would recognize a daughter as a blessing.

At the *gurdwara*, I had heard the *granthi,* the priest, say on a number of occasions, "There is delay in the house of God but never darkness. Prayer is the answer."

I visited the hospital chapel before my mother came to get me. I knew she would never approve of me going there. I wished Baksho had been with me to feel that woman's desperation for a healthy child. And I wished my mother knew how fortunate she was. But maybe it was sufficient that I knew.

Preet had not been home from the hospital for more than two hours when the parade made its way to the Dhillon residence. If she had given birth to a girl, the house would have been empty; Baksho and Preet would have been alone, crying on each other's shoulders.

While Baksho greeted guests with a large plate of sweets, Preet admired her newborn as if she had given birth to the heir to the British throne. Although she looked fatter, older and tired, she reminded me of the Preet I had met almost two years earlier at the *gurdwara*.

"Today you can ask me for anything. I will not say no," Baksho announced. "I have reaped the rewards of this long and lonely life." She looked up at the ceiling and closed her eyes.

The absence of the baby's father did not affect the festivities, and the guests were all careful to avoid the subject. I would have been more than happy to bring up the topic myself, but I knew better.

To me it seemed crazy for Preet to want a boy so badly. She expected her son to be her saviour, but giving birth to a son would not solve her problems. A boy would not necessarily bless her with a decent life. We weren't back in India where sons are valued because they can help on the farm and daughters are a burden because they need dowries. Baksho's own son was far from a shining example of success, and who knew how Preet's son would turn out? But it didn't really matter. He had already won half the battle. He was born a boy.

Preet's Diary

February 1, 1980

I saw a picture of him today, my future husband. He is from Canada. He looks handsome and smart. My uncle, the matchmaker, tells me my fiancé owns many grocery stores and a taxicab company. He is a well-brought-up boy, properly versed in Punjabi culture. He respects the values and morals of our country and believes in arranged marriages. He does not even want to see me because he trusts his mother's choice.

Since I was a little girl all I have dreamed of is the day I would be married. Never did I imagine I would marry a successful businessman from abroad.

My girlfriends are all jealous. They say I am lucky because I am fair-skinned. My mother ate a lot of eggs while she was pregnant with me, which is why I am so white. Girls who are dark-skinned are considered ugly, and it is hard for them to find decent husbands. I am very fortunate.

My mother-in-law did not ask me any questions. She just sat there and admired my beauty. She said I would fit right in with the *goray*. She wants me to call her Mummy *ji*.

My uncle tells me my fiancé has fallen in love with my picture. Although we have never met, I have been thinking about what our life will be like together. I know he will love me. I am going to make such a good wife because I know how to do all the housework. I will never argue or get angry with him. I will always listen and do as he says.

February 8

Today was the *mehndi* party. I love every tradition associated with two souls becoming one. It is an old Indian saying, the darker the *mehndi*, the more love one will receive from her husband and mother-in-law. The *mehndi* on my hands has already dried to a dark maroon shade. The intricacy of it is unique and complex. Each flower, each line, signifies the delicate relationship I will have with my husband. It is pretty to look at, but I must be careful not to smudge it or the lines will cross over and the design will turn into one big mess.

Some women get tired of all the fussing over a new bride, but not me. I love the attention. This is the only time, except when I give birth to a son, that I will be catered to by all the men and women of the house.

I am not to do any work because no lines of stress or tension should appear on my face. My wedding day is the most important day of my life so I have to look my very best. If I need anything, all I have to do is ask. My only duty is to look beautiful for my new groom and I do not want to disappoint him.

When I started college, my mother forbade me to study late at night because it would cause dark circles and bags under my eyes. When the electricity went out, which is almost daily in this part of the world, I would finish my homework by candlelight, but my mother would yell at me whenever she caught me. I was forbidden to go outside between ten in the morning and four o'clock because the sun would spoil my complexion. And never mind all the trips to the beauty parlour! My mother's main concern has always been to find me a suitable husband.

The last few days my mother has been reminding me of the strategies for a successful marriage. I am not to call my husband by his first name because it is disrespectful. My mother says if my fiancé wanted a rude wife he would have married a girl from Canada. It is my Indian authenticity he will grow to love. I am to do as he asks. I must please his masculine needs as every wife should.

If he is angry I should not question his behaviour or take it personally. Men work hard and it is natural for them to get upset, but it is my duty as his wife to always support him. And no matter what, I am never to say I am unhappy. A woman's joy lies with her husband's well-being.

If I abide by these rules, I will be able to satisfy my husband and then I too will be content.

Tomorrow my purpose, my destiny, will be fulfilled. It will be my first test as a wife.

February 9

The wedding was fantastic. I only got a glimpse of my husband because his face was covered by the traditional *sehra*. All sorts of flowers and beads hung down from his turban. He is very shy, and he did not respond to the girls when they teased him.

He is also a sophisticated man. Far too sophisticated for the old ways of the east.

I am nervous about the wedding night. My great aunty says it is shameful for women to disappoint their husbands on the first night. My married friend Binu told me not to do anything. I am to let him have his way. That is what Indian men like.

February 10

We are staying in Mummy *ji*'s family's home. Nothing happened last night. My husband was a little tipsy and passed out on the chair in our bedroom. I removed his shoes and unbuttoned his shirt so he could rest more comfortably. In Canada, I think that they must not follow all the little rituals from dawn to dusk that we do here. But the longer we wait the better it will be. Tomorrow I will seduce him. I have saved sandalwood soap just for this occasion. My great aunty once told me that seduction is a powerful tool for women. Men cannot resist temptation.

February 12

He did not speak one word to me all day. Perhaps he is not fluent in Punjabi and therefore he is embarrassed. Mummy *ji* tells me not to worry. He is just a little overwhelmed by all these new faces and traditions. I wonder if she suspects that we have not had sex.

She told me many tales about life in Canada. I cannot wait to see it all. Once I get my visa and join them, she says I will know how fortunate I am to be married to her son. And when he sees me in his own home, he will be able to accept me as his wife.

February 14

I spent the night alone again. He came into the bedroom after midnight and headed straight for the chair. Every night I bathe in sandalwood. I put on the nightgown Binu brought me from her trip to Agra. He still does not acknowledge me. Maybe I am doing something wrong.

February 16

Mummy *ji* senses the tension between us. I think she has discussed me with him, it is the only explanation. He finally spoke to me but it is as if I am a stranger.

Binu tells me women in Canada are forward, even to the point of being aggressive. She says women in foreign countries freely indulge in sexual activities with any man who offers. They have no respect for the sanctity of marriage.

February 20

My husband returns to Canada tomorrow. Mummy *ji* says they will send for me as soon as they can, but I cannot stop crying. I did not cry this much when I left my parents' home for the first time in nineteen years. My husband is my family now. He is my identity. I cannot go back to my parents' house. What would the neighbours say? They will not understand the circumstances and will blame me for being a bad wife. They will talk behind my back. They will speculate that my husband has already divorced me or assume that the dowry was not sufficient. What if he changes his mind and does not send for me? What if my visa is refused? My life will be over. Dear God! How will I face the world? How will I live? My parents will be shamed, disgraced.

April 21

Today it is exactly two months since my *jeevan sathi,* my soulmate, returned to Vancouver. Mummy *ji* has sent several letters. She writes that her son is a very busy man but he sends his love. She says they miss me very much. The house I have never lived in seems empty without me. He sent one letter earlier on but did not express his feelings for me. It was a letter one would write to a sister, not a wife. I tell myself that at least he has not lost all interest in me.

November 12

After so many long months my visa has been accepted. I leave for Canada the day after tomorrow. I can hardly breathe I am so excited.

My family wants to keep my departure a secret because someone may go to the immigration people and make something up and my trip will be delayed indefinitely. My mother says that jealous people's hearts burn when great things happen to someone else so it is always better to hide the joy and emphasize all that is going wrong so no one will jinx our good fortune. But soon I will be reunited with my love. Soon I will be happy.

November 16

Mummy *ji* and my husband came to get me at the airport. There he stood waiting for me with a bundle of bright white flowers. Mummy *ji* ran and embraced me. My love handed me the flowers with a subtle smile but turned to frown at his mother. He must have been embarrassed. True Indians are mortified to show affection in public because it is considered improper. He was so sweet to bring me flowers. He did not need to show how much he missed me. I am his wife. I can sense these things.

He smiled a lot on our drive home. I stared at his eyes in the rearview mirror. Mummy *ji* sat in the front on the passenger side. She must have forgotten that I should sit there now. I guess it was a force of habit for her to sit next to her son.

Everything in Canada is different from what I imagined. The picture Mummy *ji* painted was all sunshine and serenity, but on my first day in Vancouver I was welcomed by a rainstorm and rush hour traffic.

November 21

I was able to get a telephone connection to India today after trying for days. My family is thrilled that I am in Canada.

November 30

Two weeks have passed, and although I have familiarized myself with the Canadian culture, my husband is as much of a stranger as he was on our wedding day. When I expressed my concerns today, he said, "I do not even know you." He did not know me when he married me either, so why did he agree to it?

December 2

He has deceived me all along. He is not a successful businessman. He is a taxi driver. He does not even own the taxi. What can I do? He is my husband now.

December 10

He comes home drunk—that is, when he chooses to come home at all. He is angry with me but I do not know why. He tells me to go back to my country. We have never shared a bed and he does not want to share his home with me either. I undressed myself and stood firmly before him. He spit on me and walked away.

I have tried to be the modest wife I was taught to be. Perhaps someone's evil eye has jinxed my marriage. If marriages are arranged in heaven, why has the universe been so unfair to mine? What kind of unforgivable sin did I commit in my past life that I cannot be blessed with the love of my own husband?

When my parents call, I dare not tell them their princess has become a prisoner of loneliness. It would only hurt them to learn of my misery. And what could they do anyway? They are parents of a daughter. They are as helpless as I am.

December 19

Mummy *ji* confessed her sins today. She broke down into tears after he stormed out this morning because I offered him mittens to keep his hands warm. I guess her conscience has gotten to her.

She told me she forced her son to go to India and get married. She bribed him with a car and money and anything else she could afford, so he promised his mother he would go through with the wedding and bring home a wife.

I had no mercy, no forgiveness for this woman. I wanted to scream at her, although my mother always told me that silence is divine. Only when the truth became unbearable did I finally lash out at her. She continued to weep as if she has been the one to suffer the greatest of injuries.

"I am sorry," she said. "I thought he would change after the wedding. I thought that once he was exposed to a true Indian wife who would love and look after him, he would abandon all his addictions." She kept repeating this pathetic excuse for her actions. She thought her son would change after he realized his new responsibilities. So she decided to push me into this pot of boiling water. How dare she play with my life, my future? Does she not know what she has done? In hopes of saving her son, she has destroyed my innocent life.

"Who were you to play God? He will never forgive you. You will go to hell for what you have done!"

I had left the confines of being a good daughter-in-law. There was no turning back. My hatred and resentment for this woman grew deeper by the second.

"Please do not speak ill of me," she said. "I have loved you like I would my own daughter."

Would she really have wanted her own daughter to marry a man like her son? I think not. But maybe, since this lady has no respect for women, she has loved me like a daughter. Maybe she would have done the same to her own daughter. She went on and on about how her son may still change. She insisted that it was my duty to stand by my husband no matter what his faults because that is what Indian women do. She told me to make the best of the situation. She knows very well I will not leave. Where will I go? We Indian girls never return home once we are married since there is no greater shame for a parent than to have a divorced daughter move back in with them. A husband who has no respect for his wife is far better than no husband at all.

My mother used to tell me that every household is respected based upon the self-sacrificing reputation of a woman. I am beginning to think that she was right.

January 28, 1981

Although I want to hate her, I cannot. She treats me well. But I do not think I can ever forgive her. My marriage is a constant reminder of what I will live through until the day I die.

Perhaps if I could have my husband's child, he would love me. My great aunty once told me that when a woman's body can no longer keep her man at home, she must produce his son. In India motherhood measures the value of a woman. A woman who cannot give birth to sons may as well not exist. Binu told me tales of women who could not have children. When their prayers went unanswered, some of them turned to witch doctors, and the witch doctors were able to impregnate women diagnosed by modern medicine as infertile.

March 1

I wish I had died before God brought this moment upon me. He brought another woman home today. A *gori*. I pounded my fists against his chest and he slapped me across the face.

He took the girl into our bedroom. I immediately phoned Mummy *ji* at the store. To my dismay she was not surprised. Instead she told me to stay calm and not say anything. She would deal with it when she came home.

I banged on the bedroom door but they turned the music up to drown my cries.

March 12

Mummy *ji* told me not to mention my husband's behaviour to anyone. She says if the story gets out her reputation will be destroyed. I cannot believe this is happening.

June 22

She talked to someone today. Someone who can help me! He lives outside the city, about an hour away. She has heard stories about his miraculous happenings, but I cannot tell anyone. She will only get him to help me if I keep quiet.

July 7

We went to see Swami *ji* this evening. We had to cross over the orange bridge—the Port Mann Bridge, I think it is called. The farm was hidden behind large trees and we had to drive up a long, narrow gravel driveway to get to the house. A young boy, maybe about fifteen, answered the front door. He stepped out, quickly closing the door behind him so we could not see inside. He did not say a word and led us around the house to the backyard. He then motioned for us to follow him past the strawberry rows toward an old red wooden barn. As we crossed the pavement, he directed us to walk ahead of him. Before we got to the door, I turned to look back, but the boy was already headed back toward the house.

Swami *ji* sat in the middle of the bleak building on a chair that was covered in a yellow silk fabric. In front of the chair were white bed sheets laid out in a perfect square on the cold concrete floor. Mummy *ji* bowed at his feet and sat down directly in front of him. I nervously followed her lead and did the same.

Swami *ji* was not as I pictured him. He looked no more than thirty. He had curly dark hair that sprawled around his shoulders and blended into his dark robe. He was clean-shaven but wore a black mark of what looked like ash in the middle of his forehead. I could make out that he was wearing light blue jeans and bright new running shoes under the robe, which merely reached his ankles. He was very calm and straight to the point after he received Mummy *ji*'s five-hundred-dollar deposit. First he read my palm. He examined it closely and wrote down numbers and letters in a language I could not interpret. Then he drew a chart on the page and nodded his head several times. All this was done in silence. Mummy *ji* fidgeted with her *dupatta* while he analyzed my situation.

After twenty minutes he spoke his first words. "I can help you," he said, "but I am afraid you will have to sacrifice much."

Although I felt uneasy about giving up what little I had, I asked him to continue.

"You have two choices. I can change the ways of your husband and you will live happily as man and wife. But you will never be able to have children."

My mouth dropped open and Mummy *ji* stood up in objection. Swami *ji* waved his hand and motioned her to sit down again.

"Or you can have a child, only one child, but you will never receive the love of your husband."

Mummy *ji* pressed another fifty-dollar bill into Swami *ji*'s hand. As we got up to leave, I noticed a shelf in the far corner covered with plants of some sort and a bunch of empty bottles, but before I could examine anything else she rushed me out of the building.

August 2

What I would have done to have my husband love me. But what choice do I have? Mummy *ji* says if I cannot have children, I will never be a complete woman. She says society will taunt me. Eventually my husband will get frustrated and go elsewhere to find a woman who can give him a child to carry on his name and then he will never return home. Men only love women if they give them sons.

"I know my son. He will never stay with you, spell or no spell, if you cannot bear his children. Fertility is a status symbol for men. It proves their masculinity."

Mummy *ji* has reassured me that this is the path I must choose. She has told me a child will bring happiness to this household. According to her, one must learn to manipulate the situation and use it to its fullest advantage.

September 18

Upon Swami *ji*'s request, I have provided him with hair from my husband's comb, a recent picture of him and an item of his unwashed clothing. The rest is up to me. I never thought I would believe in this *jadu toona*, this voodoo stuff, but I am desperate. So much for having faith in God! I think He has forgotten about me, anyway.

If mother ever knew I had chosen the route of witchcraft over the path of God, she would never forgive me. But if black magic has found its way here to this new land, it must have some power in it. And I have nothing left to lose.

September 30

For the first seven days I must drink a concoction of goat's milk and a special serum of herbs. This should be done before sunrise. Between the eighth day and the next full moon I am to chant a mantra which Swami *ji* has provided. It is a bunch of mumbo jumbo but I will do as he wishes. Every Tuesday and Thursday until the full moon I am to feed my husband a different potion. I am then to tie a black thread around the muffler of my husband's car. This will lead him back to me. The toughest part is placing the red cloth under his pillow without him noticing. Swami *ji* says I cannot give up. Every step must be followed down to the last detail.

On the day of the full moon, Swami *ji* will return my husband's belongings to me and I must bury them in the backyard before midnight. According to Swami *ji*, I will conceive within the first seven days after the full moon. During that week I too must take some herbs once a day in the evening. Dizziness and hallucinations are side effects but this is nothing compared to the tests one must pass to be a good mother. During these last stages, Swami *ji* has asked Mummy *ji* to stay away from the house. She is also to leave her house key in the garden. This will allow good luck to flow into our home. But Swami *ji* has warned that no one in the household can attend any religious institutions or prayer services while the ritual is taking place. And we must remove every religious symbol from the house or it will weaken his efforts. Mummy *ji* has reassured him that we will be vigilant.

Once the baby is born, Mummy *ji* will give Swami *ji* two thousand dollars. He donates all the money to the poor because God has been so kind to him for helping those who are troubled. Swami *ji* has been blessed with a luxurious ten-thousand-square-foot home, a brand new Lincoln and a speedboat.

November 14

The last seven days have been a blur. I did as Swami *ji* asked and followed every step with extreme caution. I have made no mistakes. I am not sure whether it was a dream or if it was real, but I am sure my husband was in my bed. When I woke, still a little dizzy and fatigued, he was not there.

November 29

My husband is as distant as always. Mummy *ji* spends every waking moment when she is not at the store in the *gurdwara*, praying for a miracle. In time I will have a son and then I will be happy. I have been a noble wife and daughter-in-law. Soon I will reap my reward.

December 21

Today the floodgates of my eyes have once again been opened. These, however, are tears of pure joy. I am pregnant! Finally I will have someone who will belong to me. Someone who will be a part of me forever. I am indebted to Swami *ji* for a million lifetimes.

My mother once told me that a woman has two purposes in life. One is to get married and serve her husband. The other is to conceive his children. Other than the birth and death of a woman, these are the two most significant events that lie between. Raising a child will be my last chance at completeness.

I pray that this child is a boy. If I produce a son, Mummy *ji* will continue to provide for me. For a grandson she will take on my burden.

January 14, 1982

My husband denies the child is his. His mother tried to explain but he would not listen. He packed his bags and left for good. Mummy *ji* has been crying for days now. She says God has punished her for sins she has no knowledge of, and she believes she is innocent in all this. She says she sacrificed my happiness for the love of a grandchild. But still she thinks she is the victim.

May 26

Mummy *ji* took me to see Swami *ji* today. He is confident that I will give birth to a boy. My son will pave our way to a bright future. I will finally have my own identity.

Sunday Langar – 1984

"No one's going to tell us the truth straight out about what is happening between Preet and Jack!" Nikky whispered to the other girls sitting next to her at the table in the far corner of the *langar* hall. They could see the older women working away in the kitchen.

"They're probably talking about Baksho right now! Maybe they know who filed for divorce first! I wonder who will get to keep the kid," Kiran said.

"Well, let's go and hang around the sink and pretend we're doing the dirty dishes. One of them has to know the real story!" Raj, Prakash Kaur's daughter, although much younger than her two companions, was usually the one with all the bright ideas.

But before the girls got up to make their way to the kitchen, they noticed Jessy headed in their direction.

"Quick, pretend we don't see her!" Kiran looked away and Raj turned her back.

Jessy could see that the girls were trying to ignore her so she changed direction and headed for a different table.

"Pretend we don't see who?" Nikky asked.

"Jessy, Rani's daughter," Raj replied.

Although Kiran and Raj did not approve of Jessy, their mothers had welcomed her mother, Rani, into their lives. Rani also had only daughters. She had once been a beautiful woman, but by the time her youngest daughter turned two, Rani had been diagnosed with vitiligo. At first the white patches were visible mostly on the back of her neck and her chin, and she tried to conceal them with layers of foundation and various other types of makeup, but none of it did much to hide the discolouration. Then she had taken to covering her head with a *dupatta* at all times and shading her face whenever possible. Rani's physical imperfections along with her inability to give her husband a male heir had left her lonely and him resentful. The beautiful woman he had taken responsibility for was now just an ugly burden.

"I don't like that girl," Kiran whispered to Nikky as they passed the table where Jessy and her little sister had opted to sit. "They've been here for almost two years and she still speaks with that phony British accent. She should have lost it by now!" Before Jessy's family began calling Vancouver home, they had lived in the area of London, England, known as South Hall.

"Maybe you just don't like her because her mom looks all weird," Nikky suggested. "Or is it because she's been allowed to cut her hair short and you still have to keep yours in a braid?"

Kiran did not feel the need to respond.

"*Lorra Aagaya*!" Mrs. Gill called. "I can't believe you girls have decided to come and help all on your own! *Ajj ta mee payu*!" The other women working in the kitchen laughed at Mrs. Gill's sarcastic comment and went back to their conversation in Punjabi.

Raj smiled at the ladies and pushed the other two girls toward the sink.

"The sink is too far from the flour counter," Kiran complained in a whisper to Nikky. "And with Prakash Kaur chanting *Satnam Vaheguru* at the top of her lungs, we won't be able to hear what they're saying. That woman never gets tired of praying!"

Kiran had forgotten that Prakash Kaur's daughter, Raj, was standing next to her, but although Raj heard her, she was too embarrassed to respond.

"Well, Kiran has a point," Nikky said to cut the tension.

Raj laughed. "You're married now, Kiran, and you have a son, so you've risen in status. Why don't you go over there and roll out those *rotis* with the other women like a *good* Punjabi bride! No more dish duty for you."

Kiran's mother had not wanted her to go astray. After the trouble with Satinder, Manjeet had not let her daughter out of her sight. She drove her to school, although it was only minutes away, and picked her up in the afternoon, sometimes having to arrange her shifts so she worked nights. The *gurdwara* had also been off limits, partly because Manjeet was afraid that Kiran could be influenced by the other Indian kids but mostly because she did not want to answer Baksho's questions. Manjeet had only attended functions when absolutely crucial. But once Kiran was married, Manjeet was at peace and she and her family had slowly made their way back into the circle.

"I wish!" Kiran snapped. "Getting married at eighteen doesn't exactly make me an expert at *roti* making. I can't even make a round *pera*." She shrugged in frustration.

"Yeah, but didn't you want to get married?" Nikky, only two years her junior, knew her day would come soon as well.

"I didn't have a choice! After that business with Satinder, my parents became so strict it was like being in prison. I only agreed to get married so I could get out of the house. At least I have a little more freedom now. My in-laws are way more lenient than my parents. And it's a good thing my first-born is a boy. That's why everyone treats me so well! And I'm one up on my sister-in-law, too!" Kiran looked pleased. Marrying Onkar had been a good decision.

Nikky rolled her eyes. There was no point in saying anything. She knew the battle for equal rights was lost for her generation.

"I'm not getting married!" Raj swirled her *dupatta* around as if she was a socialite in a television soap opera. "I'm going to be rich and famous!"

"Yeah right, Raj! As if that'll ever happen!" Nikky teased. "Your parents are probably going to send you away to some *gurdwara* camp for the rest of your life! I'm surprised you're not baptized yet. You would look good in a turban!"

"But I'd hate to be you, Nikky! Any day now your parents are going to be on your case!" Kiran snatched a food tray from the hand of a child who had approached them and cleared the leftovers into the trash carefully, hoping not to spray any *daal* on her embroidered satin *kameez*.

"Now that all my sisters are married into good families, my mom is a lot happier," Nikky replied. "She doesn't sleep as much and she's even cut down on some of her pills."

Kiran laughed. "Yeah, I heard Baksho telling my mom that your mother was on drugs!"

But Nikky had shifted her entire focus to the women standing by the stove. "Guys, we have to get over there before Baksho arrives. That woman can dish it out, but when it's her turn, you can't pry her thin little lips open with a set of pliers."

But Kiran's laughter had drawn the women's attention. "*Anvay dand kadi jandian*. Why are you laughing so much?" Mrs. Gill was sounding more and more like Baksho as each day passed. "We don't need to count your teeth! Get over here and help us! Who's going to marry useless girls like you? Don't you know that girls are only supposed to smile, not laugh like donkeys?"

"These girls just don't understand, Mrs. Gill, that the more they laugh now the more they will c-cry later!" Manjeet added. "That is what my mother always told me."

"Go quickly, before Miss Perfect changes her mind." Kiran urged the girls forward so they could place themselves strategically within the circle at the flour counter.

"As I was saying, I can't believe Trudeau will not be our prime minister anymore." Mrs. Gill was speaking to an audience who had absolutely no interest in politics but they still nodded in agreement. "When he announced his retirement a few days ago, I was so sad. He was so good for *apnay lok*. And he is such a nice man. Because of him, we can live in this country with respect! Our religion, our culture, our rights, he has made sure that we are protected!"

"Yes, life is a little easier now, not as bad as it was ten years ago!" Manjeet said, recalling the violence and vandalism that had affected their lives just a decade earlier.

"*Kuray,* Nikky, where's your mother today?" Rani inquired. She was no longer working weekends as a cleaner at the airport and was happy to attend the *gurdwara* again on Sundays.

"She's gone to California for my cousin's wedding," Nikky replied. Her eyes were fixated on Rani's chin.

"It's good to see Indu in better spirits these days. Before she was always complaining and crying. And once you're married, Nikky, all her burdens will be lifted! She'll finally be able to enjoy her life!" Mrs. Gill was trying to get a glimpse of her reflection in Manjeet's new large-rimmed eyeglasses.

"Mrs. Gill, can you pass the *atta* this way!" Raj waited for a minute then, since no one had bothered to acknowledge her request, she reached past the women to get the dough.

Within minutes the women had returned to their original conversation in Punjabi, the one they had been engaged in before Mrs. Gill had suddenly switched to English and the subject of Pierre Trudeau's retirement. The women were so certain the girls did not understand the Punjabi language beyond simple conversation that they did not shade their version of the truth.

"I heard Preet has moved out and she took the boy with her." Manjeet divulged the little information she had gleaned from the limited resources where she worked. "She's filed for divorce but there's been no response from Jugga."

Rani nodded in agreement. "Yes, that's true. Someone was saying that Preet is thinking of getting re-married and Baksho is allowing it as long as Preet gives up the boy to her. In the meantime Preet's gone to live with her dad's cousin in Winnipeg."

"That's because Jugga's living in that skid road area, you know, that Hastings Street place," Mrs. Gill said.

The patting, rolling and flipping of dough all came to a halt as Mrs. Gill received inquiring looks from all those surrounding the counter. Mrs. Gill grabbed the spatula and turned toward the stove. It was obvious that she had not sworn undying loyalty to Baksho. In this circle it was every woman for herself.

"Preet's marriage is scheduled for next year," Rani said to lighten the tension.

"Already!" Prakash Kaur could not help but overhear. However, she had no intention of partaking in the gossip. "I mean, there's so much to do here at the *gurdwara*. Weddings need to be pre-booked well in advance." At that moment she was called away by her husband who needed help serving in the *langar* hall. Ignoring Prakash Kaur's interruption, the women continued with the discussion.

"How do you know all this, Rani?" Manjeet asked.

"Since Baksho has helped find grooms for Indu's daughters, I've been inviting her over more often. Maybe she'll find my Jessy a suitable husband when the time comes." Rani looked quickly around to make sure she had not uttered these words in her daughter's presence. Although Jessy and her younger daughter, Tejinder, were busy eating across the hall, she could still feel her rebel daughter's eyes piercing the side of her skull.

"*Ek minte,* Rani, one minute," Manjeet said as she picked up Nikky's Asia-shaped *roti* and threw it back into the pile of re-dos.

"You girls are making a mess. What a disgrace, look at this disaster!" Mrs. Gill pointed at the *rotis* Kiran was burning on the *dhava*. "Go and wash the dirty dishes, and don't break anything!"

"But, Mrs. Gill, how else will they learn?" Rani questioned.

Manjeet shook her head. "Thank God my Kiran is already m-married!"

Prakash Kaur returned to the kitchen, wiping the perspiration off her forehead with the edge of her handkerchief. Although it was chilly outside, the kitchen was an uncomfortable zone. "You should send all your daughters to me. I will teach them like I've taught my Raj!" She patted her competent daughter on the back. Raj rolled her eyes.

"We need Baksho here right now," Mrs. Gill whispered to Manjeet. "She would put that woman in her proper place."

Prakash Kaur smiled at them all politely. "This isn't a school where our children learn to cook and clean. This is the house of God and we should learn to treat it like one. It is here that all our wishes are fulfilled." It was straightforward yet honey-coated comments like this that did not earn her any friends. She noticed the glares, fetched a plastic container and returned to her duties out of earshot.

"Are they talking?" Manjeet asked.

"Is who talking?" Mrs. Gill had become distracted.

"Preet and Baksho, who else?"

"I think so. The child is all Baksho has, and Preet holds that over her head," Mrs. Gill replied.

"Good for her! *Baut tung keeta*! Baksho really did a number on that girl," Rani said, and Manjeet nodded in agreement. "Hopefully she'll be happy now. But he must be a good man to take on a divorced woman with a child, *hana*?"

"He's from India! To come to this country, men will marry anyone." Mrs. Gill flapped the dry *atta* off her hands.

Rani knew how true that statement was. She swung her *dupatta* around her face, pulling it high above her chin."Well, for Preet's sake, let's pray God is watching over her."

"Shh! Baksho is coming." An awkward silence fell over the group of women.

"So, Mrs. Gill, let's hope this third one is a boy!" Baksho flashed her one gold filling amid the last of her deteriorating teeth. "When is your due date?"

"Oh, I almost forgot!" Rani exclaimed. "Where are your little daughters today?"

"My in-laws are watching them, but they are threatening to go back to India soon and they refuse to take the girls along this time. I don't know how I will manage without them. I need them for babysitting." Mrs. Gill had finally received her teacher accreditation, and she was working part-time at an elementary school.

"They are probably upset that you're not producing grandsons for them!" Baksho said. "If you don't have a son soon, people will begin to talk. Before your eldest, Manohar, was born I overheard people calling you barren." Baksho put down her purse, took off her coat and tied an apron over her loud, printed, tent-like *kameez*. Her hair was a brighter shade of red this week. She had been experimenting with *mehndi* on it for years but the excessive amount of grey she was now trying to disguise was only emphasized by the uneven application of colour.

Mrs. Gill gave her a smile but whispered a few choice words under her breath. Rani and Manjeet shared a pleased glance. No one here was a real friend or a real enemy, but as long as the discussions were an analysis of others' lives, all could be trusted.

Across the kitchen the girls had almost finished the last of the dishes.

"Great plan, Raj!" Nikky said. "We got stuck doing dishes but at least we got all the dirt!"

"Shit!" The large rice pot had slipped from Raj's hands into the sink. The loud thunk echoed throughout the kitchen.

"Raj, watch your language!" Kiran said. "You're in a temple!"

"You sound like my mother!" Raj muttered.

The three girls stared at each other. The thought of becoming just like their mothers was reason enough for the two older girls to leave the oversized pans to soak in the grimy dishwater and sneak away.

Raj, however, could not leave. Her mother often gave Rani a lift home in her station wagon because Rani had never learned to drive. Raj would have to wait until her mother had gathered all the passengers, but rather than return to the dishes, she opted to find her little sister, who she had last seen playing "ring around the rosy" in the foyer.

"Just look at her!" Baksho rolled her eyes in Prakash Kaur's direction and added, "She thinks she's so *wonderful*! Running around on her tippy toes catering to everyone! She pretends to be all sweet, but I know she trapped that husband of hers. How else would someone like her get such a nice, muscular man?" Baksho peered at Prakash Kaur's husband, unaware she had made her last comment out loud.

Manjeet and Mrs. Gill giggled so quietly that they did not interrupt Baksho's train of thought.

"She's so sickening! Always smiling and laughing for no reason! That daughter of hers, she'll be trouble, too. Just you watch! You should keep your daughters away from her! She'll claw her way into some naïve young man's life. Maybe I should let Preet take my grandson away with her..." Baksho bit her lip. She had inadvertently given the others too much information.

The women were waiting for her to carry on but Prakash Kaur made another appearance. "Rani, you may want to get a ride from someone else as I have to stay a little longer. I hope that's not an inconvenience. Or I can go drop you off and come back." Prakash Kaur was apologetic.

"That won't be necessary," Baksho announced and then quickly took off her apron. "I can drive *my* friends home. Come on Rani, let's go!" Baksho grabbed her purse and coat with one hand and began pulling Rani toward the exit with the other.

"Stop!" Rani yelled. "I have to find my daughters first!"

Mrs. Gill and Manjeet removed their dirty aprons. With Baksho gone, there was nothing left to talk about.

By the time Prakash Kaur completed all the chores the others had left undone and loaded her family into the vehicle, it was time for the evening prayer.

Gian — Wisdom

Gian and her daughter, Sandy, left their home in the middle of the night and showed up on our doorstep without warning. They carried two mismatched pieces of damaged floral luggage.

My father did not approve and was adamant that we not let them stay at our house. "There is no way I will allow this, Prakash Kaur!"

"Where else will they go? Besides, the neighbours were asking this morning who our new visitors are," my mother said. She knew the only way to change my father's mind was to remind him of his image in the community.

"Yeah, Dad," I interrupted, "when you're talking to people at the *gurdwara,* you always say we should help people in need!"

"You stay out of this, Raj! Go do your homework!"

"It's already done." I waited but he didn't tell me to do it again. He seemed really perplexed over this issue.

"Raj is right!" my mother said. "We must set a good example for our children. And imagine the *shavashay,* the praise, you will get from our community." My mother smoothed my hair and adjusted my headband over my braids.

After pausing to consider my mother's words, my father said, "Okay fine, they can stay, but there's no need to broadcast the truth to anyone. Have I made myself clear, Prakash Kaur?"

Gian and my mother had lived in the same village on the outskirts of Amritsar. I had heard her tell one of my aunts that every day after school they had taken a rickshaw through the crowds of people, bicycles, scooters, buses and sacred cows all the way to the Golden Temple.

They knew they would never be allowed to buy tasty *golguppas* from the vendors or enjoy lemon-flavoured drinks and eat *samosas* at the roadside restaurants like people from the city, but every day after school they got to be girls, talking about boys, classmates, movies and fashion.

While my mother had been forced to stay home after the age of fifteen to help with the housework, after graduation Gian had been privileged to attend an all girls' college in the city. Her father was a schoolteacher and placed great importance on education, though he believed only a few months of post-secondary learning was an adequate level of achievement for a woman. More education than this and women would begin to act superior.

My mother and Gian lost touch with one another after one of my uncles married a woman from New Westminster, and my mother's entire family immigrated to this country. My mother was only seventeen at the time. Gian married a year later and moved to eastern Canada with her husband. At first they wrote letters to each other on a regular basis, but as time went on and letters were intercepted and read by other family members, they wrote less often.

Two days after Gian and Sandy's arrival in our home I overheard my mother talking to my father about her old friend. "Poor woman, she was the envy of every girl in our village," my mother lamented. "What can she do now? If she leaves him, she'll have no respect. If she stays, she'll have no respect."

"There's no need for you to get involved, Prakash Kaur," he responded. "She'll only put ideas in your head and then you'll criticize me. You already don't appreciate all I do for you." My father could always find a way to make himself the victim. As always, the real martyr would just shake her head. A husband who could not empathize with his own wife would have no sympathy for another woman.

Seventeen-year-old Sandy soon confided the story to me and my cousin Baljot. She told us that her mother and her father, Kulwant, had been married for twenty-one years. Kulwant was unusual for a Punjabi man because he didn't drink and he didn't believe it was acceptable to bully his wife. He provided a comfortable lifestyle for his family and allowed Gian to further her education once they settled in Canada. Afterwards she took a job as an assistant manager in a shoe store for a number of years.

Sandy knew she was a fortunate girl because her father had assured her she would be allowed to choose her own husband when the time came, but in the meantime education would be the top priority. Kulwant and Gian were often ridiculed by other members of the community for raising Sandy like a son, but they dismissed these comments. They appeared to be a very happy family.

Then one evening Kulwant came home with a woman and a small boy he introduced as his other wife and child. Gian stood frozen. Tears rolled down her face, but she did not utter a word. Sandy shook her mother, demanding answers, begging her to say something, anything, but Gian was not in her senses. In a rage Sandy screamed at her father, pushing and shoving him, but still there was no reaction from Gian. He ignored Sandy's pleas and accusations and told her to sit down and not to interfere in adult matters.

He then carried on as if he owed no explanations. He assured Gian he would remain married to her on paper. After all, he had no complaints with her behaviour. He explained that she had been his parents' choice, and now he wanted to be with the woman he loved—a woman who had given him a son. This Indian immigrant, not much older than his own daughter, had come to replace Gian.

"We'll all live together," he announced.

He lectured his mistress on respecting his first wife. Gian would be her new *vaddi didi,* her older sister. Gian would remain in charge and the young wife was to assist her in household chores. Then before Kulwant took his mistress into the spare bedroom, he put his hand on Gian's shoulder and said, "I'll always be married to you. I'll fulfill all the duties and responsibilities of a husband."

Gian said nothing and when Sandy challenged her she said she must continue to be compliant as her mother had taught her. She must remain silent until the thunder passed.

Sandy, however, refused to stay in the house. Gian explained in vain that staying with Kulwant was necessary. "What would people say?" She tried to reassure Sandy that nothing had changed. Kulwant was still Sandy's father and she would have to respect him.

"Not in this country and not in this lifetime," was Sandy's reply.

She threatened to run away, but for a while Gian guilted her into staying.

Gian continued to fulfill her obligations as a devoted wife. Not only did she pretend nothing had changed, she also accepted the mistress. When Kulwant offered to put the son and mother in an apartment, Gian insisted there was no need to waste money. There was plenty of room in the house for everyone.

Sandy stopped speaking to her father and ignored the mistress and her half-brother. But when she could bear it no more, she packed bags for her mother and herself and bought bus tickets to Vancouver.

"I won't let you degrade yourself in this way," she pleaded passionately with her mother. "You aren't the whore. She is!"

Her words echoed through the house and the damage was irreparable. Kulwant slapped his daughter so hard he left a mark on her face. Sandy gathered her belongings along with her mother's in dead silence. The same silence accompanied them all the way to Vancouver.

"I never imagined this would happen to my family," Sandy said, choking back tears as she relayed seventeen years of her life to Baljot and me. In a matter of minutes her own and her mother's existence had been shattered. "How could we live there? If we stayed, my father would have thought his behaviour was acceptable."

"Shit like this happens all the time in India," Baljot sighed. "I didn't think it happened here."

"This never would have happened if that other woman had any morals at all. Do you think men would cheat on their wives if other women refused to sleep with them? Do you think they would assault their wives and treat them like dirt if they knew they couldn't easily find a replacement? Women encourage this type of behaviour by putting up with it."

"And by fucking married men!" I added.

Baljot gave me the look she always gave me when she thought I was too young to be part of the conversation. But Sandy noticed her disapproval and stepped in before Baljot threatened to clean my mouth out with soap.

"It's all right if she listens, Baljot. If you want to change your life, you have to do it yourself because no one else is going to come to your rescue. You're not going to find yourself draped in a chiffon *sari* and singing Hindi love songs on top of the Himalayas with your favourite hero. Instead, some bald-headed, middle-aged old guy is going to turn up to take you as his bride."

Baljot and I laughed at the picture Sandy had painted.

"I'm not joking," she said. "If you believe you're weak, you will be."

It was because of discussions like this that my father was against Sandy and her mother staying with us. Once he caught us chatting in the driveway when he drove up, and he rolled down his window and hollered for me to get into the car. He said we had to go to my uncle's house for dinner, but he drove to the *gurdwara*, went in for a few minutes and then drove me back home. When I asked about the dinner we were already late for, he glared at me.

While my father bore the presence of Gian and Sandy like a burden, my mother seemed happy to be revisiting her childhood in Gian's company.

"So many women were jealous of me, Prakash Kaur," Gian said once while we were preparing dinner. "They said I married a modern and honourable man. But do you think he sent me to school because he wanted an educated wife? Do you think I got a job because I was free to? He *needed* me to work. The cost of living in Canada is so high that he couldn't support Sandy and me on his modest salary, but he'd never admit it. Instead, he tried to look like a film star. I struggled to work forty, sometimes fifty hours a week with a young child, a husband and a household to look after."

My mother stopped chopping the carrots to reach over the counter and hand Gian a tissue, but instead of wiping her tears Gian scrunched it in her hand and sat at the kitchen table, abandoning the potatoes she had been washing under the tap.

"I was raised to be a good wife learning how to do household chores with my mother. I wasn't allowed to go out and enjoy *lukko meechi* and *gulli danda*. There was no time for games like hide and seek or cricket. My sisters and I had to learn to make *saag* and *makki di roti*. My childhood was spent taking on responsibilities I would commit to for the rest of my life."

While she was talking, Gian had ripped the tissue to shreds and it was all over her black *kameez*.

"Why did you not tell me sooner, Gian? I would have prayed for you."

"We were taught to remain quiet and never breathe a word of the cruelties against us. But it can't be hidden any longer. I couldn't lie to you anymore. I can't lie to myself anymore."

This time it was my mother's turn to reach for a tissue.

"Did you know, when my brothers were young, my father made them memorize an old Indian proverb?" Gian said, a smile appearing on her face for the first time. "That proverb said it was a sin to inflict harm on others but it was a far greater sin to tolerate injustices."

My mother nodded in silence.

"My father didn't realize that I, too, had memorized it," Gian added.

But their smiles could not conceal the truth behind the proverb. It did not apply to the women in their world.

"I don't want this *shaddi aurat* living under my roof any longer!" my father yelled. "This wandering woman who has been disposed of by her husband can't stay in my house!"

"She left him. He didn't leave her!" I said, jumping to Gian's defence.

He turned back to my mother. "Do you see what that woman's already done? These stupid children are listening to her stories and believing them. The next thing I know she'll be telling you to leave me."

My father then began taking drastic measures to keep his family separated from Gian and Sandy. He warned his sister Shindi, who lived in Richmond, to limit Baljot's visits to our house because he said she was at a vulnerable age and could be easily swayed by Sandy. This created further misunderstandings between my mother and Shindi *bhua,* who were already bickering over minor family issues. He also paid for weekend excursions for my older brother so he would not return home from college until Sandy and her mother were gone as he was afraid Sandy would eventually seduce him with her outspoken manner.

When my mother was not home, he would sweet-talk me into helping to care for my little sister, thereby securing hours of my time away from Sandy. If he found us engrossed in conversation in the laundry room or the backyard, he would call for us immediately. Next, he spent weeks renovating the house to create a basement suite for them, claiming that it would offer more privacy and we could rent it out in the future. When none of this worked, he found Sandy and Gian an apartment closer to Gian's workplace. He was probably afraid that if my mother and I became aware that we were capable of making it on our own, like Gian and Sandy, we would have no need for him. How could he be king if there were no commoners to rule?

In spite of my father constantly expressing his disapproval, while he was at work or at the *gurdwara,* my mother continued to see Gian. "I'm so glad I can share my sorrows and joys with you," I heard her tell Gian. "Finally I can confide in someone who'll understand." My mother had once told me that people who have suffered much through life are the best confidants, and she had at last found someone to ease the pain she kept hidden from us.

The following year, however, Sandy returned east to go to college and her mother decided to go with her. My father breathed a sigh of relief, and my mother was again alone with her thoughts. Later we learned that Sandy had married a *gora* whom she met while on vacation in Florida. Gian then moved back in with her husband, the other wife and their two sons.

"This is what happens to women who think they can grow wings and fly!" my father said. "Sooner or later their wings get clipped. Look at what her daughter's done!" He smiled smugly. "That woman has already brought so much shame and embarrassment to her family by leaving her husband. Maybe she wasn't an obedient wife and that's why he brought another woman home. It wasn't a big deal! It happens all the time. The stupid woman wrecked her home and what did she gain?"

My father turned away, shaking his head. Although I could not see his face, I knew he was pleased.

Gian's Letters

May 13, 1986

Dear Bibi *ji*,

Sat Sri Akal. Greetings! I pray that you are well. I did not want to write you with such ill news, but whom else can I trust?

Your son-in-law Kulwant has brought home a young lover. I worry about Sandy's future. If I stay with him, my daughter's life is ruined. No respectable family will marry a girl whose father has a mistress. But I also worry that if I leave him, this will create even more problems for her. People will say I am divorced, and the daughter of a divorced woman can only have bad karma. I am the one who will be blamed for the demise of my family. Even if a good *rishta* comes for Sandy, they will ask too many questions I cannot answer. Divorced women are tolerated in this country, but there is still stigma in the Indian community that I cannot escape.

I have written to you because I need your honest advice. I know only a mother will understand a daughter's anguish.

Your loving daughter, Gian

July 3

Dear Gian,

I cried and cried after reading your letter. What can you do if God has written such a fate for you? You must stay with your husband! For better or worse, he is your keeper and can do as he wishes. Many husbands have concubines. All these years I have kept to myself my suspicions about your father. You should be thankful your husband has looked after you for so many years when you could not provide him with an heir. It is far more respectable to stay with a husband who has another woman than to have the black soot of divorce rubbed on your face.

I understand your pain. I am your mother. It hurts me to see you trapped in this confusion. If I was there with you, I could hold you in my arms. We could cry together. From this far away I can only give you advice that is close to my heart. A mother only wants happiness for her daughter.

If you leave him, people will point fingers at you. I cannot swallow the thought of my little girl being tortured in this manner. You are an Indian woman. Do not forget that. You must make this sacrifice.

Your *budhnaseeb*, unfortunate mother

September 30

Dear Bibi *ji*,

Sat Sri Akal. Sandy sends her love. Although you advised against it, Sandy insisted that we move to a different city. Only my close friends know what has happened, and I assure you, no one in India will hear about the separation. I will not allow my bad *kismet* to tarnish your reputation.

We like it here in Vancouver but it is not the same. Although I cannot forget Kulwant, the pain is tolerable because I do not have to see him.

I know you do not agree with my decision but I hope you will forgive me in time. Please know that your granddaughter is content. Hopefully this knowledge will ease the ache of my betrayal.

Your loving daughter, Gian

January 24, 1988

Dear Bibi *ji*,

Sat Sri Akal. It has been over eighteen months since I have received any of your letters. Perhaps they were lost when I moved from my friend's house to the apartment!

As you will see from the address on this envelope, Sandy and I have moved back to Toronto. I could not let her come back here alone, but I wish we had stayed in Vancouver. I cannot go to the *gurdwara* here without being bombarded by questions. Some people pretend to sympathize, but I hear them talking when my back is turned. My friends never return my calls. I think their husbands do not approve of me. I have gone days without leaving the house to avoid running into people I know, but I cannot take any more time off work. I am having trouble paying the bills as it is.

I need your support. Please pray that God gives me the strength to do what is right.

Your loving daughter, Gian

July 15

Dear Bibi *ji*,

Sat Sri Akal. I hope you are well. God has finally given me something to rejoice about. Your granddaughter has married. He is a *gora*, but she is happy. I tried to fix a *rishta* for her, but the boys' families would come up with silly excuses as soon as they learned that Kulwant and I do not live together. They would say Sandy is too tall, too thin, too fat or too short, and one by one they all rejected her. They assume my husband left me.

Sandy's husband is a well-respected man. He does not care about my situation, and he accepts Sandy as she is. They have offered to let me live with them, but my heart is still Indian. How can I live as a burden to my daughter? But I cannot work as much as I did. My joints ache with pain. I am old and alone now.

Your loving daughter, Gian

January 10, 1989

Dear Bibi *ji*,

Sat Sri Akal. I hope you are well. I have written you several letters, but each one is returned unopened. I have not been able to rest knowing that you have not forgiven me for leaving Kulwant.

You were right. A wife belongs with her husband, and now that I have fulfilled my role as a mother, I have decided to become a good wife and daughter once again. I am going back to live with my husband and promise to serve him unconditionally.

Your loving daughter, Gian

Sunday Langar – 1989

"I can't believe it!" Baksho clapped her hands together.

"Quiet!" The elderly woman sitting cross-legged in front of Baksho and Mrs. Gill could endure their chatter no longer. "Go outside and talk if you want to talk, but please don't ruin my meditation!" She glared at them before closing her eyes again.

Baksho took Mrs. Gill by the hand, pulling her to her feet then leading her down the stairs and into the ladies restroom. Since the new *granthi* had been hired, he did not permit conversation in the kitchen or anywhere else, and their gossip circle was disintegrating.

"Did you see her? She doesn't walk around all proud anymore." Baksho's new white dentures flashed from one corner of her mouth to the other. The Indian dentist had recommended she replace the few teeth she had left before they caused any more problems. Dentures had been the most inexpensive and effective solution.

"Who the hell are you talking about?" Mrs. Gill was losing patience with Baksho, but she was grateful that she had led her to the restroom as she wanted to fix her hairdo. Now she bent over to allow her hair to fall forward, so that she could squeeze her permed curls into a banana clip.

"Prakash Kaur," said Baksho. "Who else? Oh, stop fussing with your hair and look at me!"

Mrs. Gill looked. Baksho seemed unable to stand up straight. Either she needs to urinate, Mrs. Gill thought, or the gossip she wants to impart is kicking up a storm in her stomach. "She's really not that bad, Baksho!" she protested. "Her *akar* just lasted while her only child was a boy. As soon as she became a mother of two daughters, her attitude disappeared."

"She makes my blood boil!" Baksho said. "There's just something about her that I don't like and never will. Maybe it's because she's from the other side of the river in Punjab. I hear women from her region are very cunning!"

"Isn't that exactly what you said to Indu about the area Rani and I are from as well?" Mrs. Gill inquired.

Baksho had indeed made such comments in the past and quickly looked away to avoid direct eye contact with Mrs. Gill.

"And is that all you brought me in here to tell me?" Mrs. Gill raised her loose, oversized *patiala salwar* and tried to shake off the piece of wet toilet paper that had attached itself to her heel. "This isn't the cleanest and most pristine place in the *gurdwara*."

"No, no. I have some real news!" Baksho fanned herself with her *dupatta*. "It was just so hot upstairs that I could hardly breathe!" She was pre-menopausal but did not know it. She had missed her period again and was afraid to tell the others, afraid they would accuse her of scandalous behaviour that had resulted in an unwanted pregnancy. She was totally unaware of what was happening to her body. No one—not her mother or grandmother—had warned her about menopause.

"All right, just spill what you have to say and let's get out of here!" Mrs. Gill said.

Suddenly two little girls ran into the bathroom, slamming the door back so hard that it smacked against Baksho's head.

"*Nee marjo tusi*! You stupid brats!" Baksho snarled, wincing in pain as the girls scuttled into the toilet cubicles.

"Just hurry up and say what you have to say!" Mrs. Gill snapped.

Baksho, quickly forgetting about her injuries, pulled Mrs. Gill close. "*Well,* Prakash Kaur's *aadmi,* that tall handsome husband of hers, had a *chakkar,* an affair, with her best friend. You know, that woman whose husband left her!"

"*Randay toon,* that's utter nonsense! I don't believe it for a second. They're good people!" Mrs. Gill started for the door. She had been trying to distance herself from Baksho since the birth of her second daughter, Roop, as she no longer found Baksho's gossip amusing. Baksho, however, did not loosen her grip on anyone too easily.

"I'm serious!" Baksho blurted, taking hold of Mrs. Gill's arm. "Ask Lalita. She's the one who told me. But no, on second thought, don't say anything. I promised I wouldn't tell anyone."

"What does Lalita know? She hardly leaves the house! She's too busy phoning people, looking for her alcoholic husband day and night, poor woman! You know, she was stunning when I first met her, such beautiful green eyes, that sun-kissed skin and those long golden brown locks." Mrs. Gill stood aside to let the two little girls leave the washroom. "She looked like a *gori*. Now her whole head is grey from worry, her eyes are hidden behind those dark bifocals, and she has put on so much weight that she has two chins."

"Lalita heard it from someone else," Baksho added, struggling to validate her story. She swung her *dupatta* around her neck and then continued. "You know how these divorced women prey on married men. Well, that stupid Prakash Kaur let this one right into her home. It was only when Prakash Kaur threatened to commit suicide that her husband finally bought his mistress, that Gian, a one-way ticket back to Toronto. And if that wasn't enough, Gian sold her daughter to a *gora*, and now she's living a life of luxury…"

A few minutes later Rani barged into the washroom and grabbed Mrs. Gill's arm.

"Are you two crazy?" she demanded. "Some little girls just ran into the *langar* hall and repeated everything you were saying about Prakash Kaur and her husband word for word to their mothers! *Sharm karo*! Have some shame!" She shook her head in disgust. "What are you thinking?"

Rani left the bathroom before anyone saw her conversing with the two women and gathered her daughters, Jessy and Tejinder, before leaving the temple.

Although Rani had happily joined in gossip sessions with the ladies in the past, she had realized belatedly that it was best to keep her involvement in the community limited. She did not want anyone to dive into her own life because she had her own secret, one that no one in the community was aware of, not even her daughters or her husband: Rani's eldest, Jessy, was her daughter from her first marriage. Rani had come from England to India to marry her first husband and they had only been together a few short days when he was stricken with typhoid and died. Her mother-in-law was devastated because she had thought her eldest son would secure her passage to England, but with him gone she needed to send her other son abroad in his place.

It was a common practice for widowers and in some rare instances for widows to re-marry within the same family, so although Rani's mother-in-law blamed Rani for her son's death, referring to her as unlucky and cursed, she had convinced her younger son to marry Rani. And Rani's brother-in-law was happy to oblige as Rani was only twenty years old and fair and pretty with almond-shaped eyes. So he bedded the enchanting beauty, not knowing she was carrying his brother's child. Rani did not object to the union and sponsored her new husband so he could join her in London. He assumed the baby was his and did not question Rani when the child was delivered prematurely. Fortunately for Rani, her mother-in-law had died before Jessy's birth.

Her husband had been kind and loving toward her at first but grew distant when she produced only daughters. Then after her disease had been diagnosed and her beauty began to fade, they had gradually drifted apart, and she was afraid that, if he learned the truth, he would be justified in ending the marriage.

For several weeks after the bathroom incident Prakash Kaur and her husband denied the rumours. But when the rumours continued, he eventually resigned from his position at the temple and the family ceased to attend the Sunday prayer service. A short time later they relocated to Vancouver Island.

Jasveer – Courage

When my sister Jessy, short for Jasveer, was eleven, she placed wads of chewing gum in her long silky braids so the teacher was left with no choice but to hack her hair off to get the gum out. That was how she traded her two braids for high bangs and big hair.

My mother was devastated. "If you were older and had defied us in this way, at least we could have quickly married you off. Why didn't you just cut off an arm or a leg? Your hair is a part of your body just the same. And what about your sister, Tejinder? How will we stop her from following your lead?"

My father, on the other hand, had no words for Jessy. He just blamed my mother for not bringing her up like a proper Punjabi girl. "It's only a matter of time," he said, "before she starts dating *goray*!" My father had removed his turban as soon as he reached England because he found it difficult to cope with the racism there, yet he did not have the same compassion for his daughters. Of course, he was a man and the rules for survival were different for him.

Although it was only hair, my parents felt that Jessy had denied her heritage by chopping it off. They were trying to raise their offspring as Indians and they knew that once the culture and tradition began to slip away so would their children. But while it was so easy for them to blame Jessy for giving in to peer pressure, for exploring new worlds and opportunities, they had forgotten it was they who exposed their children to this new world in the first place.

Although her western counterparts identified my sister Jessy as an apprehensive and self-conscious girl, the people on my street saw her as defiant and unruly. She was the rebel in the family, the one who would deviate from tradition. And perhaps it was this fire inside of her that in the end would leave her engulfed in flames too resistant to douse.

I must admit that I—along with many other girls in our neighbourhood—was resentful of Jessy. Unlike her, I was the future conventionalist, easily persuaded and quickly subdued. I was the subservient daughter, and I was afraid that one day I would have to live in her shadow. Jessy would be the one to break away and bask in inestimable freedom. I would be the one who would spend my life conforming, tortured by remorse and regrets.

Jessy had been given the name Jasveer because wise elders assured my mother that the name would guarantee the birth of sons in the future. (Unfortunately, I had not been the male heir who could promise them success and prosperity.) Even though she had not been a son, Jessy was deeply cherished by my parents, but it was not any easier for her to have what she desired most: independence. She would join every club and extracurricular activity at school and take part in any venture that would abolish her role as a weak female, but my parents would coerce her into abandoning each one.

"We give you so much *khul*, so much more freedom than all the other girls in the neighbourhood, but you still want more," my father would say. "We send you to school for an education, not to parade around in skimpy little shorts in front of those *goray*."

When my father was finished, my mother would begin. "What will you get out of the writing club or the drama club? You don't get grades for those things. I didn't do any of that in school and tell me what's wrong with my life? If you have that much extra time you should be learning to cook different Punjabi meals. These are the skills that will prove useful in the future."

The fights would go on every night. As in most families, the topic would be discussed, reworded and rephrased for hours, but nothing would be resolved. My parents would hear what Jessy was saying but refused to dismiss their preconceived notions long enough to understand her. Occasionally she was able to persuade my mother to her point of view, but then fear of my father's accusations would immobilize my mother's tongue, leaving Jessy to fend for herself. So each night my father would walk away the victor. But each day he also embraced failure because Jessy's hatred for him grew stronger and stronger. My parents were trying to do the best they could for Jessy and me, but they were slowly suffocating our dreams and aspirations.

Jessy never bowed her head in defeat. Like my father, she was stubborn, but he blamed my mother for that as well. According to him, we inherited all our adverse qualities from my mother. Anything slightly deserving of praise was all his doing, although he never spent any time with us. He was always at work, and when he came home, he did not consider it important to bond with the women in the house. What could we possibly have to talk about?

Jessy, however, was able to use my father's busy schedule to her advantage. She continued to participate in non-academic activities and pursued forbidden friendships with the *goray*. At first my mother was reluctant to be an accomplice but eventually she gave in.

"Do you want me to live the same kind of life you have?" Jessy asked her.

We watched my mother as she eased her shawl up to cover her face. "There's nothing wrong with my life. It's you children that don't let me be happy—always upsetting your father with this and that. You never let this home have any peace!" Of course, she had not chosen the life she now lived, but she had been conditioned never to question it. Then at last she would say, "Fine, do what you want. But if your father finds out, he'll have both our heads."

So Jessy's plans went ahead without a glitch. My father did not suspect anything until one day Mr. Chan, the new manager of the local gas station, introduced himself to my father as Cindy's dad. Jessy's team had just won the school district volleyball championships, and above his cash register Mr. Chan was proudly displaying a picture of Jessy and his daughter holding the trophy.

My father was furious. He had not only been disobeyed by his teenage daughter but also betrayed by his wife. "How dare you lie to me, woman! What kind of fool do you think I am? Look what you're teaching them. Shame on you, Rani!"

I had never seen my father strike my mother. So when he raised his hand to beat her now, it was what she had expected all along, and she relinquished her own well-being for the sake of her daughter's *zid*, her stubbornness. Jessy had not realized that our mother would be the one to face the consequences of her determination to live her own life. When she did, she resigned from the team.

A few days later, after my father's friends had congratulated him on his daughter's achievement, he decided Jessy could return to the game. In this way he once again secured his position as the most powerful person in the house. But although he had given his consent, it was accompanied by a list of restrictions: she was not permitted to participate in overnight tournaments and she could only play in games that ended before five o'clock because late evenings and overnight stays spelled disaster for teenage girls. To spite my father, she refused to rejoin the sport. She would spare herself the lengthy explanation to teammates as well as the embarrassment. It was easier just to quit. Once she accepted her first defeat, the ones that followed were inevitable.

Since she was a little girl, Jessy had dreamed of becoming a lawyer, and the more my mother disapproved of the occupation, the more Jessy persevered with her plan.

"What kind of man will want to marry a woman who argues all day to prove her point?" my mother demanded. "You won't become a man just because you become a lawyer. Your status will still be the same."

Jessy believed she had the ability to stand up for her rights and for the rights of others as well. I don't think that she really understood that releasing women from oppression would mean fighting against thousands of years of tradition. In her fantasy world, everyone was going to be equal and everyone, including women, would be happy. But my parents would never agree to law school for her, not in this lifetime.

According to my mother, men did not like women who were smarter than them. "Look at the Manns' daughter, that Nikky. She did a six-month secretary course and now she works in Dr.Varma's office. She's a good girl, *no*? Baksho has found her a boy in Vancouver and his family originates from the same district in Punjab as Indu's family. He's an engineer. What more could she want?"

Whenever there was talk of a future for Jessy that did not include marriage, my father would remind us of all the docile Indian girls who lived in our neighbourhood. These comments were directed toward Jessy and they became more detailed the closer she got to graduation. She, however, would snicker and leave the room, refusing to let his opinions deter her from her goals. My father would then turn to my mother with great disapproval.

"*Samjala ainu,* make her understand! If she keeps dreaming these silly daydreams she'll bring misery into her life. It's entirely your fault she behaves in this way. You've overindulged her!"

"She'll learn soon enough," my mother would say, not willing to go against his wishes again.

"All women are the same," my father would continue. "I do everything for you and you still complain. What is it that you don't have? Expensive clothes, a comfortable home! If it weren't for me, you would have wasted away milking *mujjan* and gathering cow dung in India. If it weren't for me, you know very well what would've happened to you! I only stay for my children, but you can get out and go to some other man if you think he will take you!"

After comments of this kind my mother would spend her time trying to find more ways to disguise the discolouration caused by her disease. As well as the *dupatta* that had become a permanent fixture on her head, she would wear full sleeves and a high-necked *kameez* even in the sweltering heat. But she would continue going about her daily chores as if his words did not sting.

Jessy had never been allowed to attend school dances, and the dance held at her high school graduation was to be no exception.

"You're not going and that's final!" my father shouted. "Next you'll be saying you want to go with a boy like the white girls do. *Sharabee lok* and *goondas,* those are the types of people who go to parties. What will you get from associating with those drunks and hoodlums? I know what happens there. Don't forget it's me who picks up those shameless, half-naked girls and drives them home in my taxi. We're having a party for you here with all our friends."

The people invited to this function were neither Jessy's buddies nor my parent's well-wishers. Parties were never about getting together and having fun. They were all about who could outshine whom. Since Jessy would be on the home team that night, the visitors would do and say all they could to belittle her achievements.

Baksho, that fat cow, was the first to arrive. No one in the community could tolerate her but everyone felt obligated to maintain superficial relations with her. After all, she was the one who helped so many new immigrants settle into their homes and so many desperate mothers marry off their daughters.

"Look at her gawdy *salwar kameez.*" Jessy had to turn her eyes away so the glare off the multitude of tiny mirrors on Baksho's multi-coloured, embroidered outfit would not blind her.

But Baksho's appearance was just the beginning of the ostentation. The women with the most gold jewellery would be the envy of every other at the party, though most of it was compensation for loveless marriages and unfulfilled lives. Usually the most decorated was the most miserable.

"Wow! Check out Miss Perfect!" Jessy exclaimed.

Mrs. Gill's sexy chiffon *sari* and elegant diamond accessories left every girl, woman and man envious. The women wanted to be just like her and the men wanted to be married to her. Mrs. Gill was the mother every girl wished she had.

"I know, she's so awesome and she's modern like the *goray*. Her daughters are so lucky. She lets Manohar and Roop go to ballet classes and they're even allowed to wear skirts," I said.

"What I don't understand is how Mom can be such close friends with Mrs. Gill but still be so backward in her thinking," Jessy said.

"It's because Mom is also great friends with Fatso, too!" I pointed to Baksho, who was yelling at a little girl who had stepped on her foot.

After all the guests had arrived, Jessy and I collected all the purses and shawls and threw them on my bed. Then we locked the door so we could hide out in the bedroom for a while because the party was actually only for the males. The ladies were the hired help. No one questioned this practice, not even Jessy, but she did find ways to get out of doing any of the work. Unfortunately, after a few hours my mother noticed our absence and hauled us both out of my bedroom and into the kitchen. After dinner the men headed off to chat and continue drinking in the living room while the women had made their way back to the kitchen where they had spent most of the day cooking.

"*Nee* Jessy, you must be so excited! Your parents have already started looking for suitable boys." Baksho was back to her dirty tricks, waiting for Jessy to cause a scene. Surprisingly, Jessy ignored her comment and went to clear the rest of the dishes from the dining room table.

My mother pulled Baksho aside. "Baksho *panji,* please! Nothing's final and I'd like to be the one to tell Jessy."

"Why, Rani, do you think she won't agree?" Baksho asked.

"No, Jessy's a good girl. She always does what we ask of her. But this isn't the time to talk about her wedding. Let her enjoy the party."

I continued washing dishes as though I hadn't heard a thing. My mother was able to squash Baksho's curiosity for the moment, but it was obvious Baksho had gathered enough ammunition to gossip among the neighbours for the next several days.

That summer Jessy began receiving acceptance letters from colleges and universities all over Canada and England. She had set her standards high and took it upon herself to cover all her bases. There had been no more mention of suitable boys since the night of her party. It was, however, bound to come up again.

"I didn't realize choosing a school would be so difficult," she said when my father entered her room. Jessy and I had been sitting on her bed looking over her letters. "I don't know which one's better."

To my horror, my father began grabbing the letters and envelopes that she had spread over the floor and ripping them up. Jessy said nothing, she just sat on the bed, stunned. Then he looked up at her wall at the posters of Madonna, Bon Jovi, U2, Whitney Houston, Guns N' Roses and her most recent and cherished purchase, New Kids on the Block. In a rage, he began to tear them from the walls and rip them up as well.

"What did I say? No university and no college!"

My mother ran frantically into Jessy's room. "*Hai main marjan*, what's happened? What's wrong?" As she fumbled to pick up her white cotton *dupatta*, which had caught on the door hinge, she stared at the shreds of paper on Jessy's peacock print bedspread.

In the days that followed my father pointed out several times that Jessy was not yet eighteen and therefore not legally allowed to live on her own. In the meantime the only choice she had was to look for a job and hope to make enough money to give herself financial independence, and so she got herself hired at the local Safeway.

However, she had many restless nights after that. Her bedroom was across from mine, and ever since we were small children we had the habit of leaving our doors open at night. Now sometimes I would see her sitting upright on her bed praying to a god she used to claim did not exist. Other times I heard her weeping. I wanted to comfort her, but I knew her room was her only refuge. Some nights I saw her writing in a little red book, but I would never dare to read it because that would be no different than my parents intruding on her private thoughts. But through all this she never said or did anything to openly show her disappointment. She had emerged into a copy of my mother, the woman she had sworn she would never become.

Although Jessy never mentioned law school again, there was something about the way she looked at my father that made me believe she had not accepted defeat. It was the same look she would have in her eyes when she was angry with me; she had never rested until she had revenge for her headless Barbie dolls and torn magazines.

I asked Jessy a number of times what she was planning, but she did not want me to get involved.

"They'll get it out of you, Tejinder, and then you'll be in more trouble than me."

Our time together suddenly became precious. I knew we would have to make the best of it.

A few days later my mother, standing behind the kitchen table, announced, "We have a *rishta* for you."

Before my father could add anything, Jessy put her hand up to object and walked straight into her bedroom. She returned seconds later with a picture and placed it next to my mother's hand.

"What's this?"

"He's the boy I want to marry." The confidence with which she had carried herself in previous confrontations had disappeared. She held onto the back of a chair with both hands.

The boy's face was dark and slim and he had not yet grown into his nose. His hair was short and feathered in the front and long at the back. The gold *khanda*, the Sikh symbol, around his neck made his appearance even more awkward.

As my father shot up, kicking his chair behind him, my mother grabbed his arm and ordered Jessy and me to leave the room. I had never seen her touch him before. She had always kept her distance from him.

We listened quietly from my bedroom, but the loud *bhangra* music next door drowned out their voices. After a while Jessy grew impatient. She went into my closet and pulled out all the books and teen magazines I had hidden under my old clothes, but they didn't hold her interest for long. She took down the only poster I had been permitted to put up, telling me I was too old for Mickey Mouse. Then she picked up the Indian doll centrepiece off my dresser and slid it under my bed. Jessy often did this when she was stressed out...I just let her because at least she was paying attention to me.

One by one she removed all the items my mother had purchased with such pride. When she finished, all that remained were bare white walls, my homemade pink floral quilt, my bunk bed and the cherry veneer dresser, which I would have been more than happy to dispose of.

After hours of deliberation, Jessy was called back to the kitchen. No one noticed it was after midnight.

"Did you know this boy is another caste?"

Tears began to form in Jessy's eyes. Even I knew there were rules to a love marriage. According to my parents, one was allowed to find a suitable partner as long as the potential mate was a *Jat* Sikh. Not only did Jessy have to marry into our religion but the boy also had to be from the farming community in Punjab. For some reason, these practices still held relevance for Indo-Canadians.

"But he's Sikh, and that's all that should matter," Jessy replied.

Jessy was right. During last week's Punjabi lesson, Mrs. Gill had gone off on a tangent. She taught us that Guru Nanak, the founder of Sikhism, considered all people to be equal, regardless of caste or gender. And as firm believers of the faith we were to adhere by these principles. Come to think of it, Jessy had been the one to spark that discussion.

But my mother completely ignored Jessy's comment. It seemed she had rehearsed exactly what she wanted to say.

"His mother worked with me a couple of years back. He's a kind boy," my mother said firmly, reassuring my father that it was the right decision.

He cleared his throat, then with obvious reluctance stood up to say his piece. "We'll go see his parents soon. You should be extremely grateful. After this we'll lose face in the community for marrying you to a lower caste boy. People are going to think there is something wrong with you and no one else would marry you, so we had to reduce ourselves to their level." He turned to walk away and then paused. "As long as *you're* happy! We don't want anyone to think I didn't do all I could for my daughters. And what will it matter to you after you're married? *I'm* the one who will be ashamed."

I saw my parents in a different light that evening. For the first time my father had given in and a little bit of my faith had been restored.

My parents went to meet Dev and his family on Sunday afternoon. Jessy had wanted them to go sooner but my mother was waiting for an auspicious day. She had become quite superstitious and did not want anything to go wrong after all her efforts. At first she had wanted my father to go alone, fearing questions about her disease. She was afraid Dev's family would think that her skin condition was a genetic disorder and would affect Jessy, but after much persistence from my father she had no choice but to go with him.

After they left, Jessy told me that she and Dev had been working together at the Safeway. They had only known each other a short while but were madly in love. She said Dev was generous and romantic, just like the characters in the novels she read. After they got married she was going to complete her education, and then he would take her all around the world for their belated honeymoon. And once she was an established lawyer, she would start up her own firm. They had no plans for children—not yet anyway. In fact, Jessy was not sure if she wanted to be a mother.

I was still a gawky teenager with problem acne and braces, oblivious to what existed beyond my world, so I was shocked when Jessy confided in me. But who else could she trust? She'd never had any Indian friends and most of her former classmates were away at college. My father had limited her contact with these girls because he was afraid they would be a bad influence and encourage her to go with them.

"What's taking them so long?"

"It's only been an hour. Relax!"

Jessy slid the scrunchie off her hair and rather than fix the loose strands and tie it back up around her ponytail, she threw it directly at my face.

"Oh shut up, Tejinder! What do you know?"

She continued to pace the floor anxiously awaiting the arrival of good news.

Minutes later my mother walked through the front door, and my father followed, dragging his feet. Dev's family had refused the proposal. They too did not approve of their son marrying into a different caste. He was, after all, their only son. They wanted to find a more appropriate match for their family. As the groom's family, it was their right to have complete control over the situation. My parents could do nothing but accept the decision.

Dev's family had failed when it came to putting their faith to the test. They had chosen to conform to the prevailing views in Punjabi culture. It was not an explanation to God that they feared but criticism from people in the community. After all, God is forgiving, neighbours are not.

That Sunday was the first time my father hugged my sister since she was a child. My parents broke the news gently, waiting for Jessy to express her anger, but she did not. She walked out of the room and into her bedroom and closed the door behind her.

My father's eyes filled with tears as he mumbled, "She's brought this upon herself. Only God can determine her fate now." I knew that he felt as powerless and helpless as my mother had all those years. He had been able to exert his authority over three women, but in the real world he was weak because he was not the father of sons. If Jessy had been a boy and wanted to marry a girl of a different caste, he would have done as Dev's parents did. I expected my father to become more of a dictator after that catastrophe, but instead he loosened his grip. Jessy had already tarnished his reputation. A lower caste family had discarded her.

Months passed without any mention of Dev. Jessy quit her job at the Safeway and my father allowed her to sign up for classes at the nearby college. It was now very important that she get an education, as this was the only way to increase her market value as marriage material. Jessy had always been a fighter so it did not take her long to get over Dev, but her desire for a new romance seemed to remain absent.

Then one day my mother said, "Jessy, you'll be twenty soon and I don't want to upset you but it's time we started thinking about your marriage."

"Men are jerks! They don't even understand the meaning of love."

"Love is just a word to Indian women," my mother chided. "We don't marry for those reasons. We never have. Having a husband who will financially support you and take care of you is all you should wish for. That's the definition of love." When Jessy made no response, my mother added, "You can't go on like this forever. What's life without a family of your own?"

"Fine, do what you want," Jessy answered in a monotone.

The wedding was set for two days before Jessy's twentieth birthday. Ajit Singh Cheema was a *sardar,* a Sikh who wore a turban, from Delhi, and he had immigrated to Canada on a student visa. He was seven years Jessy's senior and was in his final year of medical school in Alberta. Jessy would relocate to be with him. That is the way it has always been; the bride leaves her home to live with her new husband and his family.

"What more could she ask for? She's hit the jackpot!" Baksho exclaimed when my mother told her about the wedding.

Fearing Baksho would jinx the *rishta,* my mother forced Aunty Indu and Mrs. Gill to keep Baksho occupied during the *mehndi* ceremony so she would not mention Jessy and Dev's relationship to the groom's family. Baksho's gossip would surely put an end to the festivities. The wedding day could not come soon enough for my mother.

Jessy had never agreed to marry Ajit nor had she disagreed. My parents simply interpreted her silence as acceptance. However, she seemed content during the celebrations. If she felt otherwise, it was difficult to detect. Although at first she had been reluctant to take Ajit's phone calls and had even postponed their union by a few months, in the end she and Ajit had talked on the phone almost every other night before the wedding.

A few days after the wedding festivities came to a close the newlyweds returned to Calgary. As days passed, we started to hear less and less from my sister. She never complained about her life and when we asked how Ajit treated her, she was always quick to list his attributes. Then a few months into their marriage, her mother-in-law immigrated to Canada, and after that whole weeks went by without one call from Jessy. Every time my mother or I called her house, a lady would answer and tell us that we had the wrong number.

Jessy had been married almost a year when we heard from her again. She phoned to say she was coming for a visit and asked my father to pick her up at the airport later that night. She hung up before my mother could ask her any questions. My father and I were ecstatic but my mother was worried.

"We haven't heard from her in so long and now she wants to visit.

Has she finally remembered we're still alive?"

"Oh, Mom, get over it. She's probably been busy. Can't you be happy just this once?"

"Something's wrong. I can feel it."

At first we did not notice her in the crowd of people lugging their suitcases into the arrivals lounge. She did not look like the same person who had left us a year before. She was older, thinner and tired-looking. As she got closer, I could see she had been crying, and the bags under her eyes pointed to a stream of sleepless nights. The skin around one of her eyes seemed so dark it almost looked bruised.

I suddenly felt a sharp pain in my chest, the pain I always got when things were going wrong. I knew my mother could sense something, too, because she never stood close to my father in public and now she was clutching at the sleeve of his jacket with all her might.

Jessy ran into my mother's arms.

"I'm not going back! Please don't make me."

People stopped to stare. My mother was uncomfortable with attention from onlookers, but she still held Jessy in an attempt to quiet her. When at last Jessy pulled back, I knew the dark circle around her eye was not from lack of sleep.

Jasveer's Diary

June 20, 1989

I'm graduating with honours and my class has voted me "most likely to succeed." My teachers are very proud of me. Mrs. Foster, the school counsellor, thinks I should be able to get into any university I want.

July 26

How do you tell your parents to fuck off and let you live your own life? The umbilical cord that should have been severed when I was born still remains, waiting to suck me back in. I was stupid to think I could go away to college and make something of myself.

July 29

Mom found my diary today. Good thing her English is so bad! I told her it was a school project from last term, and she believed me!

January 4, 1990

A girl that worked at the video store next to the Safeway managed to run away two years ago and her family never found her. I could take off, too. I'm sure there are people at work who will help me.

January 26

An Indian named Dev started working as a stock boy today. He's really cute.

February 4

I think Dev likes me. I like him too. He always asks me how I'm doing. He actually wants to know about my life. He says he believes women should pursue careers outside the home, and he wants to marry a girl who is independent and educated. He doesn't seem to be like the other Indian guys, but I'm not going to tell him about my plans just yet. I don't want him to think badly of me.

March 13

Dev and I went on our first date today. I lied to my parents and told them I was working late. If they find out about Dev, they'll make me quit my job and marry me off to some complete geek.

I think I'm falling in love with Dev.

March 18

The whole community attended the *gurdwara* today, and even Baksho had only nice things to say! And Miss Perfect, she should definitely go into politics! Ever since she got elected to the board of the Punjabi school, she has been totally involved with the community. Today she made a big speech about the legislation that has finally been passed to allow turbaned Sikhs to join the RCMP. Dad is so proud he even wore a red turban over his balding head; Mom said it's the first time he has tied one on since he cut his hair off years ago. He's telling everyone that if he'd had a son, he would have made him become an RCMP officer.

March 28

Dev and I went to our first movie together. We drove all the way to Burnaby so no one would recognize us. I told my parents I was working at another location. We saw *Pretty Woman*. It's my new favourite movie now!

April 25

Dev doesn't care what his family says. He isn't traditional in his thinking. He says he'll choose his own wife. I don't have to run away from home now. I'll marry Dev and live happily ever after. After we get married, I can do whatever I want, and I'll finally have the freedom my parents have denied me.

June 2

I can't believe Dev turned out to be such a fucking coward. He said he wanted to marry me. He said he didn't care whether his family accepted me or not. What am I going to do now? My life sucks! I don't have enough money saved up to take off somewhere. I don't have a choice. I'll have to get married. It's the only way I'll get to leave this godforsaken house. I hope a bus hits Dev. I hope his father goes blind and his mother becomes a quadriplegic. So much for true love!

August 6

I thought it would be easy, but it hurts so much! I hate that fucking loser!!!!!!

September 2

I still can't get him out of my head! I hope he ends up marrying some ugly bitch!

November 18

Dad says I can sign up for some classes next term at Langara College, but only if I want to. He even said I should do a criminology course. At least something good came out of the whole situation with that jackass. I heard he's dating some fat trashy girl now. Good, he deserves it! I hope he's miserable for the rest of his life!

January 14, 1991

I just couldn't help myself. It was the perfect opportunity to get back at him. When I was driving home from my evening class tonight, I saw his black Mustang parked in the gravel lot by the recreation centre. His last name is on the licence plate. What a loser! The lot is poorly lit and I'm sure no one saw me. I scratched up his entire car with my keys. It was awesome!

April 21

Today my parents paraded me in front of a bunch of people as if I had no feelings and no mind of my own. I felt like I was on a clearance stand at the department store with consumers deciding whether I was a bargain or not. This is all Dev's fault. If he hadn't been such a fucking shithead, I wouldn't have to go through this.

April 29

He's a doctor. This is the start and finish to his personality. Money seems to be his only selling feature. He thinks he's part of the upper echelons of society, though I'm sure his father works on a farm just like everyone else's. The more I listened the more I realized that everything I thought I wanted wasn't what I wanted after all. No matter how much I want to get away from my parents, I can't sell my soul to the devil.

I need to be at least attracted to the man I spend the rest of my life with, but I can barely bring myself to look at this guy. This man—the doctor, as he's referred to by my family because his name is not sufficient to identify him—can offer me everything I've ever dreamed of, everything but love.

My parents think this is a once-in-a-lifetime opportunity for a girl who's already been shamed. They think someone who's as emotionally unstable as I am should thank my lucky stars that someone wants to marry me.

May 10

Why do I let myself get hurt over and over again? First school, then Dev. Now they tell me I have to marry this man. This man I don't know. This man who talked at me, not with me, for thirty minutes. This man who assessed my qualifications as if interviewing me for a job. What gives him the right to decide if I'm acceptable or not? I don't think he's a suitable match. I can point out plenty that's wrong with him. But I'm not the customer, he is.

I honestly thought I wouldn't have to endure an arranged marriage. I thought Mom would want something better for me. She's suffered in silence in a loveless marriage. She's walked behind her husband as his veiled shadow. Yet she expects me to do the same. The past few nights she's been coming into my room to lecture me. She wants me to cooperate. She doesn't want a spinster daughter at home. It'll destroy whatever's left of their reputation. She didn't marry for love, so why should I?

September 12

Mom's been on my case all day. She's pissed off at me because I won't return Ajit's calls. I hate talking to him over the phone. I have absolutely nothing to say to the guy. How much can you really get to know a person through a few telephone conversations? I thought I knew Dev and what a fucking idiot he turned out to be!

I'm completely out of excuses. I'll have to call him back eventually. Maybe I'll just call up one of my friends and pretend I'm talking to him.

December 14

Tomorrow's the big day. I feel nauseous. I've had diarrhea for the last three days. And I've been walking around as if I have a fucking coat hanger stuck in my mouth so no one will suspect how I really feel. Not that it would matter to anyone. But what other options do I really have? This marriage is my only way out of this house!

January 7, 1992

I guess he's not that bad. He went with me to pick out my courses at the University of Calgary. He's quite boring and has no friends but I guess it's too late now to make him Mr. Popularity. At least I'm away from the prison my parents set up for me.

January 30

I've met lots of new people at school. While Ajit's at work I go out to movies, dinners, dances and even nightclubs. He thinks I sit at home and watch the clock until he comes back, and I'm going to keep letting him believe that. I'm having the best time ever!

Ajit doesn't have much time for me anyway, thank God! He's busy with school, and I'm happy with a platonic relationship for as long as possible. If I'm lucky, he'll divorce me. My parents won't want me back and I'll be rid of all of them.

He's grown on me, though. When he's around, he's quite sweet. Maybe we'll learn to love each other after all.

February 4

A new single neighbour just moved in next door. Mark seems really nice and a lot of fun. He said he'll show me around town if I want. He has lived here his entire life and claims it's the best place, minus the weather.

March 8

Ajit and I finally slept together. There's not much to write about but he's better than that fucking Dev!

April 9

My mother-in-law has arrived. Everything was perfect until she came. Needless to say, my clubbing days are over!

Ajit's so different when she's around. She's been here two days and already she's decided to change everything about me, including my name. The woman is a fucking psychopath. According to Ajit's Indian birth chart, some astrology shit, he'll prosper from a wife whose name begins with the letter H. This psychotic woman couldn't find a suitable bride with the initial H so the fucking moron has changed my name to Harpreet. Ajit doesn't think it's a big deal. He's too busy exploring my body like a baby exploring a new toy. He tastes, licks and prods, curiously awaiting a reaction. Then he loses interest and turns away to sleep. And I, hungry for a compatible playmate, fall asleep unsatisfied.

April 15

Today she forbade me to go to school. She said my outfit was "inappropriate" and men would stare. She said if I'm going to school for an education, there's no reason to put on makeup or wear short skirts because that's sending out the wrong message. She thinks I'm going to get raped because I'm showing skin. Then she had the audacity to tell me she purposely sought out a girl of average looks for Ajit because a pretty girl might stray.

She also warned me about my expenses. When Ajit came to look me over at the bride viewing, he claimed his family was very well off and I wouldn't need to worry about money. He failed to mention his cheap-ass mother counts every penny.

She also insists I quit my part-time job at the clothing store.

"People will say that we can't provide for you. You're a doctor's wife!"

I told her straight out to mind her own business. She went directly to Ajit to file a complaint against the disobedient daughter-in-law. Ajit hasn't said anything to me yet. We're continuing our charade of a marriage. It's only our bodies, not our souls, that are having a relationship. And that too has gone sour.

April 19

When Mark came over to borrow a shovel today, I invited him in. The crazy bitch stared at him and eavesdropped on our conversation from the hallway. Poor Mark was so uncomfortable that he left before I had finished making the coffee. I was actually relieved to see him go!

April 23

When she saw the phone bill this morning, she almost fell off her chair. She's going to talk to Ajit about how he's given me too much freedom. She says there's no need for me to call Vancouver. According to her, she and Ajit are the only family I need. Give me a break! When Ajit isn't around, she treats me like crap. If I complain to Ajit about her, he just laughs it off. Sometimes I hear them whispering and when I enter the room they stop. I don't know exactly what they talk about, but I've heard Ajit tell her she's overreacting. She says she's going to monitor my phone calls from now on. Her idiot, incompetent son has nothing to say about it. She says Ajit's father died of a heart attack ten years ago, but I bet she killed him with her nagging!

May 14

Today she came right out and told me to have a child because she has a right to expect a grandson within the first year. And if I don't have a child in the first year there's a chance I may become barren. Every day I grow to hate this woman more and more. She often reminds me her child is a doctor and he won't have any problem finding another wife who can give him sons.

June 30

I told her off today and she didn't respond. Instead, she ran out to Ajit's car as he drove up the driveway. Then Ajit demanded I show his mother respect. I walked away without making a comment but I could hear her from my bedroom. "I knew something wasn't right about her," she told him. "But no, you thought she was the prettiest girl you'd ever seen. Now what are you going to do with her so-called beauty? Her tongue needs to be cut off. If you only heard the things she says to me when you aren't at home."

July 10

Mark went to the stampede today with his new girlfriend. We had discussed going together back when I first met him so he came to invite me along, but Psycho turned them away from the door. She told them I had pneumonia...in the middle of summer!

July 21

Ajit stormed into our room today and pushed me against the wall. If I don't learn to respect him and his mother, he says the consequences will be worse.

August 10

She acts like my fucking warden. She's put locks on the phones. She refuses to let me talk to my parents because they're a bad influence. She thinks I'm having an affair so she accompanies me whenever I leave the house. Ajit's stressed out. He says our senseless fights interfere with his work. Not only is he incompetent but now he's become impotent as well.

September 4

Indian men are all the same! They're all fucking assholes! He hit me. Twice. He doesn't think there's anything wrong with that because it's his duty to keep me in line. I wonder how much his doctor friends would respect him if they knew he was a wife beater.

October 30

She was nagging me again. I snapped and told her I didn't want children, and if by accident I did get pregnant, I'd abort it. I told her I didn't want to produce offspring that have her poisonous blood running through their veins. She took a swing at me but I hit her before she got the chance to try again. I refuse to put up with her bullshit anymore.

I wonder what Ajit will do when he gets back from his trip. He'll never forgive me for hitting his mother.

November 9

She ran out onto the street into the wet snow in bare feet and no jacket as Ajit pulled up in his Cadillac. He put his arm around her and brought her into the house. His eyes were bloodshot. I've never seen him this angry. The performance she put on was outstanding. After her sobbing stopped, Ajit lashed out at me.

"I should never have married a woman from Canada!"

I wanted to tell him I had no desire to marry him either. I wanted to tell him I'd been coerced into the agreement. Instead I told him to fuck off and he slapped me. Hard. I packed my suitcase while they discussed my fate in the living room, and I slipped out the back door before they noticed. Mark drove me to the airport.

November 22

I didn't want to come home, but I would rather be here than with that fucking clown and that lunatic mother of his. I can't survive on my own. I have no money and no skills.

I know my parents are going to blame me for everything. Dad is going to side with Ajit. He's going to say I deserved to be smacked because I can't keep my mouth shut. Mom will tell me my place is with my husband. Maybe I should have waited until Ajit and his psycho mother had almost killed me. Perhaps then they wouldn't send me back to him. Oh God, please don't let them send me back! I can't take any more. Forgive me for wanting to run away. And please accept my apologies for wishing evil things upon Dev and his family. I'm also truly sorry for hating my parents. I'll never be selfish again. Just please don't let them send me back to that hell!

December 19

Mom says I'll have to go back. I can't hide in her house forever. Today she told me the story that her great-grandmother once told her.

"You see, Jessy, we Indian women are like glass dolls. We aren't permitted to have thoughts or emotions. That's what we're told and that's how we're treated. We're weak and fragile and pretty to look at like ornaments that are only for show. We're of no value until there's a buyer. We don't become complete until we reach our rightful owner. And if we break, when we break, it's all over for us. We can't be put back together again."

She says I'm a glass doll, too, and Ajit is my rightful owner. If I leave him, no one else will ever marry me. I'll be tarnished, but he won't have a problem finding a new wife. It'll be me who'll regret my decision, me who ends up alone and helpless.

December 24

Ajit called today. He's coming to get me. He says things will be different but I know they won't. I think Mom called him and begged him to take me back. She finds it less disgraceful to grovel in front of that asshole than to have a happily divorced daughter living at home. She's probably more worried about what Baksho and the others are thinking!

December 28

He came alone. He says his psycho mother doesn't approve of my coming back. Ajit says if I treat her with more respect, we'll be able to get along better. Even if he treats me better, I know that bitch won't. And he'll never leave her for me.

December 29

Today my prayers have been answered. There really is a God! It's truly a miracle. I couldn't believe Dad took my side. He truly does care for me.

As I was pleading with Mom not to send me back to Calgary, Ajit got angry and shoved me toward the door. Paying no attention to my family, he grabbed my suitcase in one hand and my arm with the other and pulled me down the stairs. I yelled and screamed and tried to break free, but I couldn't escape. Mom was watching in horror but said nothing. Ajit stopped long enough to tell Dad that if he'd raised a more obedient daughter, I would have made a much better wife. He accused my family of being illiterate, poor, uncivilized and dysfunctional, and he said he'd be doing my parents a favour if I were to die by his hands.

Dad, who'd been silent the entire time Ajit was ranting, stood in front of the door to block us. In a loud voice he told me to go to my room and take my belongings with me. Then Dad opened the door and asked Ajit to leave. Ajit was not willing to budge and continued to curse. By that time Dad's fists were clenched and his eyes were raging with fire. He grabbed the table lamp, which was two feet from the door, ripping the cord right out of the socket, and swung the lamp at Ajit, narrowly missing his head. Before Ajit could retaliate, Dad lunged at him, got his hands around Ajit's neck and pinned him against the wall. Mom screamed for him to stop, and he let go of Ajit's neck, but while Ajit was gasping for air, Dad unfastened his leather belt. With his belt dangling from one hand, he pushed Ajit out of the house and followed him to his car.

I am safe.

Sunday Langar – 1993

"They are everywhere! I found twenty of them plastered to my store window yesterday!" Baksho exaggerated as Mrs. Gill analyzed each of the new handmade fluorescent posters.

No Gossiping Zone, Prayer Only.
P.S. No praying for sons!

The women gathered around. It was still quite early in the morning and the *sangat* had not yet congregated in the main hall.

"When you called me about the notice boards," Mrs. Gill said as she examined the posters, "I thought you were talking about the posters advertising the upcoming Indian Cultural Night. Apparently, there will be some well-known Punjabi singers and politicians attending. I'm really looking forward to it!"

But Baksho was not listening to Mrs. Gill. Her attention was on the signs, so Mrs. Gill also pulled her thoughts back to the matter at hand. "Anyway, I wasn't expecting this *tamasha*! What drama!"

"Who do you think did it?" Baksho asked. "Maybe the *gurdwara comaity*?"

"No," Indu replied, "the *comaity-comooty* has been busy ripping them down."

"I wouldn't have put it past that Jessy girl," Mrs. Gill said, "but since her divorce, Rani and her husband have moved the whole family to Surrey."

"I can't believe Rani allowed the divorce, but I heard it was the girl's husband's decision." Baksho was utterly disgusted. "You women are lucky your daughters didn't turn out like that one. She was always hanging around while we did *seva*. Thank God, they didn't fall into her trap!"

"What about Rani's younger daughter, Tejinder? Who'll marry her now?" Indu's concern was sincere.

"Well, I'm glad they moved or all the girls in the neighbourhood would get a bad reputation!" Kamal said. Her high-pitched voice was hard on the ears.

Kamal was a recent addition to the gossip cluster. As Baksho and Mrs. Gill's old entourage had dispersed to newer and larger homes in the suburbs, the group had begun to give women they had previously overlooked an opportunity to demonstrate their allegiance to the sisterhood. Besides, Kamal was different. She was obsessed with Bollywood and subscribed to every Indian magazine available. She carried a copy of *Stardust* in her large handbag at all times, and she would recreate ridiculous costumes and get-ups from movies she had seen and wear them to the local weddings. Baksho's crew had every reason not to include her, but her husband had become a millionaire overnight because of a smart real estate investment he had made in the late 1970s. Now, although Kamal could afford not to work, she had purchased the beauty salon where she was once employed, and this meant discounted treatments for close friends. Baksho was having trouble applying *mehndi* to her roots as her shoulder joints were showing signs of arthritis and she found it difficult to lift her arms. And Mrs. Gill had tweezed her first grey hair just the other morning, so she too would be benefiting from Kamal's services in the near future.

Kamal was also well known for treating neighbours to all the new releases at the Indian cinemas. As Indu often pointed out, she also had the money to bring back expensive *suits* and *saris* for everyone from her semi-annual trips to India. So, although she had several flaws—one being her fingernails-on-the-blackboard voice—that Baksho and the others had to overlook, no one could deny that Kamal was a very generous lady. She met the criteria to be an exclusive member of their group, if only for materialistic reasons.

"I heard from Manjeet that Jessy is going to be a lawyer." Baksho's legs were beginning to buckle under her weight, and she sat down against the wall next to the poster. "So her chances of getting re-married are next to nothing now. First, that lower-caste boy scandal, then a divorce and now an education—she's a recipe for failure."

"Please, Baksho *panji, bus kar.* Stop saying these things," Shindi pleaded. "We all have daughters, so who are we to judge?" She was another of the unfortunate women who had conceived daughters but no sons.

Shindi and her family had moved into the area only a few weeks earlier, so she had never met Rani or her daughters. She was a petite woman and her frizzy shoulder-length hair, which was an uneven shade of brown that was most likely the result of a home colour kit, was always matted down with two clips on the side part. Her beady little eyes were lost behind her large hooked nose so that her face constantly displayed an expression of frustration and mistrust. Shindi had been naturally attracted to Indu and bonded with her over their mutual sorrows, and although she had already become known for her frugality and did not possess the same riches as Kamal, she had easily won the hearts of Baksho and Mrs. Gill by siding with them on many other issues. Thus, it had been only a matter of days before she and her family were bombarded with information regarding former and current inhabitants of the neighbourhood. Baksho had also taken a special interest in Shindi when she learned that her old nemesis, Prakash Kaur, was Shindi's sister-in-law. Any of Prakash Kaur's foes were soul sisters to Baksho!

"What's true is true, so it has to be said!" Kamal unfolded her arms and placed her hands on her hips. She was overacting again.

"Since when did you get the right to decide what should be said?" Baksho demanded. She did not filter her words when addressing anyone, not even Kamal, and her suspicious nature forced her to question Kamal's every action. And while on the one hand, she was still a little hesitant to let Kamal into the circle of trust, on the other hand, she didn't want a falling-out with her either because Kamal was a loyal customer of the JD Meat, Sweets, Music, Gifts and Movie Mart, and that is how Baksho preferred it. Her prices were much steeper than the other Indian stores in Vancouver, but Kamal did not bother to shop for bargains.

Kamal disregarded Baksho's comment and followed Shindi's eyes to the poster. She smacked her hand against her forehead. "So they put them up here, too?" she screeched.

"Who?" Indu asked.

"My daughter Sonia and her stupid *saheli*—or shall I say her *dear friend* Asha! Who else? It was some school project. I've been apologizing to the neighbours all morning. I've told Lalita so many times I want her daughter to stay away from my Sonia!"

Mrs. Gill was still not accustomed to Kamal's voice and was tempted to plug her ears each time she spoke.

Indu was puzzled. "I'm surprised Sonia does not behave more like her older brother. He is such a *siaana munda*, Kamal!" She paused and then asked, "But didn't Sonia and Asha's *school-schall* let out a couple of weeks ago?"

Kamal was flushed with embarrassment.

"Asha can't be *that* bad," Baksho said. "Are you sure you're not jealous? That *kuri* can make the most beautiful of girls look average." Then, realizing what she had said, she tried to redeem herself for the offensive comment by adding, "But I'm not saying your Sonia is ugly. She's okay, too."

When Sonia was fourteen, Kamal had become obsessed with Bollywood actress Madhuri Dixit, and she had enrolled Sonia in drama lessons and classical Indian dance classes. She also made her follow strict diets and analyze the movie *Dil* over and over again until she familiarized herself with all of Madhuri's expressions. But Sonia was hopeless. She was an average-looking girl, gifted in mathematics and—Kamal's worst nightmare—athletic. Sonia was, in fact, a tomboy and only interested in playing sports.

"This is exactly why we're moving!" Mrs. Gill announced.

Indu's and Baksho's jaws dropped.

"What do you mean?" Baksho was almost in tears. Mrs. Gill was her only real friend in the neighbourhood—or so she thought—and she had not once mentioned or discussed such a move with her.

"These kids today have no morals. Look at what they learn from these *goray* television shows." Mrs. Gill directed her statement to Kamal, the mother of the maverick Sonia. "We're going back to India soon and we'll open a business there. Fast food chains are becoming very popular."

"Well, I did hear some bad things about your Manohar and Roop but I dismissed them," Baksho muttered then bit her lip when she realized she had spoken out loud.

Indu glared at Baksho, but luckily Mrs. Gill had not heard the comment and carried blithely on. "My girls will be their in-laws' responsibility when they marry, but I'm worried about my boys. There are so many drugs and gangs here now."

"But what about your work with the women's organization?" Indu inquired.

Mrs. Gill had signed on to work as a women's rights advocate. "Oh, I've already handed in my resignation! It's time for someone else to make a difference." None of the women were aware that Mrs. Gill had only attended three out of the twelve mandatory meetings while she was a member.

"I think that's a great idea. Just look at Manjeet. Her daughter was married off years ago, and she's living in a big *house-hoose* with two basement suites near Scott Road in Surrey. Manjeet has no more burdens!" Indu was envious.

The women turned as one to see that a committee member had walked into the foyer and was standing laughing at the poster. As he went to take it down, he turned to them to say, "Maybe you women could learn something from the children."

Baksho was about to respond but Mrs. Gill tugged on her *dupatta*.

Instead, Kamal said, "You know these silly Canadian-born kids, Uncle *ji*. They like to joke while we must worry what will become of our culture."

The member took down the last of the posters and threw them into the trash bin.

"As you know, Uncle *ji*," Shindi added, "it's so difficult to bring the children to the *gurdwara* these days. They don't want to listen to *kirtan* or *paht*. They have no time for hymns or prayers. All they listen to is *dhol dhamaka*, that annoying loud music."

"It's your responsibility to teach them about our religion," he responded. "You should teach your children to do *seva*. But of course, you're right—this new generation has its own agenda. They are so distant from God." He excused himself and went to clear the sandals and shoes that were blocking the entrance.

"Thank God the *comaity* has changed!" Baksho said and turned so that she could watch Shindi's reaction. "The old *comaity* was putting in all kinds of new rules. They wouldn't let us breathe when the *gurdwara* was under Prakash Kaur's reign."

Shindi looked away.

"Are you settled in?" Mrs. Gill asked. "If you need any help, do ask. I can't take too much stuff with me—and by God's grace we have so much! You can keep my pretty velvet couches and my eight-piece bedroom suite if you like. Otherwise we'll donate them to the poor."

"That's very kind of you, but I'm fine." Shindi smiled politely but it was evident by the expression in her tiny eyes that she was insulted by Mrs. Gill's attempt at charity. Although she spent much of her time attending garage sales and flea markets, she refused to take handouts from other Indians.

"Just be careful," Kamal told Shindi. "Don't let your daughters befriend any of the *bad* girls. I'm going to have to send my Sonia away for college. That's the only way we'll get that nasty Asha off her back!" She paused for a moment then turned to face Mrs. Gill. "Maybe you're right! Perhaps our children should all be shipped to boarding schools in Bombay. It may be the only way to preserve our traditions and values. Just look at what they're learning in schools here!" She waved a hand toward the trash bin with the torn-down posters that had been created by her own daughter, Sonia, and probably that Asha girl as well.

Asha – Hope

The envelope was addressed to Sonia Brar in Asha's neat handwriting and I knew what was in it as soon as I took it out of the mailbox. With my house keys and the fancy envelope in one hand and my textbooks under my other arm, I plopped down on my futon. My body was burning, but not because my wool coat was too thick for the cold January afternoon. It was the anger directed toward my merciless society that was blistering my skin.

There in bright red letters was the announcement I feared:

Mrs. Lalita Kumari Uppal and the Late Mr. Harbhajan Singh request your presence at the auspicious wedding ceremony of their beloved daughter Asha to Eshaan Chopra.

The date for the wedding was set for February 7, 1996, less than a month away.

I had not heard from my best friend, Asha, in almost a year. Not a phone call or a letter. And now this. The last time I had seen her was the day of her father's funeral. Although my mother had not approved of my attending the actual funeral, she had insisted we pay our respects at the home since I had come all that way and everyone else in the community would be there.

The women had surrounded Lalita, Asha's mother, where she sat on the couch, while my mother motioned for me to have a seat on the floor next to Asha and some of the other girls.

"*Bechari,*" Mrs. Gill chanted again and again to Lalita as if every other word in her vocabulary had been exhausted. "Poor woman."

"What will you do now?" Baksho asked. "What does it matter that he wasn't a great man? At least he was around to offer you his name and a roof over your head. As long as you have a husband, you'll get by in life. People will respect you no matter what kind of *aadmi* you're married to. But what will you do now? Once you try to venture out into the world alone, you'll only encounter defeat and ridicule."

"That's okay, Lalita," Indu said, rubbing Lalita's back while the widow cried into her *dupatta*. "Just let it all out. I heard about this woman from my village who was in such shock when her husband died that she did not shed a single tear. The elders said she went *crazy-croozy* because she did not express her despair. They had to bring a live-in nurse to take care of her."

My mother nodded her head in agreement, but I knew she did not really care. She was only there because of her loyalty to her clan. The *Dukh Sukh Club,* as Asha and I called them, consisted of my mother and all her friends, but on special occasions like this their clones from neighbouring areas joined them as well to offer their unsolicited wisdom to the grieving family. The group took it upon themselves to provide Asha and her family with the inspiration and hope to move forward with their lives. But if their sympathy alone did not result in instant depression for Lalita, their solutions for salvaging Asha's dismal future most certainly would.

"Don't be foolish, Lalita," Baksho said. "Marry Asha off to someone of your own caste as soon as possible. Now that there will be no dowry, you can't be too picky. She's a half-breed— half Sikh and half Hindu— and she can't get by on her looks when it comes to these situations. She may have all the boys in our community bewitched with her green eyes and her fair skin, but marriage is a whole other story. Relieve yourself at least of this burden."

"But times have changed, Baksho *panji*," Indu said. "It may not be that difficult to find Asha a suitable groom because many people don't ask for *dowries-showries* in Canada anymore."

"Like there would have been a dowry if her husband was still alive," my mother whispered into Baksho's ear, but unfortunately she had said it loud enough for the others to hear. "Everyone knows that drunk gambled everything away."

"Lalita, you have such an awful *kismet*." Mrs. Gill took the attention away from my mother's inappropriate comment by adding her own ridiculous statement. "And now your daughter will have to waste away, too."

Asha had been quiet throughout this whole horrible ordeal. I thought she might have still been angry with me so I too said nothing and continued to listen to what was being discussed. It occurred to me that surviving the death of a husband, son, father or brother could not be as difficult as surviving the cold comfort of the *Dukh Sukh Club*.

Now I glanced back at the wedding invitation. The red letters seemed to have been poured onto the page as if Asha had slit her wrist and dripped her own blood onto the glossy paper. The cheerful language and radiant colours did not disguise the truth about her future.

Just as I picked up the phone to call my mother, my Puerto Rican roommate barged in with a bag of groceries and a bottle of tequila. She dropped her purse on the floor, placed the bags on the counter, grabbed two shot glasses, a salt shaker, two limes and a knife and squeezed onto the futon next to me. I put the phone down next to the wedding card and opened the bottle of tequila.

"What's that?" Camille grabbed the card and began to read out the names, mispronouncing each one.

"My best friend is getting married," I replied, slicing the lime on the surface of the scratched-up coffee table beside me.

"Wow, you must be excited! Are you going to be a bridesmaid? How long have you known her?" Camille took off her scarf and jacket and threw them on the floor.

"Asha and I met the first day of our afternoon kindergarten class. She was freaking out in the cloakroom because she couldn't speak much English. I was the only one in the class who was willing to translate, and we've been good friends ever since." I said, lying just a little about the nature of our relationship.

"I wish I had a long-time childhood friend. My father dragged us all over the world so we were never in one place long enough for me to make any real friends. Surprisingly, we never made it to Vancouver. It must've been cool to live there!" Camille licked the salt off her hand, took the drink down and quickly sucked on the lime. She then licked the dregs of liquor from her empty glass.

"I think it's done, Camille," I said, laughing at her.

She poured another drink and chugged it back. "So tell me, what was it like growing up in Vancouver?" She filled my glass this time and waited for me to do a shot with her but then grew impatient and put the bottle directly to her lips. Her boyfriend of three months had not returned any of her calls for the past week. She had been camping outside his dorm room earlier in the day and I was afraid to ask what had happened.

"It was anything but fun that first year we met! My mother had to get special permission so Asha and I could leave school a few minutes early because the white kids from the high school would harass us on our way home. 'Go back to your own country! Curry eater, raghead!' I've heard them all."

"Wha-a-a-at?" Camille looked amused and shocked at the same time.

"I'm serious! I remember this one time Asha's mom marched into her first grade classroom after Asha came home with a bloody nose. Chad Parker, a big-mouthed blonde kid, had been picking on me for days. Whenever we had free time, he would walk around and stop me from playing with any of the toys at the activity station. Asha was in a different class but when I relayed the incident to her, she took it upon herself to attack Chad at recess. The teacher called Chad's parents and told them Asha was a school bully who needed to be dealt with and we were both sent home for the day." I paused, took a sip, put the shot glass down and then continued, "And would you believe the next day, we saw Chad and his parents in the school parking lot and his father rolled down the window and shouted that we'd get more than a bloody nose next time. And that jerk, Chad, was leering at us smugly through the back window. So the next day we followed him onto the playground and Asha held his arms while I kicked him in the balls. He was so scared of us after that day that he didn't tell on us. I can still see his ugly face."

"Holy shit, no way!"

"Yes, way! My parents had no idea that the taunts we heard outside of school weren't half as bad as the ones we suffered within it. And we couldn't dare tell them because they would talk to the teachers, some of whom were racist themselves, and then we would just get bullied more. So from then on, Asha and I made a pact to stick together, no matter what. And now she's getting married." I finally took the shot. I could have told Camille that the pact had been broken years ago and we were no longer best friends, but I chose to keep that information to myself.

Camille tripped over her own feet as she hurried back from the kitchen with more limes.

"Once we got a little older, my mother started to blame Asha for everything. She didn't want to admit that I was a brat too, so she yelled at Asha and her mother on a regular basis. She warned me that if she received any more complaints about our behaviour at school, we would not be allowed to see each other."

"So what did you do?" Camille's eyes were half-closed from the effects of the tequila, but she had me on a roll.

"We hung out behind my mother's back. And we continued to get into trouble. I was suspended in the fifth grade for pulling down Chad Parker's shorts during gym class, but Asha was the one who dared me. I told my mother Asha had no knowledge of what I was going to do. Then in the seventh grade, we found a bottle of her dad's whisky behind the couch and we mixed it with the apple juice in the fridge. Her little brother drank it and ended up in the hospital. We both got into tons of shit that night, but my dad and my brother covered for me and made peace with Asha's parents without my mother knowing anything about the incident. In the eighth grade, I got caught passing obscene notes to Todd Collins, the most popular guy in school. When he didn't respond, I scribbled *slut* all over his girlfriend's locker. When that didn't grab his attention, I cornered him by his locker and planted one on his mouth while Asha stood on the lookout for his girlfriend. When he finally broke up with that dumb bimbo and asked me out on a date, I decided I was no longer interested. But rather than tell him straight out, Asha and I composed a long letter telling him how much of a dork he was. And when he tried to talk to me the next day, I told him if he told anyone I had ever liked him I would spread a rumour all over the school that he had herpes. A few days later Asha heard that he and his buddies were hatching a plan to get even with me. So before he could get his revenge, I walked up to him in the hall and kissed him in front of at least a dozen spectators. And then, just like I had seen in a movie, I stepped aside and announced loud enough for everyone in the school to hear that the fairytale was a hoax because he was still a toad. In the meantime, Asha had Scotch-taped a dead frog to the outside of his locker. He never messed with us again! The last I heard, people were still calling the poor guy *Toad Collins*."

Camille had just taken a shot into her mouth and now she sprayed it all over the futon. I was laughing so much I nearly spilled my own drink. I got a hold of myself, refilled Camille's glass, although she should have been cut off four shots earlier, and carried on. "Asha and I were totally crazy together! There was this house party I planned for my fifteenth birthday. It was at her place on a weekend that her parents were away for a family funeral, and the cops showed up when it got out of control. Asha knew my mother would have moved us out of the neighbourhood if she knew I was involved, so she took all the blame for that one!"

"How did you keep it from your mother?"

"For some time I made up lots of imaginary friends, but when I couldn't keep the names straight and my mother started asking too many questions, I told her I was spending all my spare time with my new best friend, Vanessa Huxtable. I don't think she ever realized Vanessa was a character on *The Cosby Show*."

Camille was laughing so hard there were tears streaming down her face.

"What? I couldn't think of anyone else, the show was actually on when she was badgering me. Anyway, I think she knew all along that Asha and I were hanging out but she chose to be in denial."

"So can I come with you? Maybe there will be some hot men at this wedding! Or are you taking Sonny?"

"Are you kidding? My mother would shit if I brought a date to the wedding and then she'd have us married in a week!" I sucked the last slice of lime dry. Although my parents had no problem with me marrying an Indian of my choice, they did not allow me to date. It made absolutely no sense and trying to explain this to a half-corked Puerto Rican girl would be impossible.

"Why not? He's pretty sexy—I'd do him!"

"Whatever! I'll only take a guy home when I'm ready to trap him into marriage. That's what my mother's definition of the perfect daughter, Vimmi Bains, did."

"Who?" Camille asked.

"This girl I went to high school with. She was dating this guy who wouldn't commit, so she set him up." I paused, thinking perhaps this was not the best story for me to tell Camille in her current state, then continued anyway. "She got a friend of hers to make an anonymous call to both of their parents one afternoon when they were together in some dodgy motel. The families were so embarrassed the two were married within a month. According to my mother, Vimmi even faked a pregnancy to seal the deal." I remember calling Asha to ask her for the real details but she had not returned my call.

At that moment Camille sprang up and ran for the bathroom. I could hear her hurling. I did consider holding her hair back while she clung to the toilet bowl as I had done on a number of previous occasions, but I was still thinking about Asha.

That night I lay awake, tossing and turning, afraid to fall asleep. Had Asha really changed so much that she would sacrifice all she dreamed of? Or had she succumbed to the pressure Indian parents used to guilt their children into anything short of sin? It was obvious her mother had arranged the wedding as Asha would never have agreed to this of her own accord.

Then it hit me. Could this be one of Asha's plans? Was she planning to build a palace for herself from the broken pieces of her mother's pride? Although the idea excited me, I also became frightened for her. As a child Asha had threatened to run away whenever she was angry with her mother. She would pack her bags and sneak into my house, but she always returned home before my mother found her in my room. But how would she pull this one off? And did she need my help? Did she even *want* my help?

Face it, I told myself. Too much had happened and too much time had passed for Asha and I to start over where we left off.

Because of my mother's interference, the Asha I once knew so well had slowly drifted away. Of course, I knew my mother was not entirely to blame. It was mostly my own fault. Something had happened to Asha. She had started acting a little strange the last couple of years of high school, and at first I thought it was family problems again and I didn't push it and she didn't volunteer any information. But then I became suspicious. She had started making other friends, mostly hanging out with the *nice* Indian girls, and so I thought she was betraying me. Activities we once found pleasurable turned obligatory. Our relationship was no longer a priority in either of our lives. She would always be busy when I wanted to get together or would make excuses to avoid me at school.

Asha knew I was applying to colleges and universities far away from home and I persuaded her to do the same because I wanted her to go with me, but it seemed like she was no longer interested in being in my life. When I finally confronted her, she tried to convince me how lonely I would be if I went away to school. She said I would not be able to survive on my own, that I would come crying back. She said a lot of mean things to me that day, so I accused her of being jealous, evil and a million other things and that was when I decided she was no longer my best friend. We did not talk after that day although she did take one last step to salvage what little was left of our friendship the day before I moved to Toronto. She had come to say goodbye, but I was still pissed at her and pretended I was too busy to chat. She left without saying much but looked as if she was about to cry.

I arrived in Vancouver the evening before Asha's wedding and took a cab from the airport to my parents' house. My mother was very obviously not in favour of me returning home for Asha's wedding, but she knew the more she opposed my decision the more determined I would be to attend.

Although my father no longer shared my mother's narrow-minded views about our society and its values, he was never able to stop her ramblings.

"Don't you think it's time you got married?" she began. Having been away for a while I had forgotten that listening to my mother's voice was like listening to fingernails scraping a blackboard. "Even the Bollywood girls start thinking about finding husbands before your age," she continued. "And look at all your friends. You think you're some kind of princess waiting for your prince to fall out of the sky, don't you? Look at me! I was so young and gorgeous when I got married, and everyone tells me I still look like Bollywood's *dream girl,* Hema Malini! But look who I got, your father, a replica of all the villains in Indian cinema!"

My mother had been really fortunate to find such a caring and loving man as my father. He shone with charm and charisma like many of her favourite *filmi* heroes, but she couldn't see that, and regardless of what she believed, she was no *dream girl*.

"You're not getting any younger, you know," she went on. "Your father and I have to listen to people constantly reminding us that most women your age already have two or three children. But no, *you* have to finish school first. So how much longer is this school business going to continue? The least you could have done was make me proud by winning a Filmfare award, but now we have no choice but to marry you off. Each day that passes is one less chance of you finding a suitable boy. Thank God your brother is happily married and living far away from here or else he'd be embarrassed, too!"

Then, after a thorough inspection of my body, she started again, "And what have you done to yourself? What's that yellow colour in your hair? You look like a zebra. And why is your hair so short like a boy's? You could at least put on a little makeup—look at that boring face! And you're so skinny. How do you expect to carry children with those scrawny hips?" She paused briefly before adding, "Why do you need to have so many muscles on your arms and legs? We sent you to Toronto to become an accountant, not a *kabbadi* or a wrestling champion."

I had no desire to listen to her criticism and advice anymore, so I stayed just long enough to change out of the new identity I had created for myself. I emerged draped in ominous black silk, woven with all the lies and disappointments of my childhood. It was the night before the wedding, the last day Asha would be in her maternal home as a single woman. It was the night her family and friends came together to celebrate and make last-minute wedding preparations.

My mother looked me up and down, and I knew if it had been any other occasion she would have asked me to change out of that "depressing and superstitious colour." Instead she said, "I still can't believe you came all this way for that girl's wedding. I tried so hard to make you understand, but you just couldn't stay away from her. After what happened in India in 1984, I thought you would come to your senses, but no, you still followed her around, wagging your tail!"

"Mom, just because Asha and her mother are Hindus, it doesn't mean they're responsible for the Indian government's attacks on the Golden Temple!"

"Well, that woman belongs to the same caste as Indira Gandhi," she argued. "And how can you forget about the thousands of innocent Sikhs who were tortured, raped, wrongfully imprisoned and brutally murdered. It was genocide, Sonia!"

"Yes, I know, Mom, I agree with you, but you can't blame Asha's mother for all those terrible crimes!"

In fact, for my mother the tensions between the Hindus and Sikhs in the 1980s were just an excuse. Although she would never mention this to any of her friends, I knew she was holding a grudge against Lalita over something that had happened more than twenty-two years earlier. My mother had wanted to arrange Asha's father's marriage to her own younger cousin in India but he had fallen for Lalita, a Hindu, instead. Despite being Sikh, he had married this Hindu woman. According to my mother, that made him a traitor, and she insisted that he had only tied the knot with Lalita to stay in the country. However, Lalita had been a breathtaking beauty with a seductive smile that froze men into statues. One look at her and any man would have forsaken his faith and family.

"Mixed blood, mixed loyalties," my mother would say time after time.

And when the riots broke out between Hindus and Sikhs in India, my mother had one more reason to hate Lalita. Then, rather than stand together and find solutions to stop the terror that was already spreading a dark cloud of sorrow and suffering over a once-bustling and prosperous Punjab, my mother and some members of the community had turned on one another. My father, who had once stayed up all night with Asha's father and her extended family to guard houses against vandalism and other racially motivated crimes, no longer spoke to any of them. Revenge and demands for justice began to consume the minds of many individuals who called Little India home. The same people who once referred to each other as *apnay* now called each other enemies.

"Don't you remember what happened to my uncle and my two cousins? They were hauled away in the middle of the night and never heard from again." My mother wiped a tear away.

I knew that if I left at this moment, she would continue the rant after I returned, so it was best to listen to it all now and let her get it out of her system. Though I would have liked to remind her that the Bollywood actors she idolized were also most likely Hindus, I kept my mouth shut.

"And I'm sure you haven't forgotten how Lalita treated you after that Air India plane went down. She blamed the entire Sikh community for the tragedy and accused *you* and made you leave her house."

Although I was too young to remember exactly what had happened in those days, my mother made sure I would never forget. She had preferred I only watch Bollywood movies when she was at home, so I had often gone to Asha's house to watch television. They did not have cable and therefore the news had been our only source of entertainment. I remember the two of us being glued to the screen after the Air India flight went down off the coast of Ireland, and we watched the broken hearts and shattered images in despair. There was no human emotion that could express or justify the grief the families of the innocent victims had to endure at that time and in the endless days afterwards.

Yet, just like me and Asha, those people on the flight were caught in the middle. We were too Indian to fit into Canada and too Canadian to return to India. We did not belong anywhere. A foreign war instigated by politics, power and greed was responsible for destroying so many families on both sides of the controversy. And if it had been up to my mother, it would have destroyed my friendship with Asha as well.

Asha's mother had lost all respect for my family and other members of the Sikh community long before the allegations about the plane crash were made public. She did not, as my mother liked to believe, actually kick me out of her house, but her aloof behaviour toward me had been enough to deliver the message, and it was then that Asha and I realized that the same skin colour did not confirm kinship. Before that time it had never dawned on either of us that others viewed us as different.

Our friendship was overridden by our parents' beliefs. Even as a child I could understand that hatred did not breed peace. Adults, however, managed to overlook this reality and we became a part of their battles. Over time many from our community were able to move on and rekindle old relationships, but the human race would never be immune to its vulnerabilities.

"I'll take it you're not coming to the wedding, then," I said to my mother.

When I heard my father calling my mother to tell her the movie was starting, I took it as my cue to leave.

There was no mistaking which house belonged to Asha. It looked like a used car lot. The vehicles were double-parked in the driveway, a large blue and white tent occupied the entire front yard and vibrant flags hung from the roof.

I arrived just as the bridal festivities were beginning. Young women were dancing in the living room while several elders stood in the kitchen singing folksongs to bring good tidings to the bride and her family. None of the women could carry a tune, however, and for me their voices only added to the sour taste of the arranged marriage.

Through the commotion and celebration I finally spotted Asha who, much to my dismay, was beside herself with laughter. She looked beautiful in a yellow beaded *sari*. Her skin glowed from all the *vatna*, the mixture of turmeric paste, rubbed on her body earlier that day. The *mehndi* on her hands and feet, which had dried to a crumbling paste, only enhanced the look of an enthusiastic bride. Asha had apparently embraced all the aspects of Punjabi culture that I had come to despise, and I was glad I had been absent during this nonsense, though perhaps she was truly content with it.

I had always assumed that Asha shared my dreams. All these years I had controlled my every action, my every thought, so I would not be like any of the women I knew. I had tried to influence Asha into believing she was no different than me. In fact, I suddenly realized she had never been anything like me. I had tried to turn her into someone she could not be.

As I stood watching from just inside the doorway, I noticed that Vimmi Bains was standing in the midst of the crowd of young women who were wrapping gifts that would be distributed to the groom's family in the morning during the *milni*, right before the marriage ceremony at the *gurdwara*. She was dressed in what must have been her own hot pink wedding *lengha* and artificial jewellery, and I remembered that Asha had disliked her even more than I did in high school. And now there she stood as an honorary member of the family. She had taken my place in Asha's life.

I placed my wedding present on the dining room table and headed for the front door again.

"Oh, Sonia, you made it!" Lalita threw her arms around me so tightly I could not breathe.

All the women turned to stare. The singing also came to a halt as Asha hurried away from her new friends to greet the one who did not recognize her.

"I'm *so* glad you're here, Sonia! I can't imagine getting married without you. The day I've always dreamed of has finally arrived!" Asha then turned to glare at her mother, and Lalita quickly looked away and scurried off.

I was surprised that Asha expressed no resentment toward me. It was

TS0333 VRA-YVR
S62313-601-1918
Depart. 3APR2017
20:31:38 3APR2017

White Wine	$6.75
Chicken Sandwich	$7.75

Total CAD 14.50
MasterCard CAD 14.50

**** **** **** 0868
Expires AUG2019

as though we were the best of friends once again. As for her dreaming of her wedding day, that was a side of Asha I had never known existed.

Still, I told her I had been thrilled to hear about the wedding. I got so carried away with my lies that I even offered to help with the cooking.

"Eshaan and I couldn't get a direct flight back to London, so we'll be in Toronto for a few days. Eshaan has always wanted to see Niagara Falls. We will be staying with some of his family, but I'll give you a call and maybe we can go for lunch or something!"

Asha seemed so excited that I promised my services as a tour guide, but I was hoping this was all just a polite gesture and that she would not call me after all.

I kept a secure lock on my tongue that night. A few rum and cokes would have helped settle my nerves, but the alcohol was being served in the garage and, of course, it was only for the men, and I did not trust any of the boys to sneak some booze from the bar in a teacup for me. But it was probably for the best as the last thing I needed was for Baksho and the other members of the *Dukh Sukh Club* to notice a drink in my hand. I am sure Asha could have also used a stiff one. I wish I'd had the opportunity to take her to Whistler for a bachelorette party, but maybe she had enjoyed the lame bridal shower Vimmi had apparently thrown for her two weeks earlier.

So with a parched mouth, I continued to quietly monitor Asha, watching for signs of unhappiness, still hoping she would rethink her decision and stop the wedding. Although I prided myself on being an advocate of change, it was something I myself resisted. Much to my displeasure the festivities continued, and I watched as Asha's maternal uncle conducted the final ceremony of the night by dipping the bangles of her *choora* one by one into milk and then placing them on her wrists. And then the women lined up, pushing and shoving to be the first to offer their monetary blessings. Regardless of what Asha said, the activities would not have ceased in my absence. I was merely a spectator, one without say and without opinion.

Although I had no desire to attend the nuptials the next day, I forced myself to go. My mother, after pointing out that she was not lucky enough to witness the same joy for her own daughter, came unwillingly and sat next to me throughout the ceremony. Then as her friends gathered around, she continued to justify my reasons for not being married. She was also able to put to rest the rumour of my running off with a *gora*.

"Why are they having a *gurdwara* wedding when there is a Hindu *mandir* she could have used?" my mother asked Baksho.

"I think Lalita wanted the wedding at the *mandir*, but the groom's family insisted on the *gurdwara*, and Asha must have persuaded her mother," Baksho replied. "That girl can convince anyone to see it her way, but Lalita claims it's because her good-for-nothing dead husband would have wanted it this way, too."

"Well, I think it's all for show," my mother said.

"Shhhhh! The *lanvs* are starting," Indu said.

"This is going to take forever!" I could not help but comment. If I had known I would be sandwiched between my mother and her friends I would have thought twice about attending.

"It's because you don't understand what's going on," my mother said.

I did not want an explanation but I knew I was going to get one.

"The four verses known as *lanvs* are read from the Sri Guru Granth Sahib," Indu explained. "Simultaneously after each *lanv* the bride and groom walk around the Guru Granth Sahib four times, and that is known as *parkarma*. Although there are several versions and translations of the four stanzas, each one signifies the progression of the blessed union, two individuals coming together as one before and with God."

Baksho chimed in when she noticed Asha's brothers and male cousins forming a semi-circle around the Guru Granth Sahib, "Back in my mother's day when brides' faces were covered and they needed someone to help them find their way around, the brothers would assist their sisters during the ceremony." Baksho shook her head and added, "There is no need for this custom anymore. I don't know why people still follow it."

"But everyone makes up their own rules now. I've even been to a wedding where the bride and groom remained seated throughout the whole ceremony..." Indu stated.

"Oh no," my mother said. "The verses are to be read while the bride and groom are standing, not sitting!"

"Where did you hear that?" Baksho asked.

I tuned them out. The lines of religion and culture had become blurred for me, and because of the oppressive views of some individuals in my community, I had my own version of the holy and humble ceremony.

I watched as Asha followed a few steps behind her groom, clasping the decorated *pallah or* scarf. According to my mother, their union would be jeopardized if she released it or it came undone, but it was securely placed over the groom's shoulder, burdening the bride with the sole responsibility of keeping their marriage afloat. Her brothers escorted her, passing her from one to the other to ensure she would not stumble in a moment of weakness, then taking her back to where she began the circuit. And in the end she sat next to Eshaan while his relatives dictated his actions from the right.

All of this re-confirmed that from then on Asha would never lead but follow blindly, nor would she journey alone on her chosen path, whether that path be right or wrong. She would sacrifice as other women had done before her, and only then would she earn the respect of her new family.

However, the wedding was a great success. After several speeches by politicians to ensure future votes, a few outcries to fight for a homeland and numerous other irrelevant issues with little or no mention about the symbolism and meaning of the actual ceremony or its origins, this wedding was finally over.

The gossips at the back of the temple had little to chatter about as Eshaan and Asha made a cute couple, but I found it difficult to assess what Eshaan really looked like under the red turban, the facial hair and traditional *achkun*. However, he did measure up somewhat to the husband I envisioned for Asha, at least physically.

Before I left the temple, I wished the bride and groom luck and said goodbye, promising Asha I would keep in touch. I felt guilty lying about hurrying back to Toronto for mid-term exams, but staying in Vancouver any longer meant my mother would have more time to focus on my lack of a husband. She believed not being married after a certain age was comparable to having an incurable disease. Two hours after the wedding, I once again boarded a plane to escape reality.

I had broken my promise to Asha to always stick together when I left her stranded in a world that would swallow her. I had been selfish and weak because I did not have the courage to stay. And now instead of being happy for her, I had hoped she too was saddened by this marriage. My greatest fear was coming true: I was alone on the path I had chosen.

On my second day back in Toronto I had just finished printing out my assignment when I heard a faint knock on the door. Someone must have let my visitor into the building. I knew it wasn't Camille and her new boyfriend as they were away for the weekend. And it was much too early for it to be any of my other friends because there had been a huge party in the co-ed dorm the night before and they would all still be hungover. I hadn't gone to the party as my flight had arrived late and I was tired. I also needed to stay up all night to finish an Economics paper because my professor had refused to give me another extension. Now it was one o'clock in the afternoon and I was still in my pajamas.

I walked to the door and peered through the peephole. Although I had never seen him clean-shaven and dressed in a sports blazer, I knew without a doubt that the man standing there was Eshaan. I grabbed a robe, flung it on and opened the door.

He sat down before I offered him a seat and did not give me a chance to speak.

"We had rented a car and were on our way to my cousin's house from the airport when we stopped in a mall parking lot to look over the directions. Asha hadn't been feeling well the last couple of hours of the flight. Come to think of it, she had been really anxious and restless. I didn't think much of it because she had told me it was her first time flying. The stores had just opened and she went inside to buy something for her stomach while I planned out a new route. Anyway, when she didn't return after twenty minutes or so I went looking for her in the pharmacy. She wasn't there. One of the clerks behind the counter told me an East Indian woman attempted to buy some medicine for her upset stomach but changed her mind and ran out the door. I walked around the mall for an hour but I couldn't find her anywhere. I waited outside the women's restrooms thinking she could have been in there, and I even asked a couple of women to look for her inside the stalls but they didn't find her either."

He paused for a moment and then continued while I sat staring in disbelief.

"And I've been looking for her ever since. She had talked a lot about you on our flight here from Vancouver. She was really looking forward to seeing you again. I didn't have your address, but Asha had kept it in her purse, so I rang up the mother-in-law and pretended that Asha was visiting with you for the morning but I couldn't reach her because I had misplaced your information. She was hesitant at first but eventually agreed to call your mother and get your address and phone number for me. I'm sorry I didn't call you first, but if Asha was here I didn't want her to take off again."

I was surprised my mother had even talked to Lalita let alone given her my number. But maybe it hadn't been as easy as Eshaan thought. Lalita must have gone through the channels, the other members of the *Dukh Sukh Club,* and one of them must have creatively retrieved my address for her. Plus, with the time difference, it would have been early in the morning. I'm surprised Lalita bought his story at all. I was sure my mother would be calling me soon!

Eshaan waved his hand in front of my face to see if I was still listening.

"I'm sorry," I said. "I'm just a little shocked."

"Me too! I didn't want to alarm anyone or have the story get back to any of my family so I came directly here. We were going to stay with my cousins, but I didn't want them to get suspicious so I've checked into a hotel instead. But I can tell from the look on your face that you know nothing of this. Here's my number at the hotel. Please call me if you do hear anything. I hope nothing awful has happened to her! And please keep this to yourself...I'm sure you understand."

I nodded, and before giving me a chance to ask him anything, he got up and left.

Asha's Diary

April 13, 1991

Yesterday my mother tried to do what she has been threatening to do for years. She had warned me so many times but I just thought she was bluffing. The noose was still around her neck when I barged into the basement and she was standing on the wooden chair. She must have tried to tie the other end to the old metal pipe which runs across the ceiling, but luckily the rope was pretty much unravelled and her attempt was unsuccessful.

She told me she could handle my father but it was me who was ruining her life. She had found some pot in a little plastic baggie in the bottom of my brother's sock drawer. He is only eight and he swore he didn't know what it was and how it got there. My mother didn't know what it was either, so she had called Uncle Gary over to investigate. Sonia had bought it from this kid at the birthday party we threw for her while the rest of my family was away, and we had forgotten all about it. We weren't actually going to try it. We were just trying to be cool like the other kids. We were going to throw it out later.

I was so scared thinking about what could have happened that I promised I would not be friends with Sonia anymore. I promised I would start acting like a good girl from a decent family. My mother has warned me that if I don't straighten out, she will try to hang herself again! And the next time she will succeed and her blood will be on my hands. She says I can do whatever I want after she's dead. She says my father will not care and my little brothers will be orphaned. And it will be entirely my fault!

April 22

I've been trying really hard to stay away from Sonia at school, and I make lots of excuses after school. I can't tell her what happened. I can't believe I'm having to do this to her. She can find a new best friend, but as my mother often points out, I only have one mother and I'll regret it when she's gone.

May 14

Sonia called. She wanted me to go to the movies with her but I told her I had to babysit my brothers. She said she would rent one instead and bring it over, so I lied again. I told her I was watching Uncle Gary's kids too and that I was going to be at his house. It's too far away so she wouldn't be able to walk over there.

June 1

Tomorrow is my sixteenth birthday. I know my father won't show up at my party, he has started drinking and gambling again, and he turns into a monster when he loses all his money. But I guess my mother is the one who suffers the most. She only stays with him because of my brothers and me. She thinks she has no other choice. She never learned to read or write in English because he didn't let her. If she left him, she wouldn't be able to raise us on her own. When I'm old enough to leave, I'm going to take my mother and my brothers with me. And maybe then she'll change her mind and let me hang out with Sonia again!

June 2

He came and he brought me a gift! My first computer! I can write all my personal stuff on it. I can save everything on the hard drive. Other than me, no one even knows how to turn it on. It must've been so expensive. My mother isn't happy with him. She thinks the money could've been better spent paying bills.

My party was so much fun! My father even danced along with me to my favourite Malkit Singh songs.

June 8

Sonia has been avoiding me for the last few days. She found out about my party and was upset because she wasn't invited. But my mother is happy these days because she hasn't heard any complaints about me from school or any of the neighbours and I'm always at home when she needs my help. And so is my father. He is working again and he hasn't touched a drop since my birthday party. But I'm so bored!

July 15

Sonia called today to say she was going to Kamloops for the rest of the summer to visit her cousins. She said she would call me from there, but I told her not to bother because my parents were going to take my brothers and me on a trip to Disneyland. I lied again. It comes easily now.

September 22

Things were going so well. He hadn't gone to the casino in almost two months, but when Uncle Gary brought him home tonight, he called my mother a whore and accused Uncle Gary of sleeping with her. Then he told me he wasn't my father, that I'm the daughter of a tramp and it's my destiny to become one, too. Uncle Gary waited around in the driveway until my father passed out.

October 10

I only talk to Sonia once in a while now. She is in different classes than me so I hardly ever see her.

December 30

He hit her today. I called the cops but my mother refused to press charges. She says it's an embarrassment having the police come to our door again. She's worried what the neighbours will think. I don't give a shit about our reputation. I can't take this anymore.

April 11, 1992

We've come to stay with Uncle Gary and his family for a few days.

May 27

I heard my mother talking to someone on the phone today, and when I picked up the receiver, I heard a man's voice. I put the phone down before I heard their conversation because, if my mother found me eaves-dropping, there would be shit to pay.

June 6

Sonia has been distancing herself from me now that I'm talking to some of the Indian girls in school that she doesn't like. She's been hanging out with other girls, too.

October 22

My father hasn't been home for days. He's probably out selling more of our possessions so he can get cash for the casino.

October 24

I left school early today because I felt sick, and as I walked around the corner, I saw a man leaving our house through the back door. I asked my mother who he was. At first she denied anyone had been there, but then she told me to shut up and stay quiet. She said my father would misunderstand and kill us all.

January 18, 1993

I ran into Sonia in the cafeteria today, hanging out with some *gori*. She still makes an effort to talk to me when I'm not with my new friends. She says she'll be applying to colleges and universities soon, and she told me to apply to the same ones because that has been our plan for years. I wrote down the names, but my grades have dropped and I'll be lucky if I even graduate. Even then, I can't afford to go. Sonia knows that I'm not rich like her, but she has no idea that my family is completely broke now. She doesn't see me enough to know that I rotate the same four outfits all the time.

February 9

I like this guy at school. His name is Ravi. He's pretty cute.

May 25

Ravi and I have been dating for three months now. There are only three weeks left of school, but I don't know how much longer I can keep this a secret from Sonia. Even though we don't really hang out anymore, I know she doesn't like Ravi. I heard her say he's a FOB (fresh off the boat). He has an Indian accent and he doesn't dress well. She called him a backward-thinking, male chauvinist mama's boy. She says he's the type of guy who gets married so he can have a maid.

June 14

I was surprised to see Sonia waiting for me after school today. She wanted to know how my exams went. She says we can live together in September. She doesn't care what her mother says because she doesn't need to know. But she has no idea what's going on with me so I had no choice, I had to tell her off. I don't think she'll ever talk to me again.

June 30

My mother asked me about the posters around the neighbourhood. She heard I was involved but it isn't true. I think Sonia did it by herself.

I was so scared my mother wouldn't believe me and try something again so I told her I had been a good girl and to ask anyone other than Sonia's mom, and they would tell her that Sonia and I weren't even on speaking terms. Eventually she believed I was telling the truth and promised me she wouldn't do anything to herself.

July 19

Ravi's talking about going away to college, too. His aunt adopted him when he was ten years old because she didn't have any sons of her own, only two daughters, and Ravi's parents were thrilled to send their son to Canada. But he says he's been a burden on his aunt and uncle far too long.

July 21

Ravi told me his whole life story today. He said that when he was a child, his father was in an accident and lost his right leg. In India it's nearly impossible to find work if you're a healthy and educated man, and there was a long line of workers ready to replace his father after he was let go. His aunt promised to send money to Ravi's family in exchange for gaining a son. Once he got to Canada his aunt became quite possessive of him. She was afraid her sister would eventually want him back. At first he cried a lot, but his aunt smothered him with love, toys and other gifts. She tried to fill the void of his mother but he couldn't forget the woman who gave birth to him.

He hasn't seen his family in nine years, but now that he's older he no longer needs to depend on his aunt. He says it's time he supported his own family.

August 12

Ravi's decided to wait a year before starting university. He's going to work instead and save money for his trip to India. His aunt thinks he's saving money to help pay for school. At least this gives me more time to convince him to stay here with me.

If Ravi and I are found out, my mother will go on and on about how I've ruined her, and she might try to take her life again.

August 30

I went to say goodbye to Sonia while my mother was out with my brothers. Sonia was packing the whole time and basically ignored me.

December 17

We haven't been using protection. I think I should go see a doctor so I can go on the pill. If my mother found out, she'd give me the same lecture she did when I asked her to buy me tampons. She said single girls don't wear tampons because it affects their virginity. If she knew Ravi and I were having sex, she would push me off a bridge and then jump herself.

If I lived in India, I'd have been married off at sixteen. Then I'd be allowed to have sex every day and twice on Sundays whether or not I was willing.

July 18, 1994

Ravi says he'll be leaving in December. He's going to live with an uncle in Edmonton…or maybe Toronto. He tells me he loves me, sleeps with me and now begs me not to get too attached because it'll only make it more difficult when he leaves.

November 18

I'm pregnant. He'll have to stay now. He has no choice but to marry me. My parents will be disgraced and his aunt will disown him. She'll tell people how she took him in and treated him better than she would have treated her own son. She won't support him because her reputation is far more important. But blood is blood and Ravi knows this. He'll have to accept our child. My father will kill us both if he doesn't. And my mother—I can't imagine what she'll do!

November 19

Ravi told me to get an abortion. He says I deceived him. Deceived him? He was the one who told me he loved me one day and didn't the next. He's the one who broke all his promises. He's worried the news may get back to his parents, although I'm the one who should be concerned for my reputation. If this gets out, no one will marry me. Apparently there are two categories for women: the ones you date and the ones you marry. And I'm not the type of girl Ravi wants to marry.

November 23

I wish my brothers were older. They would settle the score the Punjabi way with field hockey sticks. Maybe a few broken ribs would change Ravi's mind!

December 17

I miscarried at the hospital. My mother brought me there because I was cramping and when she discovered why, she started hitting me and pulling my hair. I was just lucky the nurses came in and dragged her away before she dislocated my scalp from my head. Later when she promised not to hurt me, they let her back in and she told me she faked the suicide to keep me away from Sonia, but if she had known I was going to do something like this, she would have killed herself and me, too. I was too weak and broken to care about her reputation. I can't believe my mother lied to me. How could I fall for it? How was she able to brainwash me like that? But it doesn't matter now because she won.

January 6, 1995

She told the neighbours I had kidney stones, and she says she'll rip my tongue out if I tell anyone any different. She said if I didn't listen to her now, she really would end her life! I'm not allowed to leave the house. She says I have no inkling of what she's been through all these years to keep the family together and a roof over our heads. She says I've destroyed the last bit of *izzat* and integrity she had left.

She also told me to keep my legs closed until I'm married. She thinks Ravi is a *gora,* so my foolish *kartoot* will remain hidden. If she knew he was an Indian, she would thrash me. I wouldn't be able to show my face outside this house.

March 24

My father is dead. I always thought I wouldn't cry but I did. Sometimes when he was on a winning streak, he was kind to me, but he was always good to my little brothers.

My mother cried the most. She doesn't have to live within the constraints my father set up for her anymore. She doesn't have to hear about his affairs with all the white women, nor does she have to listen to him call her a whore. She doesn't have to put up with the late-night bawling or worry about him lying drunk in some alley. But none of this matters. She's a widow and an Indian widow lives the rest of her life as a corpse. She may be better off now but she can't express this. She must live within the confines of widowhood.

March 29

Sonia came, but she only stayed for one day. I miss talking to her. I wanted to tell her everything that has happened, but I don't think she wants to associate with me anymore.

August 2

My mother went to a groom viewing and took my picture along. The boy is from England, and she told his mother she accepts the *rishta*. She told them I would agree because I never go against her wishes. This "gentleman," as my mother describes him, is going to come over and check me out, and I'll sit there like an idiot while he decides if I'll be a good wife. He will determine if and when I take orders, when I put out and if my hips are large enough to bear his children. His decision will be based on whether he can love my face and body. He has no knowledge of, nor would he like to know, the depths of my soul. If I'm fortunate, he'll say yes without any conditions. This, however, is rare and his mother, his agent, will decide her son deserves more. Then my mother will scrounge together the items on her list. She won't want to take any chances. Not with my past. I won't be good enough as I am. My mother will have to pay them to take me.

August 4

Eshaan—that's his name—was very impressive. He told his mother he couldn't choose his life partner over a cup of tea, so my mother has given us permission to meet for lunch, although she was a little reluctant at first. She doesn't want this one to get away because she thinks he's too good for me. But she doesn't have much of a choice. There won't be a line of men knocking down my door. Her options are limited and so are mine.

October 26

Eshaan and I talk on the phone all the time, but my mother doesn't like it. She thinks I'm going to slip up about my past and ruin everything, so she's been pestering Eshaan's parents to set the wedding date as soon as possible.

February 2, 1996

The wedding is in five days. There will be no reception. My mother can't afford it and Eshaan's family is already paying for a reception once we return to Birmingham. My mother has still insisted on inviting the whole world to the actual ceremony. Sonia will be coming, too. Once I'm married, my mother won't be able to stop us from being friends.

Tomorrow I'm meeting some of his family. His younger brother, his cousins, aunts and uncles are arriving from England, India and all over Canada. He says they'll accept me. Even if they don't, it doesn't matter. He says he fell for me the first day we met. He assured me there's no need to worry.

February 3

The life I buried has resurfaced. Ravi is Eshaan's distant cousin. He stood and stared at me for a few minutes, but when Eshaan introduced us he pretended we'd never met.

Dreadful scenarios have been going through my mind all day. I envision Ravi telling Eshaan every intimate detail of our relationship, from the first kiss to the miscarriage. Then Eshaan lunges at Ravi as the others make their way into the room. In the morning the telephone rings. It's Eshaan's mother, calling off the wedding. And then I see my mother with a noose around her neck.

I have to stop letting my imagination get the best of me or I'll drive myself crazy!

February 4

Eshaan called to check up on last-minute details. I don't think he suspects anything. I wonder if I should talk to Ravi and see what his intentions are. My mother once told me about a girl from her village who was having an affair with a boy from a nearby town. Her parents found out and married her off to someone else, but when she unveiled herself after the wedding, she discovered that her new husband was her lover's older brother. The lover blackmailed her for years. Her payment for keeping his mouth shut was pleasing him with her body, and because she was happy with her husband, she did what her ex-lover asked of her.

Then one afternoon the husband returned home early after he cut his hand working in the field. He thought no one was home so he went up to the upper floor of the house, to get the ointment his brother kept in the *almari*. When he opened the door, he found his brother on top of his wife. He went downstairs and grabbed a hatchet. He cut her body into pieces then kicked his brother out of the house. The police officers were easily bribed and the husband was never prosecuted. In their view the woman was a tramp and deserved to die. A few months later the husband forgave his brother, but he felt no remorse for killing his wife. He never forgave her.

February 5

Eshaan's family came over to show the *vari*, the bridal clothing and jewellery, and Ravi accompanied the other family members. I could see him looking at me. Maybe Eshaan would understand if I told him the truth. He's modern thinking. He should understand that I've been with other men long before he was in the picture. But I've already told him many lies. He thinks I'm a virgin. I know he isn't. Most Indian people believe it's acceptable for men to have premarital sex but not women.

I was hoping to tell Sonia the truth when I saw her this evening, but instead I pretended I've never been happier. And even if I did tell her, where would I begin? She probably wouldn't care about the mess I've created of my life anyway. Not anymore. But maybe when we stop in Toronto, maybe I can tell her then. Maybe we can be best friends again.

February 7

Ravi cornered me as I was leaving the ladies room after the ceremony. He wanted to say something, but before he had a chance, my entourage ushered me away to where Eshaan was waiting. I'm so relieved that Eshaan and I are leaving for Toronto on the red-eye, and then after a few days there we will be going straight to England.

February 8

I can't believe it! Eshaan told me we would be staying with his relatives while in Toronto, but I never once clued in that he meant the family Ravi lives with now. I had mixed up Eshaan's two uncles. I thought Ravi had gone to live with the one in Edmonton, not the one in Toronto. I never bothered to ask properly because I didn't want anyone to get suspicious. Eshaan told me during the flight from Vancouver. I wanted to open the emergency exit and jump out of the plane!!!

Luckily no one came to get us at the airport and Eshaan had pre-booked a rental car. I told him I was a great navigator and kept him lost for some time. Finally Eshaan pulled over at a mall and took the map from me. I told him I wasn't feeling well and needed to go to the drug store. But once I got in there, I panicked. I left poor Eshaan at the mall and escaped through a different exit. I got the cab driver to take me to the nearest and cheapest motel. I didn't know what else to do. I didn't even think of calling Sonia but it's probably a good thing because that will be the first place he will look. I've never stayed by myself before, and it is kind of scary.

I can't believe I had the guts to do this!

February 9

I had an awful nightmare last night, and I woke up in a cold sweat. I had told Eshaan the truth and he said if he'd known I was used, he never would have married me. But it was too late. It would dishonour the family name if he didn't take a wife back to Birmingham. People in the community would laugh and tease him. He agreed to carry on with the marriage, but he said he didn't know if he could ever love me.

February 10

I called Sonia today and she came to see me. I told her bits and pieces about what's going on but not everything and she didn't push it. She says Eshaan is going crazy looking for me. He came to see her the first day I disappeared. She thinks I should be honest with him because he is thinking of involving the police. He has called her a few times since then. Sonia says if he loves me, he'll understand. She wanted me to go back with her to her apartment, but I told her I need to be alone for a bit longer and sort things out for myself. I made her promise not to tell Eshaan where I am.

February 12

Sonia called three times today to check up on me. She offered to come and pick me up but I don't want to involve her any more than she already is.

February 14

I'm spending Valentine's Day all by myself in this dingy old motel room. I called Sonia but there was no answer. I'm such a cow I never even asked her anything about her life. But I know she'll understand that I'm just stressed out. I have no more money so this is the last night I can stay here. I'll have to get a hold of Sonia tomorrow.

February 15

After Sonia picked me up from the motel and brought me back to her apartment, she admitted she had told Eshaan that she had been in touch with me because he was going to call my mother and file a missing person's report, but she swears she didn't tell him where I was staying or why I ran away. She said her mom had called her a few times as well because the *Dukh Sukh Club* had heard some rumours, but Sonia didn't tell her anything either. We had a good laugh over that.

Sonia convinced me to call Eshaan at his hotel. I was so relieved to hear he was not with Ravi. Eshaan is coming in the morning. I'm so scared of how he'll react.

February 16

I've chosen to be dishonest again. After my recurring nightmare of the last few nights, I didn't have the courage to tell him the truth. I tried, I really did, but I just couldn't get the right words to come out. I told him I'd been raped when I was eighteen. Indian women never report such things because this type of crime could scar a family's image forever. I didn't mention the pregnancy. I said I was afraid he wouldn't accept me if he knew the truth, so I ran away. He was quiet for the longest time. And then I guess I was sort of in shock because tears rolled down my face, words came out of my mouth but I couldn't understand what I was saying or feeling.

Eshaan embraced me. All he kept reiterating was that I was safe now and no one could hurt me again. He said he loved me and the time had come for me to let go of the past because a new, happy life awaits us in Birmingham.

He doesn't want me to mention this to anyone. He says he trusts me and our life is no one else's business. He will take care of any difficulties that may arise if his family hears of my temporary disappearance.

For now, everyone is under the impression that he and I decided to go on a secret honeymoon. He says I'm his wife now, and together we will resolve all my problems and concerns. I'm in love.

I lied to Sonia, too. I told her that I told Eshaan everything down to the very last detail and that he is okay with it all, and she's happy that we've worked things out. Sonia really likes Eshaan. I'm actually a little surprised because I thought she would tell me to leave him and come live with her, but I guess she's more mature now. I told her I'll call her as soon as I get to England.

February 17

Our flight leaves for England this afternoon, but there's a sharp ache in my gut no amount of antacids will ever relieve. Eshaan's such a great guy and I feel as if I've betrayed him. And what if Ravi comes forward one day? I've managed to avoid him this time. I guess I can never return to Canada, that is the only way. But if Ravi does ever come forward or confront me, I'll have to tell Eshaan that Ravi was the one who violated me. But then again, maybe Eshaan will really be okay with everything.

The best solution is to get pregnant right away. I can use those Chinese birth charts to conceive a boy. If that doesn't work, I remember the tips Baksho gave Indu to pass on to her daughter regarding sexual positions. She said they guarantee the conception of a male fetus. Although I was traumatized when I eavesdropped on their conversation, Baksho's demonstrations are still etched in my mind. Once I've had children with Eshaan, it will be too difficult for him to leave me. His mother won't let him.

For now the only important thing is that Eshaan loves me and respects me. He's like no other man I've ever met.

Kitty Party – 1999

The fragrance of rose incense permeated Baksho's entire home. Although her ancient entertainment set was an eyesore, she had updated her furniture from velvet floral to burgundy leather. Pictures of her grandson were plastered on every wall of the house, some in mismatched frames and others attached carefully to the wall with Scotch tape. She had sent him to live with his mother during his vulnerable teenage years because she was afraid to make the same mistakes with him that she had made with his father.

"Why did you call us to your house today, Baksho?" Kamal was curious.

"Dear God!" Shindi could not believe her eyes. "What have you done to your eyebrows, Kamal? There is nothing there!" She wanted to rub away the black pencil liner from Kamal's brow line, but Kamal waved her hand away.

Baksho had also noticed Kamal's new look. The chocolate brown matte finish formula that Kamal had been using had sucked out the last bit of moisture from her forty-nine-year-old lips. But Baksho resisted the comment because she had much more urgent business to discuss. "Mrs. Gill called me from India..." she began but she was interrupted.

"I don't have *time-shime* for this chit chat!" Indu said. "I have to watch my grandchildren today. I can't sit around and eat *ladoos* and drink tea all day." Indu had added high blood pressure to her mixture of ailments. "First we spend our early years worrying about marrying off our children and then we spend our golden years raising theirs."

"Baksho has invited us for a *kitty party,* of course!" Shindi said. "When I told my daughter, Dharam, I was attending a kitty party, she asked me if we were using handcuffs and whips. I just don't understand these kids these days." She was genuinely confused by her daughter's question.

"What's this kitty party thing?" Kamal squeezed onto the couch next to Baksho.

"Mrs. Gill called a few days ago from India," Baksho began again. "She told me these kitty parties are all the rage there. Women get together in each other's homes and restaurants and even discos to consult on important matters. Every Sunday a different member is responsible for the entertainment and food. I've ordered vegetarian *pijja* for our first party!" Pizza had become her new favourite meal.

"That Mrs. Gill is still running the show even though she doesn't live here anymore," Shindi snarled, but the others pretended not to hear.

"Did Mrs. Gill say if she has gone to Bombay yet?" Kamal asked. "Oh sorry, *Mumbai*. I wonder if she got to meet Madhuri Dixit. Now that Madhuri is married, she will have to move to *Amreeka* to be with her husband." Then barely holding back her tears, she added, "No actress will ever be able to replace Madhuri."

Most of the women had learned to ignore Kamal's Bollywood fever. It was the only way to keep her from going on and on.

"Where's Manjeet?" Indu demanded. "Did you call her, Baksho? And what about Lalita? She doesn't attend the *gurdwara* at all anymore, especially after that whole tables and chairs issue, but she can come here, can't she? It's so sad. Our holy place where we go to find peace and God has been turned into a battleground to decide where we should eat *langar*—on the floor or at tables. The innocent *sangat* pays the price. And our children, they have found another reason to turn their faces away from *Sikhi*. Twenty or thirty years ago we had to protect our *gurdwaras* from the *goray-gooray*, and now we have to protect it from our own people. *Vaheguru*!" Indu was now in tears.

The women ignored her comment as well because, other than Indu, none of them were concerned about the unrest in the temple. For them the *gurdwara* was just a place to mingle and socialize. But Indu had lost a teenage grandchild to Christianity after the disagreements had erupted in the temples, and she had found her youngest daughter, Nikky, door-knocking halfway across town with a Jehovah's Witness.

"Manjeet and Rani couldn't make it!" Baksho said. "They've forgotten us now that they've moved. And I couldn't call Lalita." She glanced at Kamal.

"Why not?" Shindi had no idea.

"After all the stuff her daughter pulled, I do not want to be associated with that family," Kamal said, feeling justified.

Indu was getting restless, and she positioned herself in front of Baksho's large window so she could see when her second-oldest daughter arrived across the street with her two sons. "Let it alone now, Kamal." Indu could see no reason for this discussion. "That Asha girl has been happily married for years, and she doesn't even live in this country anymore—she's in *Inglaand*. She probably has no contact with your daughter! Plus, your Sonia is engaged now. What a *good* girl she turned out to be. Even at her age she was able to find a *handsome-vandsome,* rich boy. She's having a *love marriage*. So you were worried for nothing."

Kamal nodded in agreement and then reached into her purse and pulled out some samples. "Oh, I almost forgot. I didn't want to give them to you at the *gurdwara*—you know how the other ladies stick to me like leeches when I have free products—but I brought some new face creams with me. They claim to prevent and vanish wrinkles. Try them out and let me know what you think. You can have as many as you like, Baksho *panji*! Your skin is starting to look all saggy and shrivelled!"

Shindi gave Kamal a little nudge, but Baksho did not notice the insult as she was reading the back of the packaging.

"Oh, and these are for Manjeet." Kamal put several tubes aside. "They are a special formula to help lighten the skin."

"We are too old for these *creams-sheams*! More than half our lives are over—who will we impress now?" Indu's voice ricocheted off the glass. "Too bad Mrs. Gill isn't here though—she would have loved these fancy moisturizers."

"Actually, speaking of Mrs. Gill, she told me some other stuff that happens there in India, too." And Baksho giggled.

"Like what?" Shindi inquired.

"Well, it's a little embarrassing, and who even knows if it's true." Baksho scanned their intrigued expressions and then continued, "Mrs. Gill told me that some of the high society wives in her city are into swinging."

"What's so great about that?" Indu said. "I go to the playground all the time and sit on the swings with my grandchildren."

"Not that kind, *kamli na hovay*! The *other* kind." Baksho pretended to be disgusted. "Even Mrs. Gill was propositioned at a party by some rich industrialist, like the ones from the Indian TV serials. *Chi chi*!"

"I've heard those things, too," Kamal said. "Apparently, at these hoity toity parties, interested couples leave their car keys in a bowl by the front door. At the end of the night the women go home with the men whose keys they acquire."

"And Baksho *panji*, you thought only *Kanayda*-born girls were such *besharms*." Shindi shook her head.

Baksho ignored her comment.

"I don't believe it! Mrs. Gill was most likely pulling your *leg-sheg*, Baksho! And Kamal, we know where you get all your information from." Indu pointed to the Bollywood tabloid sticking out of Kamal's purse.

The women started to laugh. Other than Indu they all believed the story and wanted to know more, especially whether Mrs. Gill had taken up the offer—but no one wanted to ask.

"Will you please sit down, Indu? Just tell your daughter to come here!" Shindi yelled.

Indu's anxiety was ruining the party. She had forgotten to take her medication in the morning. Reluctantly, she seated herself on the arm of the sofa.

"Well, all I have to say is like mother like daughter. I'm sure they would go home with any man's keys." Baksho had gone back to the previous conversation as she smeared the entire supply of facial moisturizer not only on her face but her neck, arms and feet as well. The gemstone rings promising success and prosperity were sliding off her pudgy index fingers. Nevertheless, she lifted her *salwar* and rubbed the last bit of cream onto her knees. She then carried on with her agenda.

The women were looking at each other completely confused. Who was Baksho talking about?

"And since her husband died," Baksho continued, "Lalita has been keeping company with other men…but I can't say any more."

"*Hai Rabba*," Indu yelled. "No wonder people tell these crazy stories about you!"

"*Nee kasama nu kahni*, what people?" Baksho knocked over an empty glass. "What are you saying?"

"At the supermarket I overheard someone saying you've been having your own *chakkar* with that elderly refugee man," Shindi said, adding fuel to the fire.

Baksho threw the pillow on the floor and stood up. "Who said this? What refugee man? Call this person right now. Is it that sister-in-law of yours who's been talking trash? You've been chummy with her ever since she moved back to town! Call her right now! I want Prakash Kaur to say it to my face!"

"Shindi and Indu aren't the only ones," Kamal squeaked. "I heard something too."

Baksho collapsed back onto the couch and smacked her hands to her forehead. "*Satyanaas*! You help someone and this is how these people repay you. They pretend to be your friends and then the first chance they get they put a *chaku*, a knife, in your back."

"Baksho, tell us more about Lalita and her daughter." Kamal had it in for those two and couldn't care less about the drama Baksho was creating.

"What can I say now? My *baizty* has been done! You have humiliated me! All these years I only spoke the truth so you could save your daughters, but where did that get me? You can all leave now...just go!" The tears streaming down Baksho's face were clear. She had ceased wearing kohl liner since the day she nearly poked her eye out with her unsteady hand.

"But what about the *pijja*?" Indu continued to tease her.

But Baksho was in no condition to respond, and as the women hurried outside and onto the sidewalk, she could still hear their laughter.

"Shindi, are you serious about this refugee man?" Kamal asked.

"No, but I heard Baksho was talking about my daughters to Lalita. We've given her too much *khul*. She thinks she can say anything about anyone."

"*Bechari* Lalita!" Indu said. "The hardships that she faced to raise her children while that husband of hers gambled and drank away all their money! Did you know she taught herself to sew and alter men's *clothing-shothing* to pay their utility bills? Her husband never permitted her to work. He'd rather let his family starve than let his wife work in an environment where she could possibly have contact with other men. She was so scared she'd get caught. She'd stay up all night finishing pieces, stitching by hand so the noise of the sewing machine didn't wake up the children. A couple of times I helped her deliver some of the orders and that's how I know. She was afraid if the neighbours saw men coming in and out of the house, they'd talk." Indu wiped a tear from the corner of her eye.

Kamal looked away, embarrassed to have judged Lalita so harshly.

"Unbelievable, *bechari* Lalita," Shindi muttered.

"She also taught herself how to *read-shead* and write English with the help of her youngest son. She didn't tell anyone about this until after her husband's death!" Indu was proud of her friend's accomplishments.

"Well, I'm just glad she didn't become one of those typical widows and stop living like they did in Baksho's *zamana*. Her life is not over just because her husband is no more." Shindi was also pleased for Lalita. "She still wears colourful suits, and she's started taking more care of herself. I've even seen her wearing makeup!"

As her daughter's car pulled up into the driveway, Indu ran across the street in the drizzle, holding her shawl over her head. Baksho watched sadly from her living room window as the other two headed toward Lalita's house.

Lalita had just moved into her newly built home on the lot that had once belonged to the Dusanjh family. The price of the property had been reduced significantly after Mrs. Dusanjh's death from breast cancer because no Indian or Asian was interested in buying or renting a home where a family member had been plagued by a long illness. So Lalita had bought the property with the help of her extended family and had the Dusanjh home torn down and a new one built. No one really knew the whereabouts of Mr. Dalip Dusanjh or his drug-dealing son as the sale was handled by a property management firm, but the daughter, Harleen, was rumoured to have headed east for college.

Balbir – Strength

In September 2003 when I agreed to go and live with Varinderpal and Balbir Johal, my dad assured me, "It will be just until space becomes available on campus, Harleen darling." When I protested that their home in Brampton was miles from my university, he said, "It will only be three weeks at the most, Harleen." I did not want him to worry about me—he had enough on his mind—so I did as he wanted but I felt uneasy about it.

It had been almost a year and a half since Ruby, the Johals' eighteen-year-old daughter, had disappeared. It was all over the Punjabi newspapers at the time. The Johals claimed she had been abducted but the police found no proof. They recovered no body and had no suspects. Varinderpal put up a reward of twenty thousand dollars for anyone who knew the whereabouts of his daughter. When his plea went unanswered, some people began whispering that Ruby had run away from home, and her parents were so ashamed that they leaked the fraudulent story to the local media. Balbir was unable to deal with the situation and spent most of her time in a psychiatric hospital.

And these were the people my dad had decided to entrust my well-being to.

After my mom's death, many of our relatives had encouraged my dad to remarry while my older brother and I were still young. After all, it had become the latest trend for middle-aged widowers to bring home teenage brides from India, but my dad was not one of those men. He had really loved my mom, and if it had been possible, he would have given his life for her. When she was dying, he promised her he would always take care of us and that is what he intended to do. But that was a lot harder than he expected because my brother had been very attached to my mom and, unable to recover from the loss, he got mixed up with the wrong crowd and entered a life of drugs and gangs. Although my dad made numerous attempts to help him, by the time he intervened, it was too late. One drive-by shooting was all it took for him to send me off to Toronto to school and kick my brother out of the house. I know my dad would have re-located with me, but because of the promise he'd made to my mother, he felt compelled to stay behind and keep trying to save my brother.

We had not kept in close contact with the Johal family, but whenever they had been in Vancouver on business, they had dropped by for a visit. When my dad first came to Canada—long before he married my mom—it had been Varinderpal and Balbir who welcomed him into their home in a small logging town in northern British Columbia. He never forgot their hospitality, and now he had somehow got it into his head that he could finally repay his debt by sending me as a temporary replacement for their missing child.

They greeted me at Pearson International Airport and without any formalities drove me home. Their house was lovely, the expensive furnishings being the result of the successful furniture business Varinderpal had started. And other than a picture of the star-crossed lovers *Sohni and Mahiwal* on the wall, it was my idea of the perfect home, one that was much too elegant for a *desi* or traditional Punjabi family. I could see that the Johals were far more advanced in their ways than people back home in Vancouver's Little India.

My first few days there were fine. Balbir went to great lengths to make me comfortable, but although she did not mention her daughter, her every effort toward me demonstrated a longing for her only child.

Varinderpal, however, told me to keep my distance from his wife. "I don't want to scare you, Harleen *beta,* my dear child, but sometimes your Aunty says and does strange things. *Very silly things*. She thinks the whole world is against her. She doesn't even trust me, her own husband. Our family has washed their hands of her. They say she's *paagal,* crazy. I've taken her to many doctors but they can't find anything wrong with her. Some say it's denial, others depression. I don't know what to do."

Varinderpal's frustration was evident, but I was not convinced of Balbir's failing mental state. She appeared to be the same friendly and caring woman I had first met at my *masi*'s, my mom's sister's, wedding twelve years earlier. Not for a moment could I believe this petite, fragile woman could be harmful to herself or others.

"It's such a big responsibility to look after someone else's daughter," Varinderpal continued. "I'm grateful my good friend Dalip thought me worthy of this duty. I'm glad the rubbish that some people are saying did not influence him."

Then one evening well into my second week with the Johals, Balbir knocked on my bedroom door. That was when I reassessed my initial diagnosis of her emotional condition.

She looked around as if she thought someone might have been following her and then slipped into the room. It was Ruby's old bedroom, which had been left exactly as it was when she disappeared, and I had been careful not to move or touch anything. Now I quickly scanned it for a hard object in case I needed to defend myself.

After inspecting the room carefully to ensure we were alone, Balbir squeezed next to me on the bed. I glanced out the window to see if Varinderpal's car was there, but the driveway lay empty.

"Harleen, I have a secret," Balbir whispered. "You must promise not to tell or they'll hurt you, too. No one believes me. They all think I'm out of my mind."

I nodded but my hand edged toward the night lamp on the bedside table.

"I *know* where my Ruby is."

"You do?" I asked, surprised.

"Yes! *He*'s done something to her!"

In the midst of her confession we heard a car pull up and the door slam shut. Without another word Balbir darted out of the room.

That night I set my alarm for before dawn so I could be out of the house before Balbir awoke, and I didn't return until after nine because I knew that she took a sleeping pill at exactly eight o'clock every night. Varinderpal, however, had waited up for me. He looked up at the clock above the kitchen table as I put my bag on the floor. I only hoped he hadn't called my dad to say I was God-knows-where doing God-knows-what!

"Where've you been, Harleen?" he demanded. "Did she say something to you?" The calm exterior I had seen up to this time was gone.

"I'm sorry, Uncle, I was going to call, but my cellphone was dead. I forgot to charge it last night, and I didn't have any change for the pay phone. I have a sociology exam tomorrow so I studied in the library all day. I'll call next time." I did not look directly into his eyes.

He looked unconvinced but relaxed his posture a little. "Okay, okay. Fine. You must be hungry. Your Aunty made *roti* for you."

"Is she asleep?" I looked around as if unaware of her regular routine.

"I took her to the hospital. They want her to stay overnight."

"Why, what happened? She seemed fine last night."

"Well, Harleen *beta,* what do I tell you? You just never know with her. One moment she's fine, the next she throws things." He nodded toward the living room. The television set had been smashed, the oak table and large leather sofa overturned. I was sure an evil spirit must have possessed Balbir because the strength required to cause such damage was not within her means. "Are you sure she didn't say anything to you or maybe you said something to set her off?"

"No, nothing!" I was anxious for him to stop with the interrogation.

"What was the last conversation you had with her?"

I hesitated. "Oh gosh, I can't remember. We had dinner and I went into my room to study."

"Okay then, all right. You eat!"

That night I moved the dresser in front of my bedroom door. I wanted to call my dad but he already had so much on his mind. Fortunately, the next day my prayers were answered. A room became available and I moved into the dormitory on campus. I thanked Varinderpal for his generosity and never returned to the Johals' home again. It wasn't until a few months later that I understood what it was that Balbir wanted to tell me that night in Ruby's bedroom.

Balbir's Daily Journal

July 19, 2001

Ruby is still seeing that boy, Fardheen or Dean as she calls him. I have warned her several times that if her Papa finds out it will be the end of her. He will never give his blessing if he finds out his daughter is in love with a Muslim. She thinks it is okay to date him because his family is from India, and the stupid girl will not listen to me. She does not understand the history between our people and theirs.

She says I never stopped her from associating with Zara and Noor and they are also Muslim. She is right. I have been a bad mother. I did not see any harm in her having friends outside our community. But when her Papa finds out she is in love with a Muslim boy, he is going to blame me. Friends are one thing but I did not know this *behvkoof kuri*, this foolish girl, would think she was permitted to love a Muslim boy.

August 13

That boy constantly phones the house, and I thank God her Papa is not around when he calls! I wonder if his parents know he is in love with a Sikh girl. I do not know of any families that would accept this relationship. She says she wants to marry him. I cannot lock her in the house. She is almost a grown woman. If I say anything to her, I am afraid her Papa will find out. She asks to go to Noor's house right in front of him because she knows I must say yes to her or her Papa will get suspicious. She uses many excuses to go see her *yaar*, her lover.

August 29

I thought she would slowly get bored with this boy but she sneaked out of the house last night to see him. I could not stop her because her Papa would have heard. Instead I waited until this morning and I warned her that I am going to tell her Papa myself if she does not stop seeing that boy.

September 21

After the attacks in New York City, everybody is on edge. Today a woman in another car cut her Papa off on the road. He was angry so he pulled over but the other vehicle turned around and slowly drove back past him. The young lady in the car rolled down her window, cursed at him and called him a terrorist. Then she sped off. Her Papa does not think it is a big deal. He says it is an isolated incident. He thinks the backlash will be minimal in Canada because most people here know the difference between Sikh and Muslim. But I am worried about Ruby. She does not understand the difference.

September 24

I cannot do anything to help her now. I tried to stop him. Her Papa had brought home her favourite cake. I told him she was asleep but he would not listen. He went to her room and found that she had stuffed pillows under her quilt. I acted as if I too was surprised and horrified.

When Ruby returns, this house will never be the same. He has been pacing the floor for two hours. He will wait all night if he has to.

September 25

He slapped her several times when he caught her climbing in through the window. I think she will be bruised for many days, and concealer will not cover it. I will have to keep her at home. She is such a stupid girl! Rather than listen quietly to what her Papa was saying, she talked back to him. She said she would marry Dean no matter what. Her Papa told me to watch her closely. He does not realize I have known all along about this relationship and have done nothing to stop it.

October 10

He allows her to go to school but she must come straight home afterwards. Most days he picks her up himself. He even visits her classroom to make sure she is attending class, and he keeps her at home as often as he can. He listens in on her phone calls.

Ruby says we are embarrassing her. The *behvkoof kuri* does not understand how embarrassing it will be for our family if this news gets out. I have tried very hard to raise her as I would have raised a son, but she has taken advantage of our love. If I had treated her as a daughter, I would never have seen this day.

October 21

She does not eat, she does not sleep. Her teacher called today to ask if she is having difficulty at home. People are prying into our family matters, all because of this stupid girl and her *zid*.

October 30

Her Papa has a tough hand. Yesterday he hit her a little too hard with the metre stick when he caught her on the phone with that boy. The teacher must have seen the bruise on her back. I do not know how. Maybe Ruby has told those damn *goray* what savages we are. Who knows what stories she has been telling them? She does not think we love her. Ruby thinks of us as her enemies.

Today the school sent a youth worker to the house. Her Papa talked to him in private. A social worker has been assigned to the case and will be contacting us soon. I think they want to send her to foster care. Her Papa was furious. How dare they come to our house and insult us this way?

January 4, 2002

Ruby turns eighteen today. At least we do not have to worry about social workers and foster homes anymore. She will graduate soon.

January 11

Ruby has been gone a week now. Her teachers do not know where she is. They say she did not return to school after the Christmas holidays. Her Papa dropped her off at school, but when he went to pick her up, she was not there. We have been going crazy. We have not reported her disappearance to the police because all the relatives will find out and we will not be able to show our faces in the community. Her Papa said he went to Dean's house but he also has not been home for days. That filthy boy has taken her.

January 25

Ruby called today. She married him. Dean's family is furious. They will not accept her just as we will not accept Dean. Ruby is afraid of what Dean's family might do to them. They threatened their lives.

Her Papa misses her. He says she can come back, but not with Dean, not yet. Later we will have a real wedding for the two of them. She has agreed to leave him and come home. She apologized for what she has done.

January 26

There will be no wedding. Her Papa lied to her so she would come back home.

January 28

Ruby no longer leaves the house. She does not call Dean. She realized her Papa would never let them be together. Dean has left his home and wants her back. He is relentless. He calls the house at least ten times a day. Today he pounded on the front door for thirty minutes straight. Her Papa threatened to kill him if he does not leave our family alone. Ruby did not come out. She pretended she did not know he was there, but I saw her watching from her bedroom window. I know she wanted to go to him. It breaks my heart but we must do what is right for the family.

March 6

Ruby is pregnant. I cannot let her Papa find out. I must arrange for an abortion very soon. It will be extremely shameful if the community finds out. We were able to cover up the marriage but if people think she is going to be an unwed mother…

It would have been better to have let her stay with that boy.

March 28

Her Papa knows. He was very calm when he discovered she had morning sickness. He is going to fix everything tomorrow.

March 29

He came home without her. He says Ruby will stay in the clinic for a few days and will call me tomorrow when she is feeling better. But he was acting very strange. He was in the shower for over two hours.

March 30

Ruby has not called. Her Papa told me there are no phones close to her bed, so I cannot call her. But he is not acting like himself. Last night after we went to bed he got up and went to the laundry room to wash his clothes. He has never done laundry in his life.

April 1

There still is no word from Ruby. I am worried. He will not give me the number or tell me what clinic she is in. I cannot ask her friends because they are the ones who corrupted her in the first place. And no one must know what is going on in our house. All I can do is wait.

April 2

He refused to take me to the clinic with him, but he came back and told me that Ruby was not there. He says they told him she checked out two days ago, and he says we cannot report her missing because then we will have to explain her whereabouts the past few days. He says I must have patience; she will come home on her own.

April 4

I do not care if people find out. Today I finally called her friends but they will not return my calls. I told her Papa that if he does not report her missing, I will! But he says the police will find out about the marriage and then we will be ruined. They will not understand why we lied and they will send us to jail.

April 6

He told the police she went to the shopping mall and did not return. They asked a lot of questions. I do not think they believe us. They took her computer. They also found a new cellphone, hidden behind a few books on the shelf next to her bed. Her Papa was not impressed.

April 30

The police have turned up nothing. Ruby and Dean must not be legally married or the police would have discovered a marriage certificate. No one in the community is talking but I think her teachers told the police that she was unhappy at home. I keep telling her Papa to disclose the truth, but he says I am stupid. It is too late to admit the truth. And he says if I tell them, no one will believe me. They will think I am mad from the grief of a missing child.

May 1

He never took Ruby to a clinic. I phoned all the clinics in the city and there was no record of a Ruby Johal anywhere. Perhaps they used a false name.

May 2

He caught me snooping in his desk drawers. He tells me to forget that Ruby ever existed, but how can I forget my own daughter? The worst thoughts are going through my mind. But he is right. No one will believe me because I have no proof. I do not know what he did to her. Who would believe Ruby ran away, got married, and came home pregnant so her Papa killed her?

May 30

He has told everyone I am *paagal*. I think he is playing tricks with my mind. He has conversations with me and then denies having them. He makes strange noises and tells me I am hearing things. Sometimes I see things at night, and he says I am dreaming, but I swear they are real. I have not confronted him out of fear he may kill me, too.

June 4

Finding Dean is my only hope of learning where my child is. Today I went into Ruby's room to find Dean's number but I found nothing. There was no sign of him ever being a part of my daughter's world. Then I went to the phone book and called every Shah in the city. There were only seven people with that name and they all hung up on me. They said they did not know anybody called Dean or Fardheen. Maybe Ruby lied to me and Shah is not Dean's surname. Or maybe Ruby's Dean also went away and his family has disowned him. Perhaps Ruby and Dean are together and my daughter is safe.

July 20

I know Ruby is not coming back.

I am going to the police. I will tell them about Dean and Ruby's pregnancy and my suspicions about my husband. They will believe me.

I am so afraid he did something terrible, something unforgivable…

August 30

He says if I want to stay in his house, I must not go near the police again. I have to forget about everything or he will find a way to make me forget. He says I will never find her. No one will. And it is my fault it has come to this. I was a bad mother so my daughter was taken from me.

October 4

He says if I do not stop bothering him, he will ship me off to a mental asylum in India, and no one will ever see me again. I think he is just trying to scare me, but I know he will do anything to stop me from talking. I heard him making an appointment for me with the family doctor this morning. He was yelling at the receptionist.

February 2, 2003

Last night I begged him to tell me the truth. I told him I would go to the police again if he does not admit what he did to Ruby. He said he would kill me if I did any such thing. He would not let me get away like Ruby did. He said the boy was able to save her but no one will save me. He says my dear Ruby is still alive, but I will never see her again. She has disgraced the family name and must hide her face in shame forever.

April 13

I am so confused. If Ruby is still alive, where is she? Why has she not contacted me? Why have the police not located her? Is he lying to me? I do not know what to believe anymore.

August 9

He only brought me home from the hospital this time because I promised I would not act stupidly anymore. I have told him I will forget the past and remain silent. I am helpless.

September 2

Harleen has come to stay with us. She is a nice girl and I enjoy her company but I am afraid for her. I did not want her to come here but Ruby's Papa would not listen to my excuses. I have already lost one child—how will I show my face to Harleen's family if he does something to her?

I must tell her the truth about him. Maybe she will help me.

September 13

He says it is time for me to go away again because I was not able to keep my big mouth shut. He says I have brought this havoc upon myself.

September 16

He has brought me to a new hospital this time, and the nurses here say that from now on I must make this my home. Although the windows are barred and the doors locked, I feel safe here. I can speak my mind and everyone listens. When I tell people what my husband has done, they all believe me. No one here thinks I am crazy. Among the world of the insane, I have found my sanity.

Kitty Party – 2004

"Did you read this week's newspaper?" Shindi spread out the front page of the *Desi Dose* on Lalita's marble coffee table and placed her reading glasses on the tip of her nose.

"Let's wait for the others!" Lalita put the tray of freshly fried spicy pakoras on the table next to the bowl of chutney, pushing the ketchup bottle aside. Then, because the pungent odour of burnt cooking oil had seeped into the room, she opened a few windows before returning to the kitchen for the tea.

"Did you hear that Manjeet's husband finally died!" Shindi yelled toward the kitchen. "I heard she's quite relieved as he'd become quite a burden!" She took her glasses off and placed them on the table.

"Well," Lalita said as she returned with the teapot and a plate of biscuits, "the man hadn't worked in years and he was sucking up all her savings!" She was speaking from first-hand experience. "And since she has no more responsibilities, she will be able to come out more often."

"That's true. I'm sure she is happier than she's letting on. But people still have to do *absos,* express their condolences. These formalities have to be taken care of!"

Lalita nodded in agreement. "Yes, of course, that's why Indu can't come today. She and her daughters have gone to see Manjeet."

"So who's coming then?" Shindi asked. "Not Baksho, I'm sure. She isn't on speaking terms with any of us since I made that comment about her losing all that weight."

"Well, how could you have known the doctor told her that her days were numbered if she didn't lose it?"

"If I had, I would have kept my mouth shut."

"And speaking of Baksho, I heard she is changing the name of her store!" Lalita exclaimed.

"Again? What is it this time?" Shindi shook her head.

"Baksho's A-One Superstore!" Lalita said, laughing.

Shindi giggled. "Crazy old woman!" She shoved a biscuit into her mouth. "Your friend Rani's crawled into her shell since her daughter's divorce, hasn't she?"

Lalita nodded.

"And you probably didn't invite Kamal."

"Yes, I did! Kamal's much nicer to me now that her daughter is married. But she can't come because she's working at her salon today. You would think she would retire now but I guess it's better to keep busy than sit at home and think depressing thoughts!" She settled into a chair and began pouring tea. "Kamal and I are going to take *bhangra* classes. I'm tired of going for morning walks and watching the old *apnay* men play cards or roam the park in their *kurta pajamas*. Why can't their ungrateful children at least buy them track suits?" Lalita shook her head and added, "Anyway, I told her I'm ready to try something new. We didn't ask Indu because she never stops complaining about her knee, but do you want to come with us?" Lalita handed a teacup to Shindi.

"No, you ladies go ahead! I have no interest in dancing."

"We're doing it for the exercise not for fun. And it's *free* for women over fifty!"

Lalita knew this would be a selling feature for Shindi. Her husband made a reasonable income as a real estate agent, but she did not see any point in wasting his money. She was more concerned about their retirement savings since they had no sons to take care of them in their old age.

"Okay, I'll think about it." Shindi stretched her tired neck and gently massaged her left shoulder.

"Oh, and I also invited Umber and her mother, Tarsem." She glanced at Shindi for a reaction.

"Tarsem who?" Shindi questioned while rubbing her right hand slowly down her left arm.

"You know, that tall woman with buckteeth, the one from Bhatinda."

"Oh, the one the kids call 'the camel'? And since when have you become Tarsem's *saheli*?" Shindi chuckled as she took the last biscuit from the plate.

"Since my oldest son has decided he wants to work at a bank part-time. Umber is the manager at the credit union two blocks away from my son's college, and I…"

There was a knock on the door, but Tarsem had come alone.

"Umber didn't come?" Lalita, hoping Tarsem's daughter was lagging behind, walked out into the driveway.

Shindi got up to take the plate of *barphee,* a sweet dessert, from Tarsem's hand and popped a large piece into her mouth. Western pot-lucks were the latest trend and it was no longer considered an insult to Punjabi hospitality to bring food.

"What's she going to do here with us old women?" Tarsem asked. "She's at the library studying for her banking exams. I've told her to forget about the promotion, her wedding date has already been set. What is the point in working so much now?" She handed Shindi a napkin to wipe her hands and continued, "Sorry. I was in such a hurry that the *barphee* didn't mold properly."

"It's very tasty!" Shindi slowly moved the napkin toward her mouth, and when Tarsem was not looking, she spit the *barphee* into it. She did not believe in wasting food, but the *barphee* was like stone and she didn't want to chip a tooth. The dental fees without coverage would be steep.

"Where are your sons, Lalita? I don't see them," Tarsem said.

"They're at a friend's house." Lalita turned to Shindi. "So what was in the newspaper that you were so stressed about earlier?" Since her ulterior motive for holding this kitty party had been thwarted, Lalita wanted to get it over with as quickly as possible.

"Oh yes," Shindi said, returning her glasses to her nose. "My husband was glued to his newspaper as usual a couple of nights ago and he discovered a connection to our community." She had aroused their interest. "Do you remember that very kind lady who died from breast cancer? She had one daughter, Harleen, and her only son became a gangster. There were drive-by shootings, police raids and everything."

"Oh, you mean the family who lived here on this property before I bought it?" Lalita asked.

"Oh, that's right! I forgot all about that." Shindi said. "Yes, they lived right here on this very spot."

"Ah yes, yes." Tarsem reached for a piece of the *barphee* she had brought. "Poor lady. *Bechari*! Her husband didn't remarry, did he?

Nowadays the wife dies and before she is cremated the husband is on a plane for India, shopping for a new young bride."

"Anyway," Shindi interrupted, "they had these friends in Ontario that visited here a few times, and I remember meeting the lady—her name was Balbir—at the *gurdwara*." Shindi paused to clear her throat and then continued, "And it says right here that Balbir's husband was arrested for murdering their only child!"

"*Vaheguru*! Oh dear God!" Tarsem clasped Lalita's hand.

"The daughter was in love with a Muslim boy, and the girl's father was against the union. It's taken the police almost two years to gather all the evidence."

"*Hai Rabba*! What was he thinking?" Lalita was trying desperately to pry her hand away from Tarsem.

"And according to my husband's sources, that Jessy girl, your friend Rani's daughter, she's one of the many lawyers working on this case. She ended up in the same city."

"Wow, Shindi, that *is* news!" Lalita exclaimed. "And isn't that a coincidence? Rani must be so proud!"

"Well, I certainly wouldn't let my daughters get involved in something like that." Shindi flipped through the pages of the newspaper looking for the continuation of the story. "You never know what men like that are capable of. They have no hearts!"

Tarsem wiped her tears away with a handkerchief. "How could a father raise a daughter just to kill her with his own two hands?"

Shindi handed her a tissue but she shoved it away. Lalita made eye contact with Shindi. This temporary new addition to their party circuit was far too sensitive. This would be her first and final invite.

"It's almost every few months now that we hear such horrible news. Last time it was that story from up north somewhere, Prince George maybe," Tarsem said, recalling the events. "That was the one where the woman convinced her husband to kill her stepbrother's second wife. And who knows what they did to the first one..." Tarsem's voice trailed off into sobs.

This time Shindi simply placed the tissue box next to Tarsem, hoping she would put her overused handkerchief away.

"This has been happening for years with *apnay lok*!" Shindi commented. "We're just getting to hear about it now because of all the media. Who knows how many lives have been destroyed because of ruthless people like this man."

"What I don't understand is, if these children were happy, why not let them be together?" Lalita asked. "He would've suffered less *baizty* if he'd accepted the relationship or just disowned the children. But these actions, *chi chi*, are disgraceful." She had picked up some of Baksho's expressions.

"Wait! There's more! It says here that there are rumours within the community that the lover's father is an accessory to the murder. Witnesses say the two men were good friends. I find that hard to believe—after all, the other man was a Muslim—but these days anything is possible!" Shindi closed the newspaper.

"*Vaheguru*!" Tarsem covered her ears and sat swaying back and forth.

"Men are so stupid! It was inevitable the RCMP would catch up with him." Lalita took a sip of tea. "It's not like in India where you can pay them off...but what about the boy? Are they saying anything about him?"

"No, there is no mention of him." Shindi went back to the story to skim over it again in case she had missed any of the details.

Tarsem was now sobbing uncontrollably.

"*Hun bus vi kar,* that's enough!" Lalita had lost her patience watching and listening to Tarsem's emotional reaction.

"Actually, it was the girl's mother—Balbir—that led the police to the killer," Shindi clarified.

"God bless her soul!" Tarsem blew her nose into her soaked handkerchief. "But imagine turning in your own husband. Only a very strong and brave woman could do that."

"Well, if there were more women like her and less like Baksho, we could save all our daughters." Shindi smacked her hand on the table. "Baksho would probably think the girl deserved it!" She stood up to leave, hoping for Lalita's sake that Tarsem would follow her lead.

"Maybe next month we can meet at my house." Tarsem suggested. "What do you think? Umber's wedding is right around the corner, and you ladies can help me get organized."

"We'll see," Lalita responded and shot Shindi a look.

Tarsem slipped on her running shoes and laced them up, adjusting her *salwar* over the heel. She stepped outside the door. "Yes, I should get home. My younger daughter, Amrit, has taken her three brothers to some family movie—*Troy* it's called. I wouldn't let her go alone so she picked a film the young ones could watch, too. My Amrit is so responsible. Anyway, they will be home soon, and my boys are always famished when..."

Lalita closed the door before Tarsem could finish her sentence.

Roop – Beauty

My mother placed the cordless next to Umber's picture and reached into her cardigan pocket for a handkerchief.

"They're not coming, Amrit," my mother said. "Harry says it would be too difficult to travel with the baby. I thought I'd be able to convince Umber to come and visit during this year's *Vaisakhi* festival, but he didn't even let me talk to her."

"You're such a fool, Mom! You know very well what Harry is like."

"I know, Amrit, but sometimes I think he'll have mercy on me. I'm getting old, you know, and worrying about your future doesn't help any."

"If you're so concerned, why do you make Umber stay with that jackass?"

"It's not so simple, okay? I'm just thankful to God she has already given him a son. At least she can have some *sukh* later in life."

My mother was no expert at hiding her emotions, and I could hear in her voice everything she didn't have the courage to say. It had been just four months since Umber's "accident" had occurred.

My older sister Umber had been pregnant for the second time. Everything seemed to be going smoothly. Harry and his parents were pleased with the arrival of another child. They had even asked my mother to come stay with Umber for a while but she had declined the offer in fear of creating more problems in the marriage. Then one night when she was well into the seventh month of the pregnancy, Harry returned home late from a friend's house, and Umber simply asked him if he had eaten dinner. Without any warning at all he struck her and knocked her down. Concerned for her unborn child, Umber got up and ran toward the telephone, but he grabbed her by the ponytail and hauled her into the bedroom. She pleaded with him to let her go, and in the midst of the commotion she went into premature labour. He accused her of faking the contractions and struck her again. Then he unplugged the land lines while she lay crying in a fetal position on the bed. When she heard the front door slam shut, she somehow managed to crawl all the way to her purse and used her cellphone to dial for help. She remembers nothing beyond this point. The next day she woke up in a hospital to discover her child had been stillborn. Harry showed no remorse for his actions.

His parents and her little boy were in Fresno at a family wedding when the episode took place. When his mother heard the dead baby was a male, she accused Umber of purposely inflicting harm on it. She knew Umber did not want another child so soon, and it was more convenient for her to reprimand her daughter-in-law than to admit her son was at fault. When the neighbours expressed their concerns, the family referred to the incident as an "accident." Umber phoned from the hospital to tell my mother what had happened but was unable to keep in contact long enough for my mother to help her grieve her loss.

"What are you thinking about, Amrit?" my mother asked, although I knew she didn't really want to know the answer.

Most of the time I would suffer silently through my mother's pathetic analysis of Umber's situation, but occasionally I would not be able to control myself. This was one of those times. "I hope I have seven daughters," I said. "Actually, I think I want eight. And then I'm going to hand out *ladoos* to every Indian I know. I'm going to express my condolences to all the women with sons and tell them maybe next time, if God is smiling upon them, they'll give birth to daughters, too!"

"*Phitay moo tera*! How dare you say such things! *Kamli kuri*, you crazy girl! Just because we allowed you to go to college, it doesn't mean you're suddenly wiser than your mother." Then, before I had a chance to respond, she changed the subject. "If my *kismet* had been better, you and Umber would have turned out like Mrs. Gill's daughters."

"Manohar and Roop?" I said, astonished. "Why would you want us to turn out like them?"

"They're not much older than you and your sister, but they are definitely wiser. One is happily married and the other's engaged. If Harry weren't such a *nakuma banda,* such a useless man, he would have found you a husband like Manohar's husband found Roop such a suitable boy. So now Mrs. Gill has something else to gloat about while I have nothing but misery to show for my life. *Her* daughters would never say or do the things you do."

As usual, my mother's handkerchief was drenched.

Mrs. Gill had lived in the neighbourhood years earlier before relocating her family to Chandigarh in India. My mother had always considered her an arch enemy because Mrs. Gill hadn't taken a liking to her, and therefore my mother had been excluded from most community functions. Although she professed not to approve of Mrs. Gill's *modernization,* I think she envied her. Mrs. Gill was, in fact, the most knowledgeable Indian woman I knew.

However, for all her sophistication and style, Mrs. Gill was very *Indian* at heart. When her first daughter was born, she was overwhelmed with grief. Manohar was dark and fat. By no means was she of any value, so her mother did not pay much attention to her and she was left to be raised by the grandmother. She took after her father's side of the family, and by the age of eighteen, she was close to six feet tall and weighed over two hundred pounds. But Manohar was at a disadvantage with her name as well. Mrs. Gill's father-in-law named the child before she came home from the hospital, and the letter he received through a *hukamnama* from the Sri Guru Granth Sahib was an M. Of all the names he could have given her that commenced with the letter M, he had blessed her with a name that had only been popular with his own generation. And as the result of her name, Manohar was often teased at school, referred to as a *man whore* or *manure* by the *goray,* but she always remained silent.

My grandmother, or *bebe,* was once friends with Mrs. Gill's mother-in-law. She told me that after Manohar's birth, Mrs. Gill consulted several self-professed *pundits,* and they all declared she would mother two daughters before giving birth to two sons. So when her second daughter was born, Mrs. Gill was ecstatic because the blockage had been cleared and she would be able to conceive a boy. *Bebe* said that even as a baby, Roop was the complete opposite of Manohar. Everything about her was beautiful, including her name, and she blossomed into a pretty young woman, just like her mother.

Meanwhile, Manohar tried everything to gain her mother's affection. Whenever her parents spoke, she listened. She was the daughter every parent prayed for, but still it was not enough. Roop was the spoiled popular one, and wherever her mother went, she announced how proud she was of her daughter Roop.

But she was not the perfect daughter her mother insisted she was. I knew exactly what she was like because she was only two years ahead of me in school. She went through five boyfriends in two years, and one of them was a college guy. She smoked regularly—and not just cigarettes—and came to school drunk on a number of occasions. She was also infamous for staying out late and getting into bars with fake identification. I'm not saying she was a *bad* girl. She didn't do anything worse than most other high school students did. She simply did things that *good* Indian girls don't do, at least not openly.

I got the rest of the scoop from Vimmi Bains, who lived next door to one of Roop's friends. She told me that shortly after Manohar graduated from high school, her parents moved back to India with their boys. And a few months later, Roop and Manohar went to live in Montreal because their mother believed a college education in Canada would secure more promising matches for them. When the time came, Mrs. Gill arranged a marriage for Manohar, did all the paperwork and then called her to Chandigarh for the wedding ceremony. Manohar's husband, Gurtaj, eventually made his way to Montreal to live with the girls. But Roop's new brother-in-law did not approve of her boyfriends, and not wanting Roop to disgrace the family name, he persuaded his father-in-law to have her married off as soon as possible. Roop agreed because she was afraid of what her parents might do if they learned what she was up to. Her future husband, who was one of Gurtaj's relatives, was in Canada on a visitor's visa and leapt at the chance to remain in the country. According to Vimmi, Gurtaj took a substantial amount of money from this man for arranging the union. Mr. and Mrs. Gill were happy to find a groom on such short notice so they didn't care whether or not the man was a suitable match.

The Gills told everyone that Manohar's husband had suggested the *rishta* because he wanted to express gratitude to his in-laws for all they had done for him. He told them he was fortunate to have married into such a loving family and the least he could do was share their burdens. It was his duty as the eldest son-in-law.

So regardless of what my mother thought, at least one of Mrs. Gill's daughters was not perfect. Roop had a terrible reputation within the community. She had no other choice than to find an Indian guy from outside of the province or agree to an arranged marriage with a man from India. She chose the latter because he would overlook her indiscretions. Canadian citizenship would make up for his wife's sinful past.

Roop's Journal

Sept. 24, 2007

I can't believe Manohar has sex with him. He gives me the creeps. He's always looking at me weird. Today when he asked me how school was, I saw him staring at my breasts. Manohar believes I'm so high on myself I think every man wants me. She thinks her Gurtaj is just a very sweet guy.

Oct. 8

Today I got my acceptance letter from McGill. I can start my graduate degree program next term. The pig gave me a congratulatory hug and his arms weren't the only body parts I could feel hardening against me. There's no point in saying anything to Manohar. She's just going to accuse me of lying. And I can't afford to move out on my own while I'm in school full-time.

Oct. 16

He's going back to India for three weeks. I can let my guard down.

Nov. 12

Manohar was at work and I was surprised to find him home. He grabbed my butt as I walked past the kitchen on my way to my bedroom. I pushed him away and warned him I was going to tell Manohar and my parents. He just laughed. He says he knows about my boyfriend and all the other men I keep company with. He says he can do it better than them. He's such a pervert.

Nov. 13

I accidentally called him a pervert out loud in front of everyone, and Manohar kicked me out of the house. She said I was an inconsiderate, selfish little bitch who likes to start trouble. She thinks I'm jealous of her relationship with Gurtaj because for once someone loves her more than they love me. Her insecurities have finally gotten to her, and Mr. Pervert has her right where he wants her.

Nov. 17

I've been living at my friend Liz's house for the last few days, but I went back to collect my things today. His car wasn't in the driveway so I thought it was safe to go in, but there he was, sitting at the kitchen table. He told me that he saw me half-naked leaving the nightclub on Saint-Laurent with a *gora* last night. I tried to leave but he grabbed me by the blouse, ripping it right down the side seam. He said he's better than any of the white trash I'm sleeping with, and he told me I don't have to go begging for it in bars and I should just lie down at his feet. I kneed him in the groin and got out of there. I'm going to tell my parents, but what can they do? They're so far away.

Dec. 9

Manohar called me at Liz's and told me to come home. Mom and Dad are on their way to Montreal. They're coming to get us. Maybe they know the truth.

Dec. 14

Dad looks so different. He wears a turban now and he's added a neatly trimmed beard to his moustache. Mom looks exactly the same. But man, are they ever pissed at me! Before I could tell them my side of the story Mom threw me into the car. The pervert has made up stories about all the men I've slept with. I didn't get a chance to defend myself or tell them what he's been doing. I begged and pleaded with them to listen to my side but they didn't want to hear it. They think I'll say anything to save myself.

Dec. 27

Gurtaj thinks he's found me a suitable match, a friend of his from India. My parents are against it. They would rather I marry a family friend from Vancouver. I just hope they aren't referring to Baksho's grandson! I don't want anything to do with that big-mouthed, *bukvas* head. Now the pervert is very upset, and he isn't speaking to my parents. Thank God!

Dec. 31

Mom and Dad have rented a house for us in Surrey, far away from our old place in Vancouver, and they plan to stay here until I'm married, then they'll go back to India. Needless to say, I won't be returning to Montreal to attend McGill next semester. No one listens to me. I've become an outsider.

Jan. 28, 2008

Manohar called today. She was crying. Gurtaj is threatening to leave her if I don't agree to marry his friend. He promised him a bride. My parents are distraught. It seems that the pervert received ten thousand dollars from this friend as a reward for setting up the *rishta*. Surely my parents must see what a loser their daughter is married to.

Feb. 11

Manohar showed up at the house today. Gurtaj has given her an ultimatum! If she doesn't return to Montreal with an agreeable bride, then she shouldn't return at all. Manohar pleaded with me to agree to the marriage. She's in love with this loser. She's such an idiot. He doesn't love her.

Feb. 26

My parents called Gurtaj last night. I don't know what they said to him but Manohar is going back tomorrow morning.

Mar. 5

I thought my parents would realize what a mistake they'd made when they forced Manohar to marry that jerk. I was wrong. Although Dad doesn't agree with Gurtaj's actions, he says he can't destroy his eldest daughter's life. He has the power to keep her marriage afloat by having me marry the pervert's friend, and that's what he plans to do. Everyone thinks Mom is so great, but they couldn't be more wrong! She doesn't care about me or Manohar, she only cares about my brothers. She says I'm almost twenty-eight and that it's best I get married sooner than later. So she's also decided to sacrifice me.

Mar. 19

They can say and do whatever they want, but there is no way they can force me to marry a guy from India! I'll figure something out, I always do.

Apr. 12

Manohar arrived with my future husband, Navdeep. When I opened the front door, I could see she was in tears and she ran directly into the bathroom. Navdeep carried the luggage inside, but when Mom tried to go after my sister, he stopped her and suggested she give Manohar a little time to compose herself. He said they'd been through a horrible ordeal.

He told us that he'd been in Montreal for two days when he learned the truth about the pervert. Gurtaj had asked him to stay with him and Manohar until the wedding, and if he hadn't been so jet lagged and up in the middle of the night, he wouldn't have overheard Gurtaj on the phone to India arranging to take Manohar there and have her killed by a hired hit man. No one would know. It seems that he'd taken out an insurance policy on Manohar a few days after he arrived in Canada, and her death would be made to look accidental. Then he'd marry someone much younger and beautiful. His parents had already lined up prospects. Their son was a Canadian citizen now so there was no reason for him to stay with Manohar. She was just the woman they'd used to gain admission into Canada.

Navdeep had been afraid for Manohar's life and even his own safety, and he had pleaded with her to go to the cops, but she refused to believe him. And Navdeep couldn't go anywhere because all his money had gone straight into Gurtaj's bank account. Not to mention the one hundred thousand rupees Navdeep's parents had paid Gurtaj's family in India. So his only hope was to expose the plot.

It wasn't until Navdeep recorded a conversation between Gurtaj and the hit man, negotiating a price, that Manohar faced the harsh reality. Manohar and Navdeep boarded the next flight to Vancouver. Gurtaj had no idea what was happening because they had convinced him they had to leave for the wedding immediately or I would change my mind.

Dad and I are keeping the recording from Mom as he thinks she won't be able to stomach it. Even he had a hard time with it, holding his hands over his face as he listened. He turned it off after listening to just one minute of it. He couldn't take any more.

But he looks better in person — Navdeep, I mean. He's tall and well-built. Although his clothes are outdated, he's well-groomed. And when he speaks in that soothing and sexy voice, the seriousness of the subject he's discussing seems to diminish.

Apr. 14

Today I overheard Navdeep telling Manohar what happened to his cousin in India. I didn't catch the whole conversation, but it had something to do with his cousin rejecting a marriage proposal. Just days after her decision, someone threw acid on her face while she was waiting for the bus. No witnesses came forward, but everyone knew it was the guy she had refused to marry.

So that somewhat explains his concern for Manohar. I was starting to doubt his sincerity. I thought he might be acting all nice so we don't deport him back to India. People in India would do just about anything to come to this country.

I wonder what became of Navdeep's cousin.

Apr. 16

My parents are still devastated. The "D-word" they feared the most is no longer "Divorce." Mom is pushing for Manohar to go to the cops and see a lawyer, but Manohar is still in disarray, and she hasn't slept in days. Dad called Gurtaj in Montreal and threatened his life if he comes near our family. Gurtaj just laughed at Dad and told him he wouldn't be able to do anything. I don't think Dad will take this lightly; he was strangling the telephone cord as if it were the pervert's neck during their shouting match over the phone. He says he will go to the RCMP tomorrow and lodge a complaint against Gurtaj if Manohar won't. Dad's police officer buddies in India are also keeping a strict eye on Gurtaj's family, harassing and interrogating them every chance they get. At least those corrupt officers are good for something!

Apr. 17

Navdeep's been staying with us for a few days now, but there hasn't been any mention of the wedding. He stays out of the way but has been a great friend to Manohar, trying to convince her to forget about the pervert. But Mom says Manohar needs time to grieve because her life's been shattered.

I know my parents are grateful to Navdeep, so my wedding will most likely go on, unless I find a way to stop it. I must admit I do like him. Of course, I don't really know him, but I'm impressed by what I do know. He saved my sister's life.

Apr. 18

Navdeep called off the wedding. Manohar told him I was not happy with the arrangement and I had only agreed to marry him because Gurtaj had forced my parents to accept this *rishta*. He was very embarrassed and apologized for all the havoc he'd caused, so I now understand why he hasn't paid any attention to me since he's been here. I thought he was just playing hard to get.

Anyway, I guess that's over and done with. I'm so relieved! He's leaving for Nanaimo in a few days. A former classmate lives there.

Apr. 19

Today I overheard Navdeep confiding in Manohar again. I pretended to be engrossed in my romance novel but I listened while he told her about all the NRI, the non-resident Indian men who go back to India and marry young women in exchange for thousands of dollars. But when it comes time to fulfill the marriage vows and sponsor the women abroad, the husbands don't follow through because they got what they came for.

He said the runaway bride and groom phenomenon is also on the rise. People in India get married to Canadians and Americans solely to get into the country, but when they arrive at the airports to meet their new spouses, they conveniently vanish. Some leave with lovers and others with family or friends. Poor guy, he isn't in either category, but his situation is just as bad.

Apr. 21

Before he left, Navdeep wished me a happy life and placed a package wrapped in newspaper on the kitchen table. He said he had no use for it and he couldn't picture anyone else wearing it. Dad drove him to the ferry.

I keep thinking that maybe I should have given him a chance. Dad begged him to stay even after he called off the wedding, because he'll have to return to India once his visa expires and his life may be in danger since Gurtaj's family members know he's the one who betrayed them. But Navdeep insisted it wasn't proper for him to stay in my parents' home. He was very unhappy he'd been manipulated by a con man.

Manohar told me the pervert had hinted to Navdeep that, if I didn't satisfy him after the marriage, there were ways to resolve the situation.

At the time he had no idea what a mastermind Gurtaj was. Navdeep had so many dreams of a great life in Canada with a beautiful devoted wife. But in these circumstances, all the dreams have fizzled. He said I needed a husband that I love, one who's worthy of me.

Apr. 24

I finally opened the package he left for me. It was a purple *sari*. I can't believe he knew my favourite colour!

Apr. 30

I keep thinking about Navdeep. Mom has sensed my restlessness, and she says that, if I'm interested, they could always re-arrange the marriage. But I've put it off for now because Manohar is our priority. Her heartbreak has brought my family together. My parents trust me again, and they've apologized to Manohar for what she's been through because they blame themselves. They were the ones who married her off to the first man who'd take her. Not once had they considered the consequences. Back when they were having difficulty finding a suitable match for her in Canada, I can remember Mom saying, "When a daughter marries, a family cries for one day, but if she never marries, they cry every day!" But now she regrets words like these ever came out of her mouth. Her daughter was lucky her death didn't make it onto the front page of every Canadian newspaper.

May 1

Manohar has finally started leaving the house on her own, and my parents have decided to stay in Canada until she's really back on her feet. My brothers attend a very prestigious and secure boarding school in India so they'll be well protected from Gurtaj's family.

Divorce proceedings will be delayed, though. The cops haven't been able to locate Gurtaj. Dad's lawyer believes he's most likely fled to India. My grandfather in Chandigarh is retired from office now, but he has some friends looking into it. And Gurtaj won't come back for fear of being arrested, so for now Manohar is safe.

Jun. 2

Manohar's been attending a support group for victims of domestic violence. Although her husband was never physically abusive, the effects of his horrific plans for her have had the same consequences. She was surprised to find so many women from different ethnicities and backgrounds going through the same emotional trauma that she is going through. She is doing a lot better now but she still doesn't want to see anyone from our old neighbourhood. Although our community may pretend to be empathetic toward her situation, she thinks they'll make judgments behind her back. They'll blame her for everything. But that doesn't matter now—they can say whatever they want! Manohar is getting the help she needs. She's no longer alone.

Kitty Party – 2008

"Surprise!"

Mrs. Gill dropped her purse onto the pavement at all the commotion. She had been expecting to meet only Baksho for lunch, but the whole gang was standing in front of the restaurant waiting for her. The group of old friends had travelled great distances, putting their differences aside for this reunion.

"*Velcum*...!" Baksho mumbled and reached out from her wheelchair to swing her good arm around Mrs. Gill's waist.

Manjeet opened the door and led the women into Pappu's Fusion Palace. Indian-style Chinese food had recently become everyone's favourite, and the distinct sweet and spicy aroma of the two cuisines merged together and lingered around the tables.

"You must be so happy that your Roop is marrying that boy from India, Mrs. Gill!" Lalita exclaimed. "I've heard he's so wonderful to her *and* he's extremely handsome! I'm looking forward to the wedding next year!"

Mrs. Gill stared at Lalita for several minutes before she realized who had spoken to her. Since she last saw her, Lalita had lost over fifty pounds, replaced her bifocals with stylish frames and coloured her chin-length hair its original shade of golden brown. The dazzling smile that had vanished almost two decades earlier had gradually reappeared since her husband's death.

"Doesn't Lalita look *lovely-shovely*!" Indu had sensed what Mrs. Gill was thinking.

"Lalita, I've been meaning to ask, how are your sons?" Shindi inquired.

"Well, the oldest got a position with the provincial government, so I sent the younger one over to Victoria as well so he can attend the university there. My mind is at ease knowing they are together." Lalita felt she had made the right decision to send her boys away.

"Mrs. Gill, you haven't changed a bit," Kamal announced. "You haven't been getting those Botox treatments in India, have you? I heard that plastic surgery is really popular there! And it's not just the Bollywood celebrities that are getting their noses fixed and boobs enlarged. Everyone is doing it!"

Shindi glared at Kamal.

But it wasn't Botox that Mrs. Gill had invested in. She'd had a laser procedure done on her eyes, but as she had never worn her spectacles in public, the others would never need to know. She had always opted for contact lenses because eyeglasses would have spoiled her beauty.

"Well, your hair looks very nice these days, Kamal!" Lalita commented.

Kamal's hair had been thinning, and she was now wearing fake hair in her bun to make it look fuller. However, the synthetic piece was just a shade off her original dyed reddish-brown hair colour and the texture smoother, and unfortunately the inch of grey re-growth at the roots only accentuated the difference.

But Manjeet was not interested in Kamal's hair, and she directed the topic back to the chief guest of the evening. "Are you back for a visit or will you be staying permanently, Mrs. Gill? And is it true that you've been living in Surrey all this time?"

The clan had not seen Manjeet in so long that most had forgotten about her speech impediment, and after years and years of therapy, she was finally able to express herself clearly. She had held back so many times for so many years, listening while everyone else spoke, and never questioning because she had been afraid they would mock her. She was different physically as well. In fact, she looked like a young fifty-something. Her cataract surgery had been successful so that she no longer wore hideous dark-rimmed glasses. And she had continued to dye her hair so she could express her new-found freedom and revive her youth. Because on the inside, in her soul, she was different, she had aged into a confident and content woman. No one would ridicule her now.

"What about Manohar?" Indu was also curious. "Will she be staying with you, Mrs. Gill?" Indu had not aged as gracefully as her friend. She was only two years older than Manjeet but looked closer to Baksho's age. Her hair was completely white from her forehead to the nape of her neck, but she had only stopped colouring it a few months earlier, and the dark, dry ends of her shoulder-length braid were a reminder of her faded youth. A recent knee operation now kept her confined mostly indoors, and her once scrawny body had transformed into a pair of droopy breasts in constant competition with a large pot belly.

As the hostess showed them to their table, Indu used the wall and her cane for support, slowly making her way to a chair.

When at last they were all seated, Mrs. Gill was finally given a chance to speak. "Thank you for doing all this, but it really wasn't necessary to go to all this trouble." She felt quite overwhelmed by the excitement that shone on her old friends' faces.

At that moment Baksho's cellphone went off, and she motioned to the others that she had to leave. She no longer made other people's business her first priority. Her life had taken a drastic turn a year earlier.

It was Kamal who had found her collapsed on the floor in the *masala* aisle of her A-One Superstore. She had called the ambulance and informed the others, and they had all sat by Baksho's hospital bed until Preet arrived. The stroke had left her partially paralyzed, and doctors believed a full recovery was not likely at her age: she would be confined to a wheelchair for the rest of her life. Preet had moved her family back to Vancouver in order to care for her former mother-in-law, and Baksho, unable to carry on with her daily routine in the store, had signed the business over to Preet. She was now dependent on her son's ex-wife to move even a few little steps.

Rani, taking the attention away from Baksho and Preet's slow exit from the restaurant, commented, "Mrs. Gill, we heard what happened with Manohar. We couldn't believe it. She's such a nice girl."

Rani had recently returned to the club after an extended absence. Shame had led to her isolation, but Baksho's failing health had brought her back.

"Let's talk about something else," Mrs. Gill said. "What's done is done. My daughter is alive and well and that's all that matters to me." She unfolded her napkin and placed it on her lap. "And Rani! Wow, look at you! You look like a *gori*!"

Rani's skin was no longer scarred with random white patches. Over the years the vitiligo had spread, eventually causing a much lighter but even skin tone all over her body. As a result, she had shed her *dupatta* and her long-sleeved turtle neck for a trendy but comfortable, low-cut, short-sleeved *salwar kameez*.

"No, Mrs. Gill, this issue needs to be addressed in our community," Indu said, refusing to shelve Manohar's near-tragedy so easily. "In fact, I think you should run in the next election. I think this is the *time-shime*. There are so many *apnay* MLAs and MPs now." Indu was able to get a little smile out of Mrs. Gill. "So much has changed since you've been gone. Look at the *Amreekan lok,* they've just elected a black man as president."

"You never hear of women plotting to kill their husbands or sons." Rani was talking like her successful lawyer daughter now. "And it's our own fault it has come to this!" She was relieved Jessy had remarried and was content with her second husband. And her younger daughter Tejinder had accepted a proposal from Jessy's brother-in-law and was also happily married.

Suddenly Mrs. Gill burst into tears. "I keep wondering where we went wrong. We tried to do our best, didn't we? And yet I became my daughter's biggest *dushman,* her worst enemy."

"Don't think that way, Mrs. Gill. We all did the best we could for our children." Manjeet's eyes had welled up, too.

"If I'd only treated Manohar as I did my sons, she would be leading a joyful life now." Regret underlined Mrs. Gill's words. She was no longer the woman who had left Vancouver years earlier to seek a brighter future in India for her boys. The sorrow that surrounded mothers of daughters was finally present in her eyes.

"Just look at Baksho," Indu said. "Her whole *life-shife* she spent criticizing other people's daughters. But where's her *Jugga-Jack* now? It's *bechari* Preet who has taken on the duty of a son." Indu, who spent so many years obsessing over no male heir of her own, had finally come to terms with her demons.

Seeing the conversation was scratching old wounds, Lalita decided to speak. "I always thought you and Baksho would change your friendship into a *rishtedari.* Your Roop and her grandson would have made the perfect *jori*!"

"Well, what about Manohar marrying her grandson?" Rani asked.

"That's not possible," Mrs. Gill responded, fiddling with her *dupatta.*

"Baksho won't care about the divorce. This is your daughter we're talking about," Manjeet added. She placed her menu on the edge of the table.

"You're so naïve, my dear Manjeet. Manohar will only be accepted by another divorcee. But thank God times have changed. At least she'll be able to re-marry without anyone pointing fingers." Mrs. Gill looked at the ceiling, hoping God would send a new mate for her daughter soon.

"*Kuray* Shindi, and what about your daughter Meena?" Indu inquired. "She's *waaaaay* past the marriageable age, isn't she? Since she left for *New York-Shork* to study, you never mention her."

"Oh, you know kids these days," Shindi responded, reaching over to open the menu. "They're so busy with their lives. They don't want to get married young. They want to be established and successful first." She always ordered the same inexpensive dish, but she had nothing further to discuss on the subject of Meena. And since everyone knew the real story, no one pressed the issue further.

Indu shook her head. "You're right about that, Shindi! Girls are choosing to stay single well into their thirties and forties. We can't even refer to them as girls anymore. And when they do decide to marry, they're marrying *goray*. It was fine when men waited before they married, but the women, *hai hai*! Now they *date-shate* so many men before they choose a husband and they parade their lovers around in public like they're a piece of *jewellery-jawllery*!"

"What kind of parents would allow their daughters to behave in this manner?" Manjeet questioned.

"Well, I think it's great that women are choosing their own life partners these days. It saves parents the headache." Kamal was content with Sonia's choice of husband, especially since her son-in-law resembled the Bollywood actor Akshay Kumar. The others, however, did not share her views and ignored her comment.

"And Mrs. Gill, you need not worry about Manohar," Rani said. "These days it's much easier to find husbands for divorcees. It's the older, single, never-been-married category that we have to worry about. At least with divorcees, they were good enough to marry the first time around. People think those that are still single have something *wrong* with them!"

"Rani is right!" Lalita said. "Times may have changed, ladies, but we mustn't let our girls end up as spinsters. And Shindi, I think your youngest, your Dharam, will be a suitable match for Baksho's grandson! He's blossomed into such a handsome man." Lalita loved to play matchmaker. She had, in fact, become well known for it in the community.

"He's not available," Shindi responded, a hint of bitterness in her voice.

"What do you mean, is he *gay-shay*?" Indu asked. When some of the others laughed, she said, "I'm serious! My grandchildren watch these shows on cable and..."

"*Hai hai,* Indu," Lalita cut her off. "Now really, you must stop taking all that medication!"

"But Indu is right!" Mrs. Gill said. "I was still living in Chandigarh when we first heard the news. In Canada, two people of the same sex are allowed to marry now and live like husband and wife! At first I thought it was a hoax, but the Internet confirmed it. Gay marriages are legal in Canada!" Mrs. Gill had been living in India for almost twelve years, periodically returning for short vacations, but she was still well aware of what had been happening in her adoptive country.

Lalita was flabbergasted. She had yet to be approached by clients wanting her to match up same sex couples.

Kamal gave a little giggle. "Baksho's grandson is smitten with someone, but it's not a boy. It's a *girl.*"

Indu motioned the waiter to come and take their order. She had been put on a strict diet since her recent diagnosis of type 2 diabetes.

"Well, it's not my daughter Dharam, that's for sure! But you ladies will never guess who it is." Shindi put her glass of water to her lips so she would not be the one to disclose this bit of gossip.

Kamal flashed Shindi a smile and leaned in to whisper in her ear, only to move her face quickly away from the ticklish and springy hair. "Don't forget your appointment with me tomorrow," she said. "We are going to fix that frizzy bird's nest of yours. This Japanese hair straightening system works miracles—trust me, it's been around for years. And maybe we'll get rid of that salt and pepper look while we're at it." Then, seeing the look of horror on Shindi's face as she mentally counted up the cost of all this treatment, Kamal added, "And don't worry about the money. I'll do it for free!"

Shindi could not see any point to the fuss Kamal was making over her appearance. A new hairstyle was not going to disguise the creases and disappointments in the face of a sixty-year-old mother with two unwed daughters. She waved Kamal away before the others sensed a conspiracy.

Dharam – Faith

My daughter Dharam showed no remorse when she walked out on us that dreadful summer day. It was after that when I started spending most of my time in her old bedroom. I was not sure if I was drawn there because I missed her or if it relieved some of my guilt. There was so much I did not know about my daughter. She had often said there was no use holding onto items I no longer had a purpose for, but in the back of her closet under old books and toys, I found notebooks filled with drawings of clothing, self-portraits and paintings. I never knew Dharam had these interests, but I later learned that was not the only thing she kept from me. I do not know when or how it happened but somewhere along the way Dharam lost sight of who she was. She sacrificed her culture, values, and family for a world she did not belong to.

I admit being disappointed the first time I saw her. She was supposed to be a boy, one who would grow up to make his mother proud. Giving birth to a son would have completed my life's purpose. But although she had robbed me of this honour, eventually I grew to love her. She was the youngest and the *good* one. I had mistakenly spoiled the other two so I had tried to keep her under my control. I knew she would always take care of me and because of her I would find some peace.

As a child, she was easily subdued. Without much rebellion on her part, she would accept whatever decisions we made for her. She had no ridiculous ideas like her older sister, Meena, did about pursuing a career as a Bollywood actress and travelling the world. But I guess that was my own fault, too. I was so depressed when Meena was born that when Kamal called to ask if I would be attending the annual *pind* party where we had first met, I allowed her to persuade me into naming her after the legendary but tragedy-stricken queen of Indian cinema, Meena Kumari.

My husband insisted we add an *Inder,* a *Preet* or a *Gur* as a prefix, suffix or both to make it sound more Punjabi, but the paperwork was already submitted and I did not care enough to pay to change it.

Dharam, on the other hand, agreed to become a nurse as I requested. And when the time came, I was sure she would marry the man I chose for her. But I should have suspected something was not right when I suggested the *rishta* from Kiran's husband's nephew, Tony. He was handsome, wealthy and settled in Ottawa, and since his family lived in Surrey, she would never have to worry about in-laws interfering in her life on a daily basis. Dharam showed no interest in him. College, *gori* friends and western influence had poisoned her mind. I should have kept her locked up inside the house, like some of the other Punjabi parents, and we could have found a suitable match from India for our wayward daughter. I would rather she had died in this house than do what she did.

The first few weeks following that terrible day were the most difficult. I worried Dharam's father would hear what people were saying. One daughter had already ruined us years earlier and now Dharam was following in her footsteps. He was not one who could go on after so much *baizty*. He was too proud of a man. I watched him very closely during that time. I counted the pills in the bottles, monitored the booze and never left him alone, especially in our bedroom with its high ceiling fan.

Since then I have been thinking that it must have been that Bains clan who did some *jadu toona,* some black magic on my children. They were always jealous of my beautiful daughters. Their only daughter, Vimmi, never outgrew her teenage acne nor did she shed her excess weight. And if not the Bains family, there were plenty of others in the neighbourhood who would wish us harm. I was never their equal because I had mothered three daughters. One daughter married into a crazy, ill-respected family, one shamed us when she moved out to wait on tables in a bar, and now the youngest is possessed by the devil.

I forgave her for being a girl. But I cannot forgive her for the respect I have lost in the community. I try to forget as I sleep, but the nightmares leave me restless. I remember that summer as if it were yesterday. I had taken the phone call from her in the kitchen and rushed into the living room to tell my husband.

"*Oye Sundeh ho,* do you hear me? Dharam's coming!"

"What's gotten into you, Shindi? I haven't seen you this *khush* in years." He went back to his newspaper. "You should practise being happy more often!"

"Didn't you hear what I said? Our daughter Dharam is coming home from Edmonton!"

He looked up. "*Oh ho*! This isn't the first time Dharam has come to visit. You're being silly, Shindi."

"You don't understand *Ji*! She's agreed to get married."

"What?" He stood up so abruptly that his newspaper fell to the floor.

"*Suchi,* I wouldn't lie about something so wonderful."

"Well, did she say those exact words? Did she say she agreed to get married?"

"No, but she's coming home, isn't she?"

He shook his head and sat down again.

I pulled the newspaper away. "If you aren't reading this dumb paper, then your eyes are glued to that stupid hockey channel. Do you care even a little about what is happening in your own home? I'm going to get rid of that channel—it's too expensive—and I'm going to tell the fellow at the sweet shop not to give you the free papers anymore!"

He grunted at me and grabbed the paper back, but this time he kept it closed. After he retired, I'd had no choice but to subscribe to the sports channel because he would not do anything or go anywhere. He did not talk to anyone. It was the only way to occupy his time. But he knew I would eventually follow through on my threats.

"Go ahead, I'm listening."

"I think this time she'll accept the proposal. I'm serious, this is it! Why else would she agree to come home now? She knows Paul's coming to visit Lalita this weekend, and Lalita says if Dharam isn't interested, there are lots of other girls she can introduce him to. I have to convince her before this one gets away."

"How does Lalita know this boy?" He adjusted his black turban and sat upright in his chair. I could sense his concern.

"Don't worry. He's from the same kind of background as us. His family is originally from Lalita's husband's village."

"You trust anybody, Shindi. These days everyone wants to be upper class so they change their last names. Everyone thinks they're *Jat*."

"No one cares about that stuff anymore! Even people in India are far more advanced in their thinking now."

Many of these people my husband referred to as lower class were far more educated and successful than the men in his own family, but he would never admit it. He had decided long ago that Sikh men who cut off their hair when they immigrated to Canada or changed their names to hide their true identities were cowards. Being called racist terms like "turban twister" and "turbinator" had not weakened his character. Although he had relaxed a lot of his views on the modern ways of Canadian-born children, he would never approve of a non-*Jat* Sikh son-in-law.

"And we can't forget how old Dharam is now, we will have to make some compromises when it comes to her marriage," I added, but he did not say a word.

There was so much to be done. If this *rishta* worked, I would give each member of Lalita's family a twenty-four karat gold ring. But first we would have to set a meeting date. I headed for the kitchen. "Baljot is still in Hawaii with the kids so I'll take Preet to shop with me at the Punjabi Market. She knows the types of *pajami suits* the young girls wear these days."

"Don't be stupid! If Baksho finds out, she'll spread it throughout the whole neighbourhood before Dharam's plane lands. That woman can't keep her mouth shut!"

I stopped in the doorway. "The poor woman can barely utter a word. What could she possibly do now? *Bechari* Baksho! I hope she's well enough to partake in the festivities. There was a time when Baksho did *gidda* all night. Now her feet can't even feel the dance floor."

"Don't you worry about Baksho. You just focus on your daughter!" And he went back to his newspaper.

My husband was right. The day I had been waiting for since I first held Dharam in my arms had arrived. I would be relieved of my final responsibility.

The next morning before he left for the airport I brought up the topic again. I knew if I waited until after he returned, he would be all worked up about the traffic in the city, accusing people of not knowing how to drive, and my issues would become irrelevant.

"I've talked to Lalita," I told him. "Paul will be here in two days. That should be plenty of time to discuss things with Dharam. I want to set the wedding date quickly, so the least you can do is find out when the *gurdwara* is available. A father isn't dismissed from his duties until his daughters are married."

He picked up the remote control off the coffee table and sank into his recliner. "Don't you think you should at least wait for her to arrive before you start booking *gurdwaras*?"

"If you don't get off the couch and drive to the airport, how's she going to get here? You're already late. You should've left fifteen minutes ago!"

Dharam did not say much when she came in. All she wanted to do was sleep and watch television, so I put off talking to her until she had rested. The next day over breakfast I showed her the *salwar kameez* I had picked out.

"What do you think?"

"It's a little flashy. And aren't you a little too old to be wearing red?"

"Don't try to be *chilak*. This is for you."

She picked it up and, without taking a closer look, threw it down on the coffee table. "Where would I wear it? Besides, I hate red."

"It's such a beautiful colour and it's so festive. Of course, if you don't like it, you can take it back and exchange it, but you have to wear a *salwar kameez* the day after tomorrow."

"Why? What's happening then?"

She was being so naïve. Was it not obvious? I had told her several times over the phone that the next time she came to Vancouver I would introduce her to suitable boys.

"Paul's coming over."

She looked confused. "Who?"

"You know, the boy I told you about. The one from New Jersey. You wouldn't exchange email addresses with him as Lalita recommended, and you didn't want to meet him for coffee either, so you left me no option but to call him to the house!"

"Oh Mom, get over it. I told you I didn't want to get married."

"*Beta*, my dear child, don't be silly. Every woman has to get married. If you were a boy, maybe it would've been all right for you to stay single. But what will people say? How can we keep you sitting at home like this?"

"First of all, I don't live here..."

"That's another thing we have to discuss. No more living on your own in Edmonton. You're done with school, so you can just as well take a job in a hospital here in Vancouver. It's hard to find a good *rishta* as it is, but when people find out a girl's been living by herself for so many years, it just doesn't look proper."

"Mom, I'm not moving back home."

"Well, that's fine. As soon as you get married, you can go live with your husband!"

"For God's sake, Mom! Let it go or you'll regret it." She was looking at me as if she were getting ready to attack me.

"Don't you threaten me!" I raised my hand as I had when she was a child. It did not have the same effect without the wooden spoon in it, but she relaxed her posture.

"Look, I was homesick and you said you missed me so I came home for a visit. Next time I won't come." And she walked into her room and shut the door.

That night when she thought I was asleep, I heard her downstairs whispering on the phone. I could not understand what she was saying, but I knew it was not appropriate conversation for an Indian woman. But then I thought maybe she has found someone on her own. Maybe it is a *Jat* Sikh boy from a decent family. I had never even asked her. If she has found herself a suitable match that would be wonderful, I told myself. At least she would not hold me responsible if things went wrong.

The next day her father and I sat Dharam down and questioned her.

"Dharam, if there's another boy you would like to marry, it's all right with your father and me."

She shook her head. "Not this again. I told you yesterday. I don't want to get married. And there's no *boy.*"

"Well then, it's done. You've had plenty of time to find yourself a husband. We can't sit and wait forever for you to be ready. Your friends have all been married for years."

Dharam grabbed her purse and dashed out of the house, but I was not about to give up. I had been pleading with her to get married for the past two years. She had let so many perfect prospects get away because she was not *ready*. It was time for Lalita to bring Paul over to the house.

That night I heard her on the phone again. If it was not a boy, who could it be? I did not want to alarm her father, so I kept it to myself. She would meet Paul the next day and all her notions of staying single would be forgotten.

I woke early the next morning and moved all the extra furnishings I bought from the previous week's Sunday sale into the basement and Baljot's old bedroom. I vacuumed the carpet twice and set out the plate of *mittaiyee* and snacks two hours in advance. It was while I was re-arranging the furniture that I noticed her heading for the front door.

"Be ready before five. And don't think you can leave the house. I'll keep the boy here all night if I have to."

Just then Dharam's father entered the room, but I could see he did not want to interfere in the conversation. It was my job as a mother to make her understand. As a *good* Indian daughter Dharam should have readily agreed to the boy we had chosen for her, but it was obvious that I, as her mother, had not taught her well.

And then the unexpected happened. She erupted. "All my life I did everything you ever asked of me without once complaining because I thought when it came to the most important decision in my life, you'd let me decide." Dharam never had much to say but when she was angry she would ramble on until every word was imprinted on our brains.

"What nonsense are you talking? We've only done what's best for you. How dare you talk back like this?"

"What's best for me, huh Mom? So tell me—why am I supposed to marry some guy I don't know so my life can be as horrible as everyone else's?"

"What do you mean?"

"You know very well what I mean."

Her father stood up, knocking over the cactus with his newspaper. "What's this *bukvas,* this nonsense?"

"Sit down, *Ji,* there's no need for you to get upset. You need to watch your blood pressure."

Dharam rolled her eyes at me. She must have learned this technique from the *goray*.

"Don't you do that to me! I'm your mother!"

"Oh yeah, a mother who wants to see her daughters miserable. Look what you've done to Baljot! And what about Meena? You don't even mention her name. It's as if she doesn't exist. All she wanted to do was be an actress. And she was really good at it, Mom, and she would've made it. But rather than supporting her, you acted as if she wanted to be a hooker or something. You shut her out because it just didn't fit into your little guidebook for *good* brown girls!"

"Don't you dare utter her name in this house!" her father shouted.

"It's parents like you who bury their daughters in graves of shame and then taunt them until they stop breathing. All these years you've been saying how you've sacrificed to keep your daughters happy when really all you care about is your precious reputation! Had we been sons, you never would have thrust the guilt of sacrifice upon us."

I was dumbstruck at the image before me. My daughter had become a monster. I needed to sit down to keep my body from shaking.

"You'll marry your daughter off to anyone who'll take her just so she won't become a burden to you. And in the end she'll come to believe the role of brown women is to remain inferior and dependent upon men—just as you do."

"*Chup kar*! Be quiet! You don't know what you're saying!"

Her father's face had turned red but he chose to sit back down.

"Do you have any idea what exists beyond your own reality? What woman do you know that's happy? Take a good look around your neighbourhood."

"Everyone's comfortable in their own homes. They're..."

"That's crap! The names and faces may have changed over the years, but it's still the same old story. Is that what you want me to be, just another story?"

If she had been a child, I would have slapped her senseless for saying whatever trash came to her mind.

"*Bus kar*, that's enough!" I said, beginning to cry. "What do you want from us?"

I had never cried publicly like this before. Dharam's father did not move from his chair, and for a moment I thought he had passed on.

"I need you to just let me be," Dharam said. "Just accept me as I am." She looked like a teenager standing there in her t-shirt and blue jeans.

"But your life can only be complete when you marry and have sons. That's the only way you'll be happy." I pleaded with her. But then she shook her head and I said angrily, "But you're so ungrateful you don't appreciate all we've done for you. If I'd known you would turn out this way, I would've strangled you at birth! Or better yet killed you in my womb!"

"For God's sake, Mom, look at yourself. Look what your life has become."

The anguish on her face told me that it pained her more to say those words than it pained me to hear them. But all I could think at that moment was that I thought I had kept my unhappiness hidden so well. I had consciously forgotten who I was because it was too unpleasant to remember.

When I was young, I had always done as I was told. When my mother fell ill, I stayed home to look after my six younger siblings. I had hoped to further my education like my brothers although I had always understood it was more important for the boys to learn. At nineteen they told me I was to marry a man eight years my senior so the whole family could immigrate to Canada. I did not object, but my heart broke when I told Gopi, the boy next door, that we could no longer see each other. I cried silently so no one would hear after I explained to him I belonged to another. Not once did I tell my family there had been another man in my life. I never breathed a word about our forbidden love affair. Instead, I wore my fancy wedding outfit and did what was expected of me.

When I disappointed my husband time and time again because I could not bear him sons, I still kept quiet. I listened to his taunts. I put up with his verbal abuse. And not once did I question my duty as a daughter, wife or mother. My happiness was always dependent on everyone else's happiness as it should be for a *good* Indian woman. Dharam would never understand what it meant to be an Indian woman.

The ringing of the doorbell later that afternoon had prevented further memories from resurfacing. It was much too early for Paul and Lalita to arrive. Dharam stopped her father from opening the door as I rushed to the window to see who it was.

And there he stood beside his fancy car wearing a white cotton shirt and khaki pants on that smoldering hot day. He looked much older than Dharam; perhaps there were even hints of grey hidden in his blond mane. He had a cigarette glued to his lips.

Before we could speak or ask any questions, Dharam spoke. "Fine. You want me to get married, I will, but not to the guy you want! I'm thirty years old. You can't make my decisions for me anymore. This is the man I'm going to marry with or without your blessing!" She turned toward the door that stood between our world and his.

Her father had no choice but to interfere. She was bent on humiliating the family. "We can forget this ever happened. Just send him away. Stay here and do as we say and we'll dismiss this *paagalpan,* this madness!"

It was the first time I had ever seen him clasp his hands and plead to be heard.

"I can't." She looked directly into his eyes.

Her father tightened his fists and crossed his arms. His teeth were clenched. After a long pause he continued, "Fine! But if you leave here today, don't ever return to this house. Our doors will no longer be open to you. You'll be dead to us if you marry that man."

He looked at me, waiting for my reaction. This was the time for me to perform my wifely duty, and as irrational as his decision was, I had no choice but to follow. I had never done otherwise.

As she turned to walk out the door, the cruelest words I had ever spoken to one of my daughters slipped off my tongue. "You'll never be happy. You'll never be able to build your dreams from our ashes. You may as well have danced on our open caskets."

For an instant I thought a tear had formed in the corner of Dharam's eye, but then it was gone.

"You're right, Mom. I probably won't be happy. Maybe I'll be more miserable than I am now. But you've left me no other option!"

Not once did she look back.

The house became a graveyard. We walked around like strangers, her father and I, barely conversing with each other. When we did communicate, there was never any mention of the child who had stolen our lives. We did not speak of her because we were never able to forget her.

Every time the telephone rings I still think it might be Dharam. I imagine she is calling to tell us she is returning home. She asks for forgiveness and her father grants it. But each time I pick up the telephone the voice is not hers.

I have nothing to show for this life's work. Worst of all, I may never see two of my daughters again. I am a mother. My heart yearns for my children no matter how much grief they have caused me. One day when Dharam herself becomes a mother, she will understand how difficult it is to raise a respectful and dutiful daughter in this country.

Dharam's Journal

June 16, 2007

I was always afraid to keep a journal when I lived at home. When we were young, I found Baljot's diary hidden in her school backpack, and I blackmailed her for months, making her take me everywhere she went. Baljot tried to beat it out of me, but Meena was tougher than her and always protected me. She eventually found where I'd buried it in the dirt underneath the swing set and she burned it. She knew if my mother read it, she would have been in huge crap! But now that I live on my own, I have no worries. Plus, I sound silly when I try to share my family problems with my *gori* friends. And I can't tell my private problems to the brown girls because you never know who knows who or who is related to which gossiping aunty. It is best to write it down and get it all out of my system!

July 24

Some days I think I have a split personality. When I'm at home with my family, I feel like a completely different person than who I am at work or with friends. My parents will never understand how difficult it is to be Indian and Canadian at the same time.

August 9

The girls at work have been asking if I'll have an arranged marriage. I told them arranged marriages are no longer common. But I didn't bother to tell them that arranged marriages are now referred to as arranged introductions.

They had watched some documentary on TV and now they're worried. Apparently an Indian woman's mutilated body was found on a raspberry farm in Abbotsford. The mother-in-law's been arrested. Investigators believe the woman was eight months pregnant with her fifth daughter. I told them it isn't always like that. All brown people aren't the same, and I told them about some of the great aspects of my culture. Sometimes I can even forget the bad stuff myself. Sometimes I wish I could forget about Meena, too.

September 28

Just when my two personalities were learning to happily co-exist, my mother called. She says that all the brown girls who went to high school with me have married. I'm the only single twenty-eight-year-old my mother knows, and she's beginning to panic. She's given me a three-month deadline to find my own husband, and then she takes over.

December 19

My parents have started matchmaking. My mother constantly calls to remind me I'm on the brink of spinsterhood. My value on the marriage market peaked at twenty-four and now I'll only experience diminishing returns. She says I should settle for whoever will take me because all the nice guys were married off at an early age. I wish I could talk to Meena. She would know what to do. I haven't seen or heard from her in so many years.

January 2, 2008

My mother is mailing me pictures and so-called "bio datas" of suitable boys.

January 9

I told her the package got lost in the mail but really I threw it away. I can't marry a guy I don't even know just because everyone else is getting married! Times are different now.

January 17

With her friend Lalita's help, my mother emailed the pictures to me. When she phoned to see if I got them, I told her my computer has a virus and won't turn on, and I can't afford to get a new one.

January 20

She deposited money into my bank account this morning. I can now purchase two new laptops and a printer. Calling my mother stingy would be an understatement, but when it comes to getting her daughters married, money just doesn't matter!

March 8

My mother called again, but it wasn't what I expected. There's been another woman murdered. This time it was in Surrey and it was front-page news right across the province. "South Asian Woman Found Dead in Surrey Ditch."

At first all brown people in this country were classified as Hindus, then we were East Indians, followed by Indo-Canadians and now all brown people are being lumped together as South Asians. I guess white people think we all look alike. When they finally realize all people are the same and crime is everyone's problem, regardless of colour, maybe then we can just be classified as Canadian!

No one ever inquires about the remarkable things our community contributes to mainstream society, but as soon as anything awful happens, people at school, work or on the street want to learn more about the SOUTH ASIANS.

March 20

Baljot called this morning. She was laughing so much she could barely speak. Her brother-in-law found my profile on punjabiaashiqui.com. I am mortified! My mother has posted a picture of me from my nineteenth birthday party. I can't bring myself to read the ad she wrote. I've closed the email account she provided.

April 18

Neil Martens, a doctor at my hospital, has asked me out for the third time. He's been pursuing me for almost six months now. He's a nice guy but I can't picture myself with him. My mother would go into cardiac arrest if I dated him, and if he were the only cardiologist alive, she wouldn't let him revive her. There's no future for Neil and me. Not in this lifetime.

April 22

My mother called to inform me that Vimmi Bains has given birth to her third daughter. She wanted to abort the fetus as soon as she discovered it was a girl, but for some reason she didn't. Maybe someone in her family convinced her not to. The child is four months old but my mother only found out about it today. There were no celebrations to announce the births of any of Vimmi's daughters. Her in-laws are so disappointed in her that they're forcing her to adopt a cousin's son from India. These people are so ridiculous. They don't understand it's the male who determines the gender of the fetus, not the female. They keep blaming the poor women for everything!

My mother's afraid that my fate will be worse. I may not be able to have any children at all because I've waited so long to marry.

May 12

My mother wants to know if I've had intercourse with any of the guys from the Internet. I think she meant to say interaction!

May 30

My mother called to wish me happy birthday, but mostly she just cried on the phone. She can't get over the fact that her single daughter is twenty-nine!

July 6

My mother is so caught up in my oldest sister's problems these days that I hardly hear from her. Not that I mind. But I feel bad that my peace has to come at Baljot's expense. My parents are threatening to disown her, too, if she doesn't stop fighting with her in-laws. Baljot doesn't want to live with the extended family anymore but her husband won't leave them for her. It was her choice to marry that idiot. They dated for eleven months before they got engaged. According to my parents, her reasons for divorce are not legitimate.

October 1

Baljot's current dilemma must have blown over because mother dearest is at it again. She's been calling up people from the matrimonial section of the *Desi Dose* newspaper, and she's threatening to send prospective matches directly to my door. Although she's miles away I can feel her breathing down my neck.

October 17

My mother called today to tell me she thinks Vimmi Bains's youngest sister-in-law is a druggie. Who can blame her with all that pressure and all those double standards? And the nosy aunties, like my mother, only make the situation worse. First the aunties are on your case to get married. Then they pester you to have kids! And then they wait until your kids are grown so they can harass them about their daily activities. I'm surprised more girls from my old neighbourhood aren't addicts and alcoholics!

November 13

Neil and I have started dating. I still think of him as a friend but he says he's waiting for our relationship to progress to the next level. I don't know what to tell him. It seems so silly for me to say my family would never accept him and I'd be disowned if this relationship became serious. He'd never understand. Plus, I'm older now and I don't want to date just anyone. But Neil is so much better than some of the guys I've dated in the past, especially better than a couple of the brown guys. One of them was mooching off his parents the entire time we were together because he was unemployed. And I'm pretty sure the other one was dealing drugs.

December 2

I'm not sure what to do about Neil. I just keep thinking that if I'd been ten years older, if I'd been Baljot, I'd be living the doomed life she is living. My parents have come a long way since then, and I can't throw all this progress away. I don't have to have an arranged marriage—they'll accept anyone I want to marry as long as he is a *Jat* Sikh.

But they'll never accept a *gora*. I can't risk their disapproval, not even for Dr. Neil Martens. All I need is a little time.

February 1, 2009

She called today. I love my mother but she'll never understand that she's going to ruin my life. If she only lived in a world outside her home and her little circle, she would know there's so much more to life than marriage and children. It's all right that she never believed in me or encouraged me, but she needs to understand she's not in India anymore. Things are different here. She doesn't need to be a victim of her unjust society any longer. If she continues to think that way, God help her, but I won't marry when and whom she decides is best.

February 13

She called again. Mrs. Gill's youngest daughter's wedding is going to be held in Chandigarh next month, but my mother refuses to go because she says they are just having it there to show off. But I know the real reason she isn't going is because of the expensive airfare.

March 3

Neil's smoking is really starting to bother me. I think he's the only doctor I know who smokes. He promises he'll try to quit.

March 13

Brown people were the topic of discussion again in the staff room. This time it was a magazine article about the male to female ratio in Punjab that put my cultural background in the limelight. Apparently women there are aborting female fetuses in record numbers. I remember Baljot mentioning something similar when we talked on the phone a while back. Her sister-in-law wanted to know the sex of her second child so she could set up the nursery accordingly, but she was told by her doctor in Surrey that he had a new blanket policy. He would no longer disclose the gender of a baby to his patients. Then just three weeks later her sister-in-law heard the same doctor had told a *gori* friend of hers the sex of her child. Baljot thinks that this is happening because some of the new Indo-Canadians want to know the gender of the baby while it is still safe to abort the fetus. Many of these women are so desperate that they are going across the border to visit private clinics. If this is true, I hope the people I work with never see that report!

March 21

Sometimes I think I want to be with Neil just to defy tradition. He makes me feel like I'm someone else. He only knows the Dharam or Dee, as my co-workers call me, that he met three years ago because other than the colour of my skin, I've kept everything else about myself hidden. Sometimes I think that, if I run fast enough, I can get away from all the pain and hurt I've seen growing up.

April 28

Yesterday my mother arrived unannounced. I hate those damn Air Miles! I told her I got called in to work for an emergency surgery and that there was a gas leak in the apartment building so she couldn't stay there. I tried to rush her out from the door but she needed to use the washroom. I guided her directly to the toilet and back out of the apartment, not giving her a chance to snoop around. Neil left in a hurry this morning and forgot his shaving kit on the counter, but I was able to hide it before she noticed. Luckily he didn't leave his cigarettes lying around.

And thank God she didn't glance into the kitchen! There were empty wine bottles lying all over the place.

I dropped her off at West Edmonton Mall until closing time. She wandered aimlessly, lost for hours, while I removed all traces of Neil's presence from my apartment. She wasn't too impressed when I finally answered my cellphone. She said she also called the hospital but they said I wasn't scheduled to work yesterday. I reassured her that I was working on a different floor than usual and the clerks don't always know the names of the casual nurses. If my mother finds out about Neil, she'll take me back to Vancouver and set me up with some brown boy. I know my parents love me, but they'd never accept my relationship with Neil. In their community interracial marriages are acceptable as long as they involve someone else's children.

May 18

Now my mother is determined to introduce me to some guy in the States. She says she understands times are different now so we can meet and date for a while, but not too long. I can't afford to take my time at my age. And if I do like him and if we do go out for more than a few months, then we have to get engaged. She seems very excited. I don't want to disappoint her, but I don't want to get married either, not yet. I'm not ready for that kind of commitment.

May 28

The boy is coming to Vancouver, and my mother wants me to return home. She's positive it'll work out. He's seen my picture and can't wait to meet me.

I broke it off with Neil. I don't love him and it's unfair to lead him on. As for this new draft pick, I'll find a way to get rid of him too.

May 30

She forgot to call me on my birthday this year. I think she's pretending it didn't happen because I am thirty now! But Neil sent me a bouquet of my favourite flowers.

June 8

Neil called again, but I didn't answer. I haven't returned any of his calls. I've been avoiding him at the hospital, too.

June 15

My mother called today to tell me Lalita had found Mrs. Gill's oldest daughter, Manohar, a suitable match but Manohar refused it. She said she is content being single for now. And Mrs. Gill is not pushing her into it as she says it's entirely Manohar's decision. I don't think my mother realized that she probably shouldn't have told me this bit of information until after the words were out of her mouth. She quickly hung up, afraid she had put more rebellious ideas into my head.

June 19

Neil proposed. He knows I don't feel the same way about him, but he says he doesn't want to lose me. I don't know what to do. If it's not Neil, it'll be someone else. I told him I need time to think. I've also booked a flight to Vancouver. I'm going home next month.

July 11

My flight is tomorrow. I hope everything goes okay.

July 14

I called Neil tonight. I told him everything. I told him what happened to Baljot and Meena. I told him what happens to a lot of brown girls. If he still wants to marry me, he has to come and get me.

July 15

I can't believe what I did today. I broke off all ties to my family for a man I don't even love. If they'd just given me more time! Neil is trying to be supportive, but he doesn't understand why I'm pining away for a family that doesn't want anything to do with me. He just doesn't get it and he probably never will. Family is everything in Indian culture! Thirty years of pain and joy have been washed away, just like that.

September 10

Neil is waiting for me to set a date. I don't know if he loves me or if he's just infatuated with me because I'm different. I always thought my parents would set the wedding date and book the *gurdwara*. They would have been so excited. My mother would have called all her friends over to look at my clothes and jewellery. She would have spent days cooking and cleaning in preparation for that one day, and she wouldn't have complained about the tedious work or expenses at all. She's been waiting for this moment since the day I was born.

September 22

We've decided to get married at the courthouse. It'll be less agonizing that way. I'm all alone now. All the nurses at the hospital think Neil's a great catch. They can't figure out why I was being so picky! I guess they're right, he does treat me well. Marrying Neil seems to be the right thing to do.

January 9, 2010

The Olympics are in Vancouver this year. A few of us from work had rented one of the nurse's grandparents' house just outside Whistler for a weekend. I wasn't going to tell my mother or Baljot that I was coming, but I decided to tell the others to go without me because I can't risk running into anyone I know. I've asked Neil to go in my place, but he doesn't want to go if I don't join him.

February 5

Neil is going to Vancouver for the Olympics. I think he feels guilty but the tickets are already paid for so why waste them? And it's only for a few days. My mother would pass out if she found out how much money we spent on those tickets.

February 18

He's gone. I don't even want to watch it on television. It makes me want to cry!

July 15

It's been a year. It seems like it was just yesterday. I miss them so much. They probably don't even think of me, although I'm sure the neighbours and my aunts have brought my mother to tears on a number of occasions.

I'm a completely different person now, but there are days when I think I'm only fooling myself. Today, for instance, I went to the bank and the lady asked for several pieces of identification—I guess I didn't look like a Dee Martens to her.

Of course, deep down inside I'm still Dharam Sandhu. I can alter my identity but my past won't set me free. But at least I don't have to hear anyone call me by that name anymore. I've always hated being called by my first name. I don't care what my mother says, it was and always will be a boy's name! I've yet to meet another brown girl with this name.

September 2

Our new house is gorgeous with a view of the golf course that is amazing. The exterior is a palace of glass and the decorator has outdone himself inside. My father would love it! It's far more stunning than any dream home I imagined.

But I feel trapped. I don't belong here.

January 14, 2011

Baljot just called to tell me that Umber Rai was murdered two nights ago. They found her body in a dumpster down the street from her work place. The police aren't saying anything but everyone believes her husband is the prime suspect. I feel so bad for her family. How could this happen? Umber didn't have an arranged marriage. She and her husband dated for years before they married. I thought they were in love.

Baljot says Umber moved back to Vancouver with her family just last year from Kelowna and everything seemed fine. She even had three sons with her husband and the youngest was only three months old. But Baljot thinks that maybe she was just having kids to try and fix the marriage. She says she has friends who've done that. Apparently the whole community is in shock, my mother included. Baljot says my mother's been asking about me, but she hasn't let on that we've been keeping in touch. That information could create more problems between Baljot and her in-laws, just when they're finally treating her well. I can't even console my mother. I can't call and empathize with anyone.

January 30

Baljot called today! Her mother-in-law got the new Indian channels on TV, and Baljot swears that Meena is playing the role of a mother to an adult child in a popular television series. She even looked her up on the internet, and she says that Meena is going by the name Meenakshi Malhotra. But she's only five years older than me—how could she be playing a middle-aged woman?

February 2

This Meenakshi Malhotra does look a lot like Meena. But when Meena left home, she had a short pixie cut and she was a little on the chubby side. This woman has long, gorgeous hair halfway down her back and her body is to die for. And those breasts—if that's Meena, those are definitely implants. I remember when Meena was sixteen, Baljot told her not to waste money on fancy push-up bras because a Band-Aid was enough to cover her two little pimples.

March 6

It's been almost a month since Baljot added herself to Meena's fan page, but there's been no response. She wants me to set up a Facebook account and contact Meena, too, as she thinks Meena will respond to me because we were always closer. I'd rather not. I don't want to field questions from all those people from my past. I'd rather stay anonymous!

March 24

I'm pregnant. Neil was quiet at first but then he seemed happy about it. The baby wasn't planned, but early in our relationship Neil had mentioned he loved children. I hope it's a girl. I always said I would partake in all the festivities only the birth of a boy allowed: the *ladoos*, the *gidda*, the dances and folk songs and my most hated of all, the *lohri* festival. In Punjab it's a yearly celebration for various reasons, though in Canada it is mainly associated with the delivery of a son. I've waited my whole life to celebrate the birth of my daughter.

April 18

Neil's edgy all the time and when I ask what's wrong, he brushes me off. Ever since he opened his own practice, he's been extremely tense. I planned a vacation two months ago but he says we have to cancel it as he has a medical conference that weekend.

April 20

Baljot still hasn't received a response from Meena, but she has a new plan. She is going to get the Indian channel, ATN, for our mother for Mother's Day. My mother is way too cheap to subscribe to it herself—she would rather get pirated Bollywood movies for a dollar at Baksho's store.

April 23

I talked to Baljot again today. I really wanted to tell her what was going on with me and Neil but the words just didn't come out. I pretended everything was perfect!

April 28

I'm sure he's smoking again. I could smell it on his breath although he tried to hide it by shoving two pieces of gum into his mouth. I didn't say anything. Maybe work is stressing him out.

May 9

I think Neil is having an affair. He denied it but I'm not convinced. Yesterday I called the office instead of his cellphone and the receptionist told me he was off for the afternoon. He didn't return home until late in the evening. He brought flowers. He hasn't given me flowers since we've been married.

May 14

I almost lost the baby today. The doctor has put me on bed rest for now. He thinks I have too much stress in my life. He suggested I call my mother or a relative to help out with things around the house. I burst into tears in his office.

May 19

Neil came home with a diamond pendant for me last night. He only buys me jewellery on special occasions. I want to trust him but I don't know what's real and what's not anymore. I'm sick most of the time and the rest of the time I sleep. I'm not even sure when he leaves and when he comes back. He has hired a housekeeper to do the cooking and cleaning. All I know is this isn't how it's supposed to be. This was meant to be one of the most memorable times of my life.

May 28

I confronted him again but he denied that anything was wrong. He says I'm being paranoid and I need to be calm. He says if anything happens to the baby, it will be my fault because I'm getting worked up over nothing. Maybe just my hormones are all out of whack.

June 5

Erica from the hospital came over today. She was extremely quiet and sympathetic and insisted I call her if I need anything. This confirms that something is going on. Erica knows everything about everyone—she reminds me of a very young and *gori* Baksho! I played dumb, but I could tell by the things she was saying she knew what Neil was up to and wanted to see if I did, too.

June 16

There was a riot in Vancouver after the Canucks lost in the Stanley Cup finals! It was all over the news. And Baljot, the idiot, had taken her kids downtown to watch on the big screen at Georgia and Hamilton. Thank God she had enough sense to leave after the second period.

My father must be devastated by the Canucks' loss. Ever since we were kids, he's been a huge Canucks fan. Baljot told me he went to the *gurdwara* to pray before each game in the final series.

June 18

The doctor has taken me off bed rest but I can't return to work and must try to take it easy.

June 29

If I hadn't been craving a gelato, I would never have seen them at the intersection. He says he didn't want it to be this way, that he was going to wait until after the baby was born to tell me. He kept asking me to say something, but I couldn't. I don't feel anything, not pain, not hurt, not betrayal. I'm numb. I wonder if my fate has led me directly into a future I thought I could escape.

July 2

I never thought it would happen to me, and I always said that if it did, I would leave. But it's not that simple.

July 9

Neil left today. He didn't even look at me. He just said we would work out the legalities after the baby was born, then he quietly packed his bags and walked out. And I didn't do or say anything to stop him.

July 12

I still haven't told Baljot I'm pregnant. I haven't told her about Neil either. What would I possibly say? The guy I left everything for has left me!

Plus, the entire family is smitten with Meena's performance in this Indian soap opera. Baljot said that our parents were really upset at first when they saw her in the role of the villainous mother-in-law, and our mother wouldn't let anyone turn on the new flat screen (also a gift from Baljot) for days. She even threatened to throw it out the window. Then she found my father watching the show on Baljot's old laptop in the basement. And that was the moment she forgave Meena. Baljot thinks that our parents will get over my betrayal now, too. She says they have changed a lot!

The neighbours are also praising Meena's acting skills—in front of my parents anyway! Who knows how much those women trash talk behind their backs? Baljot is still blogging and tweeting, trying to get a response from Meena.

July 14

I called Baljot to tell her the truth today, but I never got in a word because Meena had phoned home! Then Baljot set up Skype for my parents, but she said the first time everyone just bawled, even my father. Meena is happily married to one of her former co-stars. They have two sons, a three-year-old and an eleven-month-old baby. Needless to say, our mother was thrilled! Meena asked about me, but Baljot says my father just teared up and changed the subject and our mother left the room.

Baljot says I should try to patch things up with them. Meena is coming to visit in December with her family and Baljot really wants me to be there, too. But they have no idea what's going on in my life. They think I'm happily married, and they will be expecting my "wonderful" husband Neil to accompany me.

July 27

Neil came home today. He wants me to take him back. He says everything was his fault and he's willing to take the blame. He gave up on us and it was stupid of him. He says it's because I never let him in, because I'm always distant, as if I'm lost. He says he'll give me time to think about it.

I know I married Neil for all the wrong reasons. Regardless of what lies ahead, I can't silence the little whispers eating away at my soul. If it had been me who'd been unfaithful, would he have forgiven me?

I've spent my whole life fighting who I was expected to be and I've lost sight of who I am and what I want. Maybe it's not about him or them anymore. Maybe it's about me!

August 11

I wonder what people in the community would say if they knew what was happening in my life right now. I'll bet they would say I'm being punished for my crimes. I betrayed my parents when I married a *gora*. And why would God give me the opportunity to be a wife when I couldn't fulfill my first and foremost obligations as a daughter?

I know it shouldn't matter what they think, but it does. If they could only see inside me, maybe they would understand how I torture myself far more than I could ever suffer at their hands.

September 13

I know I have to stop running but I don't know how. I can never go back home. Meena may have gone astray a long time ago, but in the end she married a brown guy and is still married to him! She can be forgiven but I married a *gora* so I can't be.

October 15

I signed up for some wellness workshops at the community centre in the city. Maybe it will help me clear my mind and teach me how to meditate. I even went to the *gurdwara* yesterday for the first time in three years.

October 23

Today when I was sorting through some of my stuff, I found an old photo album. When I saw Baljot's wedding pictures, I remembered how my mother had reminded her not to look back during the *doli* ceremony, the bride's departure from her maternal home. The newlywed is to leave the house facing directly toward the door to her future. As she left, Baljot threw rice over her head, which landed behind her, promising prosperity to the home she was leaving behind. She had paid her dues as a good daughter.

I remember asking my mother what would have happened if Baljot had turned around or come back. She scolded me and told me not to say such bad things because disaster would strike our home!

I would never get the chance to perform this ritual and perhaps that is a far greater sin then merely turning around.

October 30

I have to make a decision soon. Neil called again. He wants to know how much more time I need. I couldn't give him an answer. Not yet. I just can't hate him. I always find I'm angrier with myself than anyone else. And as this baby grows inside of me, I feel I have a responsibility far greater than to myself. I want this child to grow and experience life without labels and expectations. I don't want her to be like me. I want her to be at peace.

November 3

I started packing this morning. I don't know where I'm going yet but it keeps me distracted. I still haven't reached a decision. Maybe if I stop thinking about what I have to do the answers will come to me.

November 6

Baljot keeps calling. I have ten missed calls and eight text messages. She wants me to call our parents.

November 7

I don't know what time it was when I finally dozed off last night and entered the territory of endless hauntings. There was a lovely young woman standing in a field surrounded by every type of flower imaginable. But when I moved closer, the sun began to fade and the flowers began to wilt. She grew old and wrinkled as I watched. Her body became weak and fragile. The flowers turned into weeds, caging her in. It was impossible for her to breathe. Then I looked into her eyes and I knew who she was. My unborn daughter.

As the weeds grew and grew, they wove a thick wall between us, and I could no longer tell if it was my daughter's shadow that peeked through the spaces between them. The last thing I saw before I awoke was my mother's face staring back at me.

November 9

I told Baljot today. She was shocked then pissed off because I hadn't told her earlier. I didn't go into all the details. She says she'll support me whatever my decision. But now she thinks I should hold off on contacting our parents.

November 12

I've made up my mind. I don't know if it's the right choice, but it's what I really need to do. I'm going to go back to my family. I won't tell them everything immediately. I'll ease them into it. Baljot thinks it would be wiser to wait until Meena's visit. She thinks with all the hype around Meena they may not take my disappointment to heart. But I can't wait that long. I am due in December.

November 17

I've been preparing myself with affirmations from the self-help books I've been reading. I doubt they work, but I'm desperate. I know it's not going to be easy to return to that life. I would be completely delusional to think that. But I have to be strong. I will have to take the first step. I'll have to go back before I can move forward. If Neil wants to follow, he can. I won't keep him away from his child. I don't know if I could love him again—if that's what I want to call it. All I know is that I need to love me first.

November 21

I will have to wait until after the baby is born. I was crazy to think I could travel in this state.

December 1

My c-section is scheduled for next week. I'm a little scared. I talked to Baljot and she said she could make up some excuse and come for a few days, but I told her it wasn't necessary. A couple of friends from work have offered to help me out for the first two or three weeks after the baby's birth. Neil wants to be with me during the delivery and I told him I would think about it.

December 12

I've decided that I won't apologize for living my life. I won't hang my head in shame because my husband wasn't faithful. I won't feel weak because I may live my life as a single mother, the mother of a daughter. They can point fingers, they can talk, but I won't let it get to me, not anymore. I'll go back to where I belong and share with them where I've been. And I'll do it with courage. I can no longer be afraid. I have to do this, for me, for my mother and for my daughter.

The Wedding – 2012

The *gurdwara* glistened with magenta and white ornaments. Fresh roses, floating candles and silver tablecloths lit up each wooden table along the back wall of the *langar* hall. A buffet of sweets, *pakoras* and *cha* enticed the long line of invitees. Guests poured in, men in dark suits and brightly coloured traditional *achkuns*. Women dazzled in the latest styles of *lenghas*, *Anarkali suits*, *churidaars* and *pajamis* or tights paired with *kameezes* so short they barely reached mid-thigh. The vast array of warm colours inside the building was a stark contrast to the cold and wet, late January morning.

This was the wedding of the decade and everyone had been invited—mothers, daughters, grandchildren, and even the former neighbours. Anyone who had ever lived in Little India was present because Baksho's grandson was to be united in matrimony with Prakash Kaur's youngest daughter.

The group of old friends was all seated along the back wall. At their age it was difficult for them to sit near the front, cross-legged and without any support for their backs for the duration of the wedding.

"It's karma!" Lalita exclaimed as she watched the bride dressed in a heavily embroidered, sleeveless, silver *kameez* with a matching fuchsia, fish-cut, long skirt follow her nine bridesmaids down the aisle.

"If you ask me," Kamal said, her voice grating on everyone's ears, "this event has almost as much glamour as the royal wedding. I was so excited I stayed up all night to watch it. What a romantic fairytale! Now if only I had followed my heart and made my way to Bollywood, I would have been a director, producer or a famous actress like Meena by now!" Her interest in the rich and famous had now spread from east to west.

Shindi blushed. Then she burst into laughter and gave Kamal a firm pat on the back.

"Prakash Kaur is thrilled that Meena decided to stay for the wedding. Everyone in the community is raving about her show." Mrs. Gill directed her attention toward where Meena was sitting with some of the other girls from the neighbourhood. They were listening carefully to Meena's every word.

Shindi smiled proudly.

"Well, how did they meet?" Rani asked, taking the attention away from Meena. "Baksho's grandson went to live with his mother in Winnipeg while he was still young, and Prakash Kaur took her family to live on the Island."

"They met on-line in the chatting rooms," Shindi said. After her youngest daughter, Dharam, had abandoned her, Shindi had turned to her family for guidance, and her sister-in-law, Prakash Kaur, had reached out in support by merely keeping her mouth shut. In exchange for that kindness, Shindi was more than happy to partake in the festivities for the marriage of Prakash Kaur's daughter.

"It's not *Rab* who makes couples anymore. It's a *dubba*, the box with buttons," Lalita said, chuckling.

Lalita had become such an expert with technology she now had a web page for her matchmaking business. And it was because of this new venture that she had gotten her own second chance at love. Her new secret companion had been betrayed by his three spoiled sons, sons for whom Lalita had found suitable matches, who had somehow persuaded the rich widower to sign over most of his property. Fortunately, before he became absolutely penniless, he had realized what they were up to and was able to retain some of his wealth. Lalita had comforted him, and he had told her how he regretted the fact that he had not fathered any daughters. A daughter, he said, would never have taken advantage of a lonely father in such a cruel manner. Lalita and this gentleman became very close during his ordeal, but fearing the community's condemnation, they had not shared the details of their romance with anyone. Meanwhile, he bought a studio apartment in White Rock and got a part-time job as a security guard. He worked graveyard shifts so they could spend their afternoons together. They had thought of everything. Their liaison would remain private.

"Well, this business really suits you, Lalita," Manjeet exclaimed. "You are always glowing these days!"

Lalita had wanted to tell Manjeet about her gentleman friend as she wanted the same for her, but she did not have the courage to say anything. Even with the prospect of spreading happiness among her dearest friends, she could not risk losing her own.

"Did you know it was Baksho who approached Prakash Kaur with the *shagun* to bring the two *families-shamilies* together?" Indu had watched the events unfold from her living room window.

"*Suchi,* really?" Mrs. Gill adjusted her *phulkari dupatta.*

"Baksho must be dying inside right now! I think the bride is a little older than the groom," Kamal could not help but comment. "At my daughter Sonia's wedding, Baksho ridiculed her for finding a husband who was five years her junior."

"Why would age matter?" Mrs. Gill inquired. "I think it's time women started marrying younger men. When men marry girls fifteen or twenty years their junior, there's not a peep out of anyone! Besides, women live way longer than men. That's why there are so many more young widows than widowers. I say good for Prakash Kaur's daughter."

What Mrs. Gill did not mention was the fact that she was two years older than her husband. Baksho had promised to keep this to herself but disclosed the information soon after she acquired it, though most people had long since forgotten. Now even in her late fifties she had a sparkle none of the younger women in the community could compete with. She was often seen around the neighbourhood wearing skinny jeans and Indian style *kurtas* or tunics. Mrs. Gill still looked perfect.

"Actually, going back to Baksho, I heard Jugga came back when he found out about the stroke," Rani said. "He's living with some *chini,* some Chinese girl. She has two kids from a previous marriage. But he came back for the money, *not* for Baksho." The bride and groom were exchanging rings, but Rani had the complete attention of the women.

"Thank God, she's not a stupid woman," Manjeet said, "and was able to see through his charade! Baksho would never stand in the way of her grandson's happiness. Perhaps it's a way to repent for her sins."

"God has a funny way of resolving things. Everything happens for a reason!" Mrs. Gill rearranged the turquoise and gold bangles on her right wrist to match those on the left then folded her hands in her lap.

The colourful accessories, anti-aging products and cosmetic procedures assured her of remaining a picture of renewed youth, but she had been unable to bleach out the age spots on her hands.

"Since when did you become such a philosopher?" Lalita asked, laughing. "You haven't been caught up in that yoga craze too, have you?"

"Of course, I have to take care of my body," Mrs. Gill replied then quickly changed the subject. "By the way, Indu, congratulations on the newcomer. I hear she's beautiful!"

The others were surprised at Mrs. Gill's comment and a bit hesitant to pass on a congratulatory greeting for the birth of a granddaughter but nevertheless decided to follow her lead.

"That's wonderful news, Indu. *Vidaiyan,* congrats!" Rani exclaimed.

"Wow, Indu! That makes fourteen grandchildren for you!" Manjeet was overwhelmed with just the thought of so many kids. "I was already a grandmother at Nikky's age! But I guess times really have changed." Mrs. Gill passed her a dirty look.

"Oh, don't listen to her!" Lalita gave Manjeet a playful shove and added, "Indu, I'm sure your *doti,* your new granddaughter, is as pretty as you!"

Indu stood and found herself a crate to sit on. She could no longer sit on the floor like the others because she was having trouble with both her knees. Once settled, she pulled a water bottle from her recycled bag and began popping pills into her mouth—first a multi-vitamin, then a calcium pill, two vitamin D tablets followed by a glucosamine capsule.

Manjeet stared.

"What? I take so many *pills-shills* for all my *dukh dards,* my aches and pains. And I have to spread them out through the day. You should all take them, too!" Indu leaned down and placed the bottles of vitamins in front of the others on the carpet. When no one responded to her offer, she snatched them up and shoved them back into her bag.

"I don't know about the rest of you," Kamal said, "but I think we should plan a party to celebrate Indu's new granddaughter! The last time I remember being this excited was when I first heard that Ash and Abhi had a baby daughter."

"Who?" Rani was puzzled.

"Don't tell me you don't know Aishwarya Rai and Abhishek Bachchan.

They were even on *Oprah* way back when! Such a lovely *jori,* just like my Sonia and her husband!" Kamal was ecstatic but the others did not share her enthusiasm.

"I think you have completely lost your mind. You talk about these celebrities as if you really know them," Shindi told her. "You should re-open your salon to give yourself something to do rather than sit in front of the TV all day long! And then you can drive your clients crazy instead of your friends!"

Although Shindi did not appreciate it, Kamal's antics were, in fact, solely for her entertainment. The group was well aware of her situation with Dharam, but they tried to avoid the topic in the hope of keeping her distracted. And though she was not as vocal as she once was, from time to time she could stop thinking about her own problems and join in conversation with them.

"If I didn't get this evil tendonitis in my wrists, I wouldn't have sold my salon in the first place!" Kamal's smile turned upside down as she rubbed her wrists.

"Who do you keep texting with that fancy phone, Lalita?" Manjeet grabbed Lalita's BlackBerry. "Put it away!" And she threw it into Lalita's silver clutch.

Lalita blushed and closed the latch on the purse.

"Actually, I was thinking we should all go to visit Tarsem this week," Indu said solemnly. "I heard she's not doing well. I was hoping to see her at the wedding, but it must still be very *hard-shard* for her." Although the group had not shown any interest in Tarsem's life before the tragedy of her daughter's murder, it had been Shindi, Lalita and Indu who were the first ones to comfort her when the news was released.

Mrs. Gill choked back tears and nodded in agreement. They observed the rest of the ceremony in silence.

After the wedding ended and the invitees rushed to line up for lunch, a very frail and seventy-something Baksho slowly rolled her wheelchair toward Shindi. She had withered away after the stroke, and other than the sagging flesh slumped in the wheelchair, there was no sign of the once obese and outspoken woman. Her thinning grey hair was loosely tied in a small bun at the back of her head, and her floral *suit* had been replaced by a dull beige *salwar kameez.*

Baksho's brittle hand grabbed the bottom of Shindi's simple brocade top to prevent her from disappearing into the crowd of well-wishers. She motioned Shindi to kneel beside her and listen carefully.

"I invite. Dharam comes, Baljot gone to get," Baksho managed to mumble. She tried to simultaneously squeeze a smile from the right side of her face.

Shindi could taste the salt from her tears. She threw her arms around Baksho and clung tightly to her for what seemed like minutes. After she had dried her eyes, Shindi wheeled the old woman out to where the others were waiting to bless the couple with gifts of cash via the groom's mother. But before she reached her destination she was halted by some loud laughter.

At the end of the *langar* hall sat a group of four women not much older than Shindi had been when she first arrived in Canada. In between conversing with each other and gesturing at other guests, the women would pause to slip a *burki*, a bite, into the mouths of the six boys seated next to them on the floor mat.

Shindi did not recognize any of these women as many of the old residents had moved out of the community after their children were grown, and young families had taken their place. New immigrants had also flocked to the area and the borders of Little India had become vastly expanded. Even the *gurdwara* had changed. In order to accommodate the growing *sangat*, a new temple, twice the size of the previous one, had been built next to the old structure. Little India was no longer little and there were now more strangers than friends in the community. And these young women, women with only sons because scientific developments and improved technologies had answered their prayers, were just a few of the newcomers that had replaced Shindi and her friends on the community's social scene. Unfortunately they had adopted the sisterhood's old narrow-minded beliefs and values. But perhaps they too would learn their lessons with time as all the others had before them.

Baksho tapped Shindi's arm and motioned for her to keep moving. As Shindi positioned the wheelchair next to Preet, Baksho once again tugged at her *kameez*. Shindi bent down to listen carefully to what else Baksho needed to say.

"Pra..." Baksho managed to grunt with the little energy she had left, but she could not get the complete word to flow from her lips. Shindi understood but before she could turn the wheelchair around and take

Baksho toward Prakash Kaur, Preet gently grabbed the handles and began to push Baksho on her way.

Preet smiled. "Thank you, Shindi *panji*. I'll take her in the right direction from here. She is my responsibility."

The *langar* hall buzzed with spirit that day. And from the kitchen a mature and content Prakash Kaur could be heard, once again, chanting hymns.

Epilogue

I am a woman. This time I have come to earth wrapped in a brown exterior. They say I am fortunate because I have been allowed to live. I am identified in this lifetime as a Canadian, an Indian, a Punjabi, and a Sikh female. I have no face. I have no name.

I belong to a religion that empowers me. I am consumed by a culture that imprisons me. I have come to reside in a new land that vows to set me free.

I have been well versed in the worth of a woman. There are three significant stages in my life; the rest are minor details. I am born into a family I must serve unconditionally. I am obliged to marry a man I must worship unconditionally. I will give birth to sons I promise to love unconditionally. Threads of shame and sacrifice weave my body together.

Although I have many labels, I still do not know who I am. My life knows no purpose and my soul knows no home. I live among shadows, a prisoner of my own thoughts. I hope one day I will learn to breathe, to emerge from the darkness and be free.

Acknowledgements

With much appreciation and gratitude to:

My parents, Beant and Harjit, for their love, understanding and ongoing support. Jas, Darshan and Jessie for taking care of all the little things that mean so much. Josh and Saira for their optimism and enthusiasm.

Gurmeet for always believing in me. Karen for reading each word as it made its way onto paper and encouraging me to keep filling the pages until the last line was written. Sukhinder and Charanjit for their knowledge and insight. Tanya and Yonah for believing in this book and the possibilities. Kuljeet, Sunil and Aman for their advice and expertise.

Vici Johnstone at Caitlin Press for the opportunity to tell this story the way it was meant to be told and Rebecca Hendry for the finishing touches. My editor, Betty Keller, for sharing my vision and making it better with her brilliant remedies. Lisa Rector for taking an interest in this manuscript many years ago in a creative writing class and editing the initial draft. Raqiya Khan for the beautiful henna illustration used on the book cover.

The many friends, relatives and colleagues who graciously shared their experiences, listened, read, edited, translated, defined, researched, typed, discussed, inspired, encouraged, debated, recommended, promoted, suggested, assisted, planned, organized, shopped, travelled, dined, cried, prayed, healed, imagined, wished, cheered, danced, laughed, hoped, dreamed…and celebrated with me on this journey.

The Divine Power that guides us to write and rewrite our own stories until we get it right.